OPERATION
MOCKINGBIRD

OPERATION MOCKINGBIRD

LINDA BALETSA

Spratt & Co. LLC

Boston ● Miami

Operation Mockingbird may be purchased online at
amazon.com, barnesandnoble.com and at your local
bookstores.

ISBN: 978-0-9894461-0-5
Cover Design by LogoWizards.com

Spratt & Co. LLC

November 11, 2013
Boston, MA

To Trey and Megan

CHAPTER ONE

Kandahar, Afghanistan

A THUNDERING EXPLOSION ripped through the night. Matt Connelly's heart jumped and then began racing. He pressed his back and arms against the wall, bracing himself, as he looked down one end of the alley and then the other. Dust filled the air, obscuring anything farther than a few feet in front of him. He began to choke and waved his hand in front of his face, trying to clear the air. The crescent-shaped moon he had seen just moments before perched above the building across the alley was now only vaguely visible through clouds of dust.

There was another huge blast, and the building behind him shuddered violently against his back. Matt leaned forward and pushed himself off with the toes of his boots, propelling himself away from the structure. He landed face down in a pool of putrid water. The liquid assaulted his eyes and nose.

He pushed himself up, gagging and spitting, just as a third explosion tore through the air. The ground trembled beneath him as the reverberating undertow of the explosion rolled past. Chunks of plaster and small rocks rained down from the sky, pounding his body and the ground around him. He covered his head with his hands and arms. Without support, he fell back into the water.

He held his breath as he braced himself against the assault on his body. The objects falling from the sky continued to pummel him, purposefully pushing him deeper and deeper. A searing pain tore through his left shoulder. He tensed but couldn't move. His eyes burned. His lungs were on fire.

Matt uncovered his head and, reaching forward, pushed his head and torso up. He gasped for air and then, breathing deeply, filled his lungs. The fog before him slowly began to clear. The water beneath him began to settle. In it, Matt saw the reflection of flames licking the sky. He vaguely registered a cacophony of sounds around him. With his arms beneath him, supporting his upper body, he started to twist around. His shoulder screamed in protest. The weight on the back of his legs and lower back grew heavier, pushing him down farther and farther into the filth.

The terrible screams and cries from those in the rubble behind him were the last sounds Matt heard before he fell into the murky abyss of unconsciousness.

Miami, Florida
Two Months Later

THE HOT AIR GREETED Matt with a wet and familiar kiss as he strode off the plane and onto the main concourse of Miami International Airport. The blinding South Florida sun streamed through the large windows lining one wall of the newly renovated terminal. As he made his way through the busy terminal, Matt used his right arm to gingerly swing his carry-on bag over his shoulder. Nonetheless, pain shot up and down his left side. More than two months since the original injury and one month since he had been reinjured, the shoulder still served as a painful reminder of his time in the Middle East.

Photographs of Miami were plastered on the walls. Pictures of strawberry fields and citrus groves. A scene of the Miami skyline at night lit up with brilliant colors. A row of Art Deco hotels on South Beach. The Freedom Tower beckoning from the center of Downtown Miami. Matt smiled at the memories these pictures evoked.

At Passport Control, the TSA agent's eyes flickered over Matt before he swiped the passport through the reader connected to the computer. As the computer retrieved the appropriate data, the agent examined the passport carefully, flipping through the many pages of stamps. Matt saw the computer screen flash, and the agent started scrutinizing the monitor, scrolling through the data and then typing very slowly on the keyboard. Matt expelled a sigh of relief when his passport was returned and he was sent on his way.

Weaving his way through the crowd, Matt dodged people embracing amid piles of luggage. Locals greeted long-lost family members in Creole, Spanish and Hebrew in the chaos that was the third largest American airport for international passengers. Occasionally, a word of English could be heard, but in most cases greetings were delivered in a heavy accent. He smiled as visitors from the Northeast, in town to escape the cold, appeared to be checking signs to make sure they had in fact arrived at a United States airport and not in some foreign country.

The appreciative glances he garnered from the women he passed did not go unnoticed. Matt was 6 feet 2 inches tall, leaner than when he had started his journey and, after months in the desert, deeply tanned. His light brown hair was bleached practically blond by the sun. Matt figured he was probably being mistaken for a lawyer or an accountant returning from a relaxing vacation in the Caribbean. Nothing could have been farther from the truth.

Baggage. We all have it, read the Kenneth Cole advertisement on the luggage carousel. But Matt felt rather light in the baggage department. Sure, he had some issues but, after what he had just been through, he figured his baggage was completely manageable. *Baggage. We all have it.*

But it doesn't necessarily need to weigh you down, Matt thought, finishing the advertisement from his own perspective. He grabbed his bag, walked out of the airport and hailed a cab.

Twenty minutes later, the cab pulled up at Matt's childhood home in Coconut Grove, the oldest neighborhood in Miami. It was a small, two-bedroom Florida bungalow originally built in the 1950s and dwarfed now by the McMansions that had popped up on either side during the last real estate boom. He paid the cab driver and smiled as he walked up the path leading to the front door. His neighbor Pierre had been true to his word and maintained the lawn while Matt was gone. The dense foliage that had laid claim to the yard for even longer than Matt was somewhat contained.

After getting settled in, Matt loaded the washing machine with clothes heavy with dust and mud before grabbing a beer from the fridge. He sat down in front of the computer and booted it up. While he waited, he twisted off the bottle top and tossed it into a nearby trashcan. Going straight to email, he quickly deleted all the spam emails and other garbage that had accumulated in the months since he had last been able to check his email. He was left with several inquiries from friends concerned about his whereabouts. He sent out a brief message to everyone on his buddy list to let them know he was fine, was back in town and would catch up with them later.

There was a message from adoren1105@hotmail.com that survived the purge. Alex Doren identified himself as a fellow writer and asked for a personal interview with Matt to speak about his experiences in Afghanistan. No way, he thought to himself. If anyone was going to write about his experiences, it was going to be him.

Matt had written a few pieces while he was at a U.S. Army base hospital in Afghanistan recovering from his injuries, and he wanted to get those published. Then he wanted to take a six-month sabbatical and write a book. A book would give him a lot more breathing space for more details and his own opinion, stuff that probably wouldn't be considered appropriate for a daily periodical. All of this, he would need to clear with his boss, Dave Kagan. Matt deleted the message without responding.

He had saved the best for last and settled down to read the three messages from his old friend Stephen Cross, a Pulitzer Prize-winning journalist from *The New York Times* who had always been encouraging and helpful when Matt was just starting out. He and Stephen had been in Iraq together but had separated when Stephen had left Iraq and headed to Europe for a much-deserved vacation before returning to the United States. Matt decided to make the trek to the Kandahar Province in Afghanistan before his own return and they hadn't communicated directly since.

The first message brought a chuckle:

Hey, buddy, I'm back. I arrived last night. Four weeks since I left and I'm still cleaning Iraqi sand out of every orifice. I'm not sure where you are and when you'll get this, but when you do, give me a call or shoot me a text.

Matt smiled, tipped his beer to the computer monitor screen and leaned back to enjoy the second message:

Matt, I've been getting settled back in town. Tomorrow, I meet with my boss. I'm going to try to sell her some of my material, regroup for a while here, and then head back out. Since my return, I've been checking out the competition. Man, I can't believe how far off the mark these guys are about what's going on in the sandbox. Our stuff's going to blow people away. Call me!

The third message, dated just two week before, intrigued Matt:

Matt, I heard what happened to you. By now you should be on your way back to the states. We need to talk. Call me as soon as you get this.

Matt grabbed the phone and punched in Stephen's cell phone number. His call was directed straight to voice mail. A computer-generated voice told him that Stephen's voice mailbox was full.

"Damn," Matt muttered.

He hung up and turned back to the computer to type a reply email.

Hey, Stephen. Great to hear from you! I just got back. I tried to reach you but no luck. Tomorrow I start to make the rounds myself. I'm meeting with my boss in the morning. Other than that, I'll be around all day. Call me.

Matt headed off to bed.

Just as he started to succumb to the comfort of clean sheets, soft pillows and a real mattress, he thought about Stephen's emails. That last one had sounded like he was onto something. Knowing the man as Matt did, whatever Stephen had gotten himself involved with would be good, with no small amount of danger and intrigue ~ if not in reality, then certainly by the time Stephen finished telling the tale.

CHAPTER TWO

THE NEXT MORNING Matt got his Jeep and drove down to *The Chronicle* Building. Parking in the basement garage, he took the elevator up to the lobby where the first thing he saw was Ana Lopez. Her face lit up the moment she saw him.

"Hola, Matt. ¿Como estas?" she said, walking up to him quickly.

In Miami, where even strangers were greeted with a kiss on the cheek, Matt also received an embrace lasting long enough to communicate a familiar undercurrent of attraction.

"Very good, Ana," Matt replied. "And you?"

"Excellent now," she said looking into his eyes. Subtlety was an art wasted on Ana. Flirtation and sexual innuendo, on the other hand, she had long since mastered.

Ana had been one of four in a secretarial pool meant to service the over-eager young journalists working for *The Chronicle,* one of them being Matt. She had since moved up the career ladder exponentially. Now, she was the executive assistant to Dave Kagan, the editor-in-chief and Matt's boss.

The job change definitely agreed with her. She was wearing a red dress that hugged her full figure in all the right places. She moved easily in shoes that most women would consider impossible for walking. Her ears and fingers shimmered with gold jewelry, glistening like the thick auburn hair hanging long and straight to the middle of her back. Her dark eyes were heavily lined and her lips were moist with freshly applied lipstick.

"Ay, Matt, I'm so glad you're back," she continued. "It's been so boring here without you. And I've missed my happy hour buddy."

Her bottom lip pushed out into an adorable pout. It was a look Matt had been the recipient of many times in the past, one that completely enthralled him. He sometimes sought to disappoint Ana just for the fun of seeing that sad face and then replacing it with one of sheer delight. He wasn't the only one, though, who appreciated Ana. Back in the day, Ana had most of the single guys in the office vying for her attention ~ which was exactly the way she liked it.

"I'm glad to be back," Matt replied. "And I'm definitely looking forward to one of those happy hours."

"Well, I'll put you back in the loop," she said beaming. There it was ~ the smile.

As they walked through the hallways and toward Dave Kagan's office, Matt could feel the energy bouncing off the walls of the newsroom. He had missed it. The phones ringing, computer keyboards crackling and reporters huddled together along the tight row of desks. The smell of burnt coffee from the morning and leftover Cuban food from lunch and then dinner for the journalists working late to meet the dreaded deadline. Finally, they got to Dave Kagan's corner office. Ana stood back to let Matt go in first.

"Matt," Kagan said warmly as he rose from behind his enormous antique desk. "Welcome back."

"Thanks, Dave. It's good to be here."

His boss may have put on a few pounds, his blond hair may have thinned a bit, but the time since Matt had first come to the paper ten years ago had otherwise been good to the man. He was dressed in freshly pressed khaki trousers. He wore a starched white shirt that was in sharp contrast to the deeply tanned skin visible at the neckline and where his sleeves ended. A navy sweater was tied loosely around his neck. A gold Rolex glittered on his wrist from underneath the French cuffs fastened with monogrammed cuff links.

"Sit down, Matt," Dave said as he gestured to the empty seat in front of his desk. "And, Ana, could you get us both some black coffee?"

Dave settled into the deep leather chair behind his desk. Out the picture window behind the editor, Matt could see all the way across Biscayne Bay to the Venetian Islands and almost the entire length of South Beach. On one side of Kagan's desk sat a flat-screen computer monitor hooked up to an ultra-thin laptop in a cradle. Advertising layouts covered the flat surfaces of the otherwise immaculate desk.

Dave Kagan had been the paper's editor-in-chief since before Matt had joined the staff fresh out of college. He had been a very hands-on editor, involved in every story line as it developed, and reviewing every article before it was permitted to be included in the final edition. He had been more diligent than any of the copy editors, and Matt had been the recipient of many pages bearing the red Sharpie evidence of Kagan's dissatisfaction.

"So, Matt, how are you?" Dave gestured with his chin in the general direction of Matt's shoulder.

"Fine," Matt replied, shrugging off Dave's concern. "A little sore, but the doctors tell me I'll be fine."

"That's good to hear. I was worried about you. You took a lot of unnecessary risks in Afghanistan," Kagan continued. "What the hell were you doing skipping out on the embed program? You were supposed to stay with all the other approved reporters, not run off to Fallujah and then Kandahar where you didn't have any military support. That was risky, Matt, and could have ended up much worse than it did."

"It wasn't that bad ..."

"Not only was it bad, Matt," Dave interrupted, "but it was also against *The Chronicle*'s orders. You should have stayed in the embed program instead of running around Afghanistan by yourself. You could've gotten some good stuff and we would have been able to keep you safe."

"Good stuff?" Matt snorted. "Come on, Dave, those embeds got crap. They only got what the Defense Department wanted them to get."

In 2003, the Bush Administration created the "embed program," which allowed only approved journalists to be in Iraq and Afghanistan and only if they agreed to be attached to military units. Nearly 600 reporters working for news agencies from around the world agreed to the terms and traveled alongside U.S. and coalition forces. Administration officials hailed the program for permitting access to the front lines and soldiers' daily lives. Media watchdog groups, on the other hand, criticized its often restrictive nature and publicly worried that reporters would become indoctrinated into the military culture, develop relationships with the soldiers and then deliver stories from a military point of view instead of an objective one. Some journalists -- including Matt -- believed that the program rules only enhanced the military's ability to limit the release of undesirable news and eschewed any involvement with the program.

"Listen, Matt," Kagan replied, "we were one of the first participants in the embed program. From that program, we were able to get a bird's-eye view of what was going on over there. In Iraq, we got stories and pictures of GI Joe and GI Jane on the front lines. Videos of the most sophisticated fighting machine in the world bombing and shootin' the shit out of the bad guys. In Afghanistan, we got pictures of people proudly displaying their purple fingers on Election Day. That stuff was priceless."

Matt sat up straighter in his chair. "That stuff was Pentagon propaganda. Those guys were essentially acting as the government's stenographers, starting with the reporting on the search for WMDs that didn't exist and then on to how great the war was going even as more and more military personnel and civilians were being killed."

"Maybe," Kagan interrupted with a small smile. "But our readers love that so-called 'Pentagon propaganda.' That stuff sold papers. Folks don't want to hear the doom and gloom -- negative news or reports of tragedy or failure. And we're struggling for survival here. We have to give the people what they want."

"Dave, that's bullshit," Matt protested.

His comment drew a surprised look from Ana who had just arrived with two mugs of coffee. As she set the coffee mugs down on the desk in front of Matt, she shot him a warning look before she turned and walked out the door.

Matt continued despite Ana's warning.

"The embed program lost all credibility after the truth about Jessica Lynch and Pat Tillman came out. You would have thought they would have killed the program after that. But, instead, several years later, the program is still going strong. I couldn't stomach getting involved."

Matt was referring to the extreme measures the U.S. government took, at first to win popular support for the wars in Iraq and Afghanistan and then later, when the wars weren't going so well, to avoid negative backlash. In the case of Private First Class Jessica Lynch, the military tried to capitalize on the capture and ultimate rescue of the first U.S. prisoner of war since World War II and the first woman prisoner by issuing press releases describing her heroic actions before she was ultimately captured. It was later determined ~ and confirmed by Jessica Lynch ~ that the reports were incorrect. The reports of her actions were highly inflated and attributed to the Pentagon's attempts at manipulating the media.

The Pat Tillman story was slightly different. In the aftermath of September 11th, Tillman left a successful professional football career to join the Army Rangers. He served several tours in Afghanistan before he died in the mountains of Afghanistan. When he was killed, the Army figured out relatively early on that he had died from friendly fire but reported that he had been killed by enemy fire in order to avoid having to admit to the human error and to be able to exploit the memory of a beloved celebrity.

"Well, Matt," Dave finally said as he clapped his hands. "Either way, the war in the Middle East is finally coming to an end. Military operations in Iraq have been terminated and the troops in Afghanistan will be gone by next year. Thankfully."

"I'm not so sure about that," Matt said. "There's still a lot going on in the Middle East. The U.S. government may have declared formal military operations over and may have set a timeline for troop withdrawals, but we're still going to have a presence over there -- in some form or another. And that presence is going to have some serious implications here and internationally."

"Maybe," Kagan replied. "I've certainly heard talk of that. But, folks are more focused on the economy now and on jobs. Those are the issues our readers want to hear about."

"Since when does a newspaper filter the news based on what it believes its readers want to hear?"

Matt tried to keep himself from shouting as he pressed on. "With all due respect, Dave, our job is to inform people, tell them what's really going on -- even if it's unpleasant and not necessarily what they want to hear."

"Still the idealist, I see.

"Matt, let's get serious," Dave continued. "When you were here, *The Chronicle* was a privately held local paper owned by the Walker family. About a month after you left, the Walkers threw in the towel and sold the paper to the Armstrong Media Corporation, a public company. Now, we're accountable to a board of directors and to our shareholders. John Armstrong ~ our CEO, Chairman of the Board and largest shareholder ~ expects us to consistently exceed Wall Street's earnings expectations. Armstrong calls me twice a day to remind me that in order to do that we need to cater to a much broader audience. As a result, I'm constantly commissioning these surveys that tell us what our readers are most interested in."

"Our readers must have some interest in what's going on outside of our little Banana Republic," Matt replied.

Dave smiled at the local reference to the City of Miami and its crazy politics. "Yes, they do. Right now, the average person is interested in jobs and how they make up all the money they have lost as a result of the worst market crash since the Great Depression."

An awkward silence filled the room. Matt knew he had screwed up. Once again, he had let his temper get the best of him. The conversation was headed downhill quickly and he wasn't sure how to apply the brakes, let alone turn the conversation around.

Finally, Dave took a deep breath and leaned back in his chair. "But, listen, that's not to say we're not interested in what you've got."

Matt felt like Dave was throwing him a lifeline.

Dave glanced at his watch. "Go home, email me all your drafts and story ideas, whatever you're thinking about. I'll see if maybe we can use some of your material."

Dave started to rise.

"Thanks, Dave." Matt said taking his cue and standing up. "I appreciate that."

When they got to the door, Matt hesitated before asking the question that had been weighing heavily on him. "What about Commissioner Suarez?"

A few months before he had left for Afghanistan, Matt had written a series of negative ~ but well-researched ~ articles about City of Miami Commissioner Carlos Suarez. The articles described how Suarez had violated campaign finance laws by taking contributions from convicted felons, some of whom were partners in his own real estate ventures. Suarez, himself a man with a questionable past, hadn't appreciated the embarrassing allegations and had publicly threatened to destroy Matt's career.

"It looks like he's going to return the contributions and get away with a slap on the wrist for questionable campaign finance activities. Thanks to his brother the Senator, of course." Kagan opened the door as he continued. "As you may have heard since you got back, the commissioner is running for re-election and, despite all the controversy, it looks like he'll win."

Kagan signaled to Ana who looked up from her desk.

"Don't worry, Matt," Kagan rested a firm hand on Matt's shoulder. "The commissioner likely has more important things on his plate than his vendetta against you. But I'm not going to lie to you. You're going to have to promise to keep him out of your sights. Think you can do that?"

"I don't know, Dave, he's an awfully appealing target," Matt replied honestly. "But, I really want to focus on the Middle East. So I'm sure I can play nice ... at least for a little while."

"That's the spirit, Matt," Dave said as he slapped Matt on the back and ushered him out the door. "Play nice. Life will be much easier that way."

CHAPTER THREE

JUST ANOTHER DAY in paradise, Matt thought as he headed down to Scotty's Landing to meet his old friend and neighbor Pierre Baptiste. Palm trees planted along South Bayshore Drive swayed in the gentle breeze coming off the bay. The sky was a cloudless sapphire blue. The black asphalt street gleamed from the effects of the sun. The air-conditioning was going at full blast but the sun beating down on the roof of Matt's CJ-5 Jeep Renegade created a sauna effect.

Matt arrived at Scotty's Landing just before 1 o'clock. He parked, went in to sit at the bar and ordered a beer. Despite the heat, the marina deck and restaurant were packed. The locals were accustomed to the weather, and the tourists were not to be deterred in their pursuit of fun in the sun. The bayside restaurant was situated in the middle of a busy marina filled with boats, but had a casual laid-back atmosphere and serene setting. Every seat in the place enjoyed a view of Biscayne Bay where manatees floated by and occasionally pushed their snouts up to the surface for some air. Women in bikinis strutted their stuff between the various boats, the marina and the restaurant.

"Hey, stranger."

Matt felt a heavy paw land on his right shoulder and turned to see Pierre grinning widely even as he sweated from the heat and the extra eighty pounds he carried. The man was clearly losing his ongoing battle with vaca frita and black beans and rice but that didn't seem to affect his disposition at all.

Matt rose and allowed himself to be enveloped into a bear hug. Pain shot through Matt's left shoulder and he gritted his teeth.

"Hey, buddy. How you doin'?" Matt said clapping Pierre on the back while at the same time trying to steer his face clear of the dark crescents in the armpits of his old friend's shirt.

"I'm hot as a pig on a spit. That's how I am," Pierre said, finally letting Matt go. The bigger man ran his forearm across his glistening brow. When his round face emerged, he was still smiling. His coal-black face, dark eyes and bald head were a welcome sight for Matt's tired eyes.

"Have a seat, my brother!" Matt said gesturing to the stool beside him. "You look like a man in desperate need of some refreshment." He waved to the young girl behind the bar.

"Janie, a Bud Light for my friend here and another for me, please."

Pierre and Matt proceeded to engage in the male version of conversation, covering all the important points such as frustrating sports team performance and attractive women, peppered with brutal assaults on each other's masculinity.

"So, how was it over there?" Pierre finally asked.

"Intense. Really intense," Matt replied. "You wouldn't believe the shit those people have been through ~ still go through every day."

"Are you gonna tell me about it or should I just wait to read about it in *The Chronicle*?"

"I met with my boss yesterday, but he didn't seem real receptive to my material. Seems the news business has changed a little since I've been gone. They think more 'happy news' is going to help them increase their circulation and me going in to the nitty-gritty about what's going on in Afghanistan these days doesn't fall within that category." Matt paused. "I'm not sure they're going to run my stuff."

"I'm sure you'll work it out," Pierre replied. "*The Chronicle* is lucky to have you ~ and your material."

"I appreciate that, but I gotta tell you, Pierre. They didn't seem real eager to have me back."

"You think that may have something to do with your exposé on Commissioner Suarez?"

"I don't think so. They're trying to convince me that people around here aren't interested in what's going on in the Middle East."

"Well, the military does seem to finally have things under control."

Matt scoffed. "Yeah, I wish, Pierre." Matt took a drink. "Based on my experiences, the situation is worse than ever. I saw Americans and Afghan noncombatants get blown to bits ~ in broad daylight no less. I also saw a lot of new construction over there ~ military bases ~ and that seemed to be a pretty strong indicator that the U.S. presence there is going to be significant and permanent. Don't you think people want to know about that?"

"I don't know. Probably not. I don't," Pierre admitted. "People are tired of hearing about the war and the money that's being spent over there. I know I am. I read about the big bags of cash that the CIA was dropping off at President Karzai's office and it just made me sick. Sick to my stomach thinking about how that money could be used over here." Pierre shook his head. "And while the U.S. government is handing over that kind of cash, I have to worry about how I'm going take care of my parents as they get on or what happens if I get sick since I don't have health insurance."

An uncomfortable silence fell between the two old friends. Matt was surprised to hear the big man's confession, although he shouldn't have been. Pierre's parents were Haitian and had come to the United States back in the 1970s through the Dominican Republic. With only limited education, his parents had raised four children in the United States. Pierre was the oldest and ran a successful landscaping business from which he supported himself and a few other guys. Business had always seemed to be good, but Matt imagined that he struggled with making enough to provide for himself and still help out his parents who lived nearby. Both men stared out into the Bay as they sipped their drinks.

"So have you called Dana to let her know you're back in town?" Pierre asked.

"Nah, man." Matt said shaking his head firmly. "You know we left it on bad terms. She was pretty upset I was going."

"Well, I think she might have recovered from her grief."

"What are you talking about?" Matt said turning in his bar stool to look at Pierre directly. "Have you seen her?"

Pierre nodded. "I was at Monty's about a month ago. You remember that place?"

Matt nodded yes.

"It was late in the afternoon and she came by boat." Pierre turned toward Matt and smiled. "Get this. It was a Cigarette Tiger Twin Step called 'Dr. Feel Good'." Both men grimaced. "The guy at the wheel must have been about fifteen years older than Dana and looked it. But Dana," Pierre shook his head slowly from side to side. "Mmm, mmm, mmm. That girl sure looked fine."

Pierre paused and looked off into the distance.

"And ..." Matt finally prodded when it seemed like Pierre had gotten lost in his thoughts.

"I spoke with her briefly," Pierre continued quickly. "She asked about you." Pierre shot Matt a meaningful look. "You should give her a call."

"Bad idea, my friend. You know I really didn't have a chance with her. She was just slummin' it with me until someone better came along. It looks like she found her man. And a doctor no less. I bet her mama sure is proud."

As Matt drove home from his afternoon with Pierre his thoughts drifted to his ex-girlfriend Dana Fried. She worked for the agency formerly known as the Immigration and Naturalization Service, or INS, until after September 11th when it had been absorbed by the U.S. Department of Homeland Security. She was a lawyer specializing in immigration issues in several key regions including the Caribbean. They met when Matt was researching a story on the U.S. policy on Haitian immigrants compared to the policy on Cuban immigrants. Dana had been recommended by a friend as someone he could talk to and who could help provide some background for his story.

Dana and Matt hit it off immediately and began dating just after his article was published. Their relationship was fun and passionate and, Matt had to admit, the closest thing to a real relationship he'd ever had.

After they had been dating for several months, Dana started talking to Matt about his career. It started as questions about how his day went and he couldn't help but be flattered she was interested in what he did. But Dana quickly moved from asking general questions about his job to offering specific career advice and then to pushing him in directions designed to advance his career down a sensible path. A path that required daily shaving, networking at various events and a new set of friends.

He soon found himself being directed down a road he did not want to travel. She didn't take it very well when Matt started ignoring her guidance and any discussions about his "professional progression" as she liked to call it.

Matt began to realize just how driven Dana was, professionally and socially. She already had the successful career, having established herself as an expert on U.S. immigration policies. She was at a point in her life when she wanted to establish herself in the center of the Miami social scene, a place her parents had long occupied. She served on several strategically chosen charity boards. She got invited to all the right events and attended most of them, mingling easily with the Miami elite. She had enough ambition for the two of them plus half the slackers in Matt's own social circle.

Matt was being dragged to those networking events and fundraisers that made it to the top of Dana's pile of invitations. Once there, he was awkwardly rubbing elbows with Miami politicos, international businessmen and professional athletes. At first, it was pretty exciting stuff, but Dana approached these events as she did her career ~ with a singular focus on cultivating the relationships that would enable her to be accepted as a member of the group of professionals known as much for their connections as for anything they may have accomplished.

His aspirations were a lot less grand ~ a hot wife, a couple of kids and an interesting job that enabled him to travel occasionally to exotic locations to report on the latest political scandal or civilian uprising. Sure, he wanted to make enough money to support his family, maybe even enough to own a boat and a house in the Keys. That was about the extent of his dreams. Aside from the occasional Art Deco pub crawl on South Beach or some random international street festival, he had little interest in the Miami social scene.

His decision to leave for Afghanistan just when the problems between Dana and him were coming to a head didn't help matters. Dana saw Matt's decision to run off to the Middle East, without the support of an embedded team of other reporters and heavy army escort ~ and knowing his views on the situation and guessing the nature of the stories he would be writing ~ as a very career-limiting move. She had always accused him of being politically tone-deaf. In a moment of clarity, just days before he left, he realized that while she meant this as an insult, he did not consider her accusation a slur upon his character. He thought the opposite was true. Being politically tone-deaf was a condition he cultivated. It was, he believed, what made him a hell of a good investigative reporter.

One evening as they were getting ready to attend yet another fancy charity event, she gave him the ultimatum most men were faced with sooner or later. Fish or cut bait. Get engaged or it was over. Matt immediately identified the bait and the sharpened hook from which it was dangled. He didn't go for the lure. Instead, he used his impressive communication skills learned from years of interviewing reticent witnesses ~ and the avoidance techniques learned from years of bachelorhood ~ to manage the situation.

He paused and took her slender, well-manicured hand into his own. He glanced at her mouth, set with determination. He looked into her brown eyes, fierce with resolve. He held her stare for several seconds before bringing her hand to his lips and kissing it tenderly. He then turned her hand over, pointed to the diamond encrusted Rolex her parents had given her for her 21st birthday and finally spoke.

"The gala started ten minutes ago. We should get going."

Dana shot him a withering glance, pulled her hand away and then surprised him with a powerful punch to the shoulder before storming out of the room.

The temperature in the car on the way over was below zero on the emotional interaction gauge. By the time they arrived at the charity event, Dana still hadn't spoken. As they walked through the door, Dana fixed the first smile of the evening on her face, made her way through the crowded room and toward the table her parents were sharing with a prominent local attorney and his wife. The wife was a regular in Miami social circles and the current star of the latest *Housewives of Miami* series. Matt took one look at the table and then around the room and quickly determined he was in dire need of some anesthetic. He made a beeline for the bar.

Several single malt Macallans later, he was still standing at the bar when Miami Commissioner Carlos Suarez showed up, accompanied by a woman Matt quickly identified as the flavor of the month. Matt watched the very married commissioner weave his way through the crowd shaking hands, slapping shoulders and kissing the cheeks of the beautiful and powerful people. Matt scowled as he watched others around him practically genuflect to the commissioner as he moved through the room. His companion followed at a discreet distance.

The week before, Matt had done a series of articles about the former bad boy turned local politician. He described the commissioner's associations with convicted felons, some of whom were partners in his current business ventures. He detailed the charges recently brought against commissioner Suarez for violation of campaign finance laws for receiving contributions from criminal elements. In his articles, Matt argued for the need to hold public officials if not to a higher standard, then certainly to the same standard expected of city workers.

Yet, Commissioner Suarez now made his way through the crowd with the confidence of a man who felt no such compunction. He was unwittingly headed straight for Matt, a journalist the commissioner had once suggested should commit a sex act upon himself. This was proposed in the most unseemly of terms and while the seasoned politician was unknowingly being recorded by a major network. For those who missed the seven o'clock, ten o'clock and even eleven o'clock news, Matt proudly recounted all the details of the encounter in an article that appeared the next morning in *The Chronicle*.

The commissioner arrived at the bar and nodded to the bartender, who proceeded to prepare the commissioner's regular drink. Suarez caught sight of Matt for the first time and stopped, the smile frozen on his face. The two adversaries stared at each other for several seconds, neither saying a word, neither moving. Matt finally smiled slightly. The right corner of the commissioner's mouth twitched. The crowd around them, aware of the significance of this chance encounter, grew quiet. The woman accompanying the commissioner bestowed a wide smile upon the bartender and Matt as she caught up with her date.

"Matt," the commissioner said as he took the drink proffered by the bartender.

"Commissioner Suarez," Matt replied, nodding politely before turning to introduce himself to the politician's companion. He filed her name away for research later.

The commissioner ordered a drink for "the lady" before turning to greet the couple standing behind Matt. The bartender scrambled to find a white zinfandel while the commissioner schmoozed with the president of a regional construction company, the recipient of the largest government contract in Miami-Dade County history, which was recently jammed through the system by none other than Commissioner Suarez.

Several moments passed when Matt didn't say a word. But soon the temptation became overwhelming. Dana was nowhere in sight, and Macallan was doing the thinking. As the commissioner reached for his companion's wine and turned around to pass it to her, Matt called to him.

"Excuse me, Commissioner Suarez." His voice sounded loud, even to himself.

Some people around the bar turned to look at him; others averted their eyes even as they stayed conspicuously within earshot.

Matt lowered his voice but continued. "Is it true that your office spent $28,000 at the Organ Grinder in South

Miami and, in particular, on a professional dancer by the name of Kiki Calle Ocho?"

Matt could see the horrified looks on the faces of those in the crowd. The onlookers alternated between shooting glances at Matt to stealing looks at Suarez. The commissioner's date was smiling, basking in the attention and the glow of the warm bodies pressed around them, oblivious to the fact that this might not be the type of attention that one should crave.

Suarez turned slowly toward Matt as he continued.

"I spoke with Ms. Calle Ocho. She says she's a close personal friend of yours."

The smile became a grimace as the right corner of Commissioner Suarez's mouth began to jerk. The right eye joined in and there was a veritable concert of uncontrolled activity taking over the man's face. Matt offered his nemesis his most engaging smile and took another sip from his own glass. Matt briefly looked away as he returned his glass to the napkin on the bar and reached for a small notepad in his suit jacket pocket.

Matt turned back toward Commissioner Suarez just in time to see the man throw his head and glass back, inhaling the liquid. He flung his glass to the ground and he lunged at Matt, slamming him against the back of the bar.

Matt stumbled and then pushed back. The two men fell into the crowd. A woman screamed, and the onlookers in the crowd scrambled away. The men crashed to the floor. Suarez punched and kicked from underneath, as Matt tried to deflect the blows while at the same time pushing himself up and off the other man. Matt was suddenly struck in the back of the head by a blunt object.

Everything after that was a bit of a blur. Matt was jerked up to his feet, escorted to an exit by two very large men and was unceremoniously thrown out of the building. Out on the sidewalk, Matt inspected the damage done to his rented tuxedo. One torn pants pocket. Missing bow tie. His head throbbed and he felt an egg rising on the back of his head but he supposed it could have been worse.

He looked around, not surprised to see that Commissioner Suarez wasn't standing on the street with him. He thought briefly about going back inside but quickly acknowledged that none of the socialites inside, including his date, would be missing him.

The next day *The Chronicle* published Matt's story reporting on the events that had transpired the night before. The day after that, though, after receiving several phone calls from Senator Suarez, the commissioner's older brother and a powerful statesman, the paper put Matt on temporary leave. Management was impressed with his gutsy recklessness, or so they said behind closed doors. But the paper was the subject of intense pressure from several local politicians and many loyal constituents of Commissioner Suarez who all suggested that Matt was harassing a prominent politician who was being unfairly persecuted by the federal judicial system, a system that was clearly biased against Hispanics.

Matt didn't know when things would die down. For some time he had been thinking about traveling to the Middle East. Right now was looking like a really good time.

He wasn't sure how long it would be before some politician or star athlete found himself embroiled in a very public scandal and for Matt's rather public "interview" of the commissioner to be forgotten. Matt started to make the arrangements.

He tried to speak with Dana before he left. He left messages on her voice mail. He sent emails. He had flowers delivered to her office. He harassed the doormen of her apartment building, who had apparently been instructed not to let him up the elevator. He sheepishly dropped by her work where he was met with an icy stare from the receptionist. Dana wouldn't see him or take his calls.

Finally, the time came for him to leave and he did without having made amends. He hated to admit it now – but from her perspective Dana had a right to be pissed off. His altercation with Suarez and his decision to go to Afghanistan may have been yet another in a series of career-limiting moves.

CHAPTER FOUR

MATT WOKE TO THE FEELING of someone pushing heavily against his chest. He tried to catch his breath, but the weight kept pressing him down. He tried to reach up, but his arms were pinned. He struggled to free his arms, his efforts more frantic as the pressure became more suffocating. The vise grip of the restraints seemed to tighten, squeezing the last drop of air out of him. But then, suddenly, he was free. He shot up to a sitting position, his heart pounding as though it were trying to break out of his chest.

He scanned the room for his attacker as his eyes slowly adjusted to the dark. The moonlight streaming in from the window behind him bounced off the walls. Familiar walls. Matt recognized the worn wood table in the corner and the threadbare rug covering the floor.

Home.

His sheets, tangled and soaked with sweat, lay in a heap on the floor beside his bed. The house was quiet except for his ragged breathing. He swung his feet onto the floor and slowly rose. Walking around the house, touching familiar objects, he tried to shake his mind free of the enormous weight that had been crushing his body.

Matt returned to bed and lay back down. His mind began grabbing for threads of the nightmare still lingering in his subconscious. Perhaps trying to remember the specifics would be helpful. At least that's what all the psychobabble he had seen on television suggested.

Funny how he couldn't remember Dana's birthday or where they shared their first kiss, but he could still recall every detail, the sounds and even the smells of those last days in Kandahar up to the moments just before the explosion that changed his life. Sometimes he woke to the memories of the screams that brought him back to consciousness. Other times his dreams were filled with the details of his escape from his captors.

When Matt regained consciousness after the bombing, he was alone in a dimly lit room. His body ached all over. When he drew a deep breath, he felt what seemed like the jagged edges of his ribs scraping across his lungs. He slowly sat upright, his body screaming from the effort. The room spun around him. He gingerly swung his legs over the side of the bed and pushed himself up off the bed. For several seconds he stood there, swaying unsteadily on his feet. His head throbbed, and he reached up to find the source. His hair was greasy but also matted and stiff in places. Drawing his hand back, he saw flakes of dried blood on his fingertips. Like a blind man, he took inventory of his own face and didn't like what he felt.

A single light bulb hung from the ceiling. He tapped it, and the globe swung slowly in an arc. The weak light provided a glimpse of his surroundings. He took a slow turn around. It was a small room, containing nothing but a steel-framed bed with a stained mattress, a threadbare blanket and a wooden chair. The only window in the room was boarded up. Slivers of light came through the spaces between the boards covering the window. He tapped the bulb again. He noticed a crimson stain on the wall behind the bed, and a chill ran through him.

He walked toward the door, turned the knob and pushed. Nothing. The door was bolted from the outside. He banged on the door, shouting for someone to let him out. He heard voices on the other side, but no one came. He strained to make out what was being said. There were no discernible words but he caught the unmistakable sound of Arabic.

Matt found out later that the coalition forces had been using unmanned aerial vehicles equipped with infrared cameras to monitor the neighborhood. They had identified some people in the area as potential insurgents and believed the house in the neighborhood where he was staying hid a huge cache of weapons. The building was located in a "no-go zone," an area the military considered too dangerous to send in troops. So they sent in Predator drones equipped with AGM-114 Hellfire missiles.

The attack had lasted only a few moments. But when it was over, the house and two neighboring buildings had been destroyed. He had been knocked unconscious, but the lives of many Afghan civilians ~ men, women and children ~ had been tragically cut short. Later he found out that they did find weapons parts in the basement of the empty warehouse next door. It turned out to be an abandoned munitions factory that hadn't been used since the Russians had fled Afghanistan in 1989. There weren't enough antiquated parts to create one full weapon of any significance, but those facts never made it in the press. Weapons were declared to have been destroyed, and with only Afghan casualties, the mission was considered a success.

That would have been difficult to explain to the families of the people who had perished in the attack. Eleven people had died ~ blown to bits or crushed under the weight of the collapsed walls. Several others were pulled from the rubble barely alive. Had the bombing happened ten minutes earlier or ten minutes later, Matt would have been counted among the dead.

Shortly after the attack, Matt, partly covered by rubble, unconscious and bleeding, had been spotted by Taliban patrolling the area to assess the damage. They were furious about the deaths of so many of their own people and the fact that Matt was still alive. They dragged him into the street, kicking and pummeling his body in front of the crowd that had gathered. The onlookers cheered his attackers and shouted for his death. Matt only vaguely recalled this, but the markings on his body and the aching in his bones confirmed the story.

Ultimately, the Taliban leader of the patrol realized Matt was of greater value alive than dead and the public assault was abruptly terminated. They dumped him into a car and took him to one of their houses in another part of town. Matt was thrown into a room, and a local doctor was sent for to check on his condition and tend to his wounds.

Matt recognized the doctor. His name was Aamir. Matt had previously met him as the doctor made regular rounds to the various clinics in the area, administering to the sick and injured. He and Matt renewed their acquaintance and, over a period of time, became friends. Aamir came to visit him every day, long after his wounds warranted such attention.

Aamir was a middle-class Afghani who had been educated in the United States at Tufts University School of Medicine. After interning at Mount Auburn Hospital in Cambridge, he became a resident at Boston's Mass General Hospital and then joined the staff as a surgeon in the trauma unit. He married Sofia, an Afghan woman who had also been educated in the United States, and they started a life together there. When the rebuilding in Afghanistan began, Aamir and his wife thought they could help in the efforts by returning to their homeland. Aamir explained to Matt that since he had been back, he had been able to accomplish much, using his connections and foreign aid to build clinics in some of the rural areas. The clinics were equipped with only a bare minimum of equipment and supplies, but the staff was still able to care for the sick, most of whom traveled many days and over many miles to see him.

Originally, Sofia shared her husband's enthusiasm and was optimistic about the family's future in their homeland, but the redevelopment had been far slower than they had anticipated. The multibillion-dollar opium trade had begun to flourish again, and the violence among the Taliban and the regional warlords overshadowed Afghanistan's attempts at democracy and threatened the lives of Aamir and Sofia and the future of their two small children. They both yearned for a better life for their children and wanted to return to the U.S. But it was not that simple. They were not U.S. citizens, and the U.S. was making it difficult for them to immigrate legally.

One night a couple of weeks after the bombing, Aamir arrived at his usual time in a state of extreme agitation. While inspecting Matt's wounds, he whispered that coalition forces were closing in on the Taliban group holding Matt. The fighters knew and were preparing to pull out. They were planning to retreat to a smaller village farther south where they still maintained a stronghold. Some of the guards wanted to execute Matt and leave his body in a conspicuous place as a warning to other Americans who dared to trespass upon their holy lands. A minority was in favor of taking Matt with them as a hostage. Either way, the outlook was not good.

Aamir had a plan to bring Matt to safety, a plan that might even allow Aamir and his family a chance to start over. Matt remembered that last night clearly. They huddled together in that dank room and talked quietly into the night about what they needed to do. Together, they formulated a scheme to escape. It was risky, but they had few options. The nightmares that plagued Matt tonight, the nightmares that he would probably endure for the rest of his life, were about the day Aamir and Matt executed that plan.

Later that morning, Matt's front doorbell rang. The two men standing in his doorway eclipsed the sun behind them and momentarily gave Matt the uneasy feeling that he was trapped in his own home. They were dressed identically in dress slacks, pressed white shirts and navy blazers. Both had neat short hair, cropped closely on the sides. Dark sunglasses hid their eyes. With their rigid postures and lips pressed firmly together, it was clear they were not here for a social call.

The younger man spoke first.

"Good morning. Are you Matt Connelly?"

"Yes. What can I do for you?"

"My name is Cole Harrison. My partner Jack Rabin and I work with the Department of Homeland Security. We need a few minutes of your time."

"What's this all about?" Matt asked still blocking entrance into the house.

"We know that you just returned from traveling in Iraq and Afghanistan and need to speak with you. May we come in?"

"I don't know," Matt said haltingly. "I've never heard of such a thing."

"Matt, we keep track of Americans who have traveled to high alert areas and interview them upon their return. These exit interviews, which are now standard operating procedure, are designed to gather information that may be helpful in the war on terror."

"It would be better if we did this inside, Matt," the older man said. "And we only need a few minutes."

"All right," Matt reluctantly agreed. "Fifteen minutes. That's all I've got."

Matt hadn't wanted to be difficult, but he worried that the exit interview was not really standard procedure but instead had something to do with his being considered persona non grata with the coalition forces and the U.S. military by the time he was finally permitted to leave the country. It was possible that these guys were merely here to harass Matt for what had happened in Afghanistan. Matt tried to shake the feeling of dread as he stood aside and the two men filed past him, each stopping to formally shake his hand.

He gestured to the couch and suggested they make themselves comfortable. A few moments later, Matt returned from the kitchen with two glasses of water. Harrison was sitting on the edge of the chair situated to the right of the sofa. The other man, Jack Rabin, was leaning against the low entertainment center positioned directly across from the couch. Both men still had their jackets on, but they were now unbuttoned, revealing the guns in their holsters. They faced the sofa and Matt took a seat there, shifting uncomfortably.

Rabin began the interview with small talk. Matt listened politely and responded in kind as he mentally evaluated the two men. Harrison removed a pen and notepad from his shirt pocket. He flipped the pad open and, with the pen poised, alternated between looking at his partner and Matt. Harrison was in his early thirties, tall and very well built. He had blond hair, blue eyes and a chin that seemed to be cut from the mold of a Terminator action figure.

Despite Matt's fifteen-minute deadline, Harrison's partner didn't seem to be in any hurry to get the interview started. Rabin was settled on the edge of the entertainment center, his arms loosely crossed and his extended legs hooked at the ankles. The older of the two, he was also well built but leaner and taller. Even leaning back against the entertainment center, he seemed to tower over the two men in the small living room. He had a scar above his right eye and another one on his chin. He talked about his recent relocation to South Florida, his first hurricane season in South Florida and the Miami Dolphins season Matt had missed while he was gone. Matt found himself falling into the familiar rhythm of exchanging anecdotes with a new acquaintance even as his experience told him he was being lulled into a false sense of security.

Matt glanced over at Harrison. The man's eyes bore into his partner, as if willing him to make eye contact. His pen now tapped what seemed like an urgent Morse code message against the pad. The intensity made Matt anxious to get to the point as well.

When Rabin paused for a moment, Matt took that as his opportunity.

"So I thought the Department of Homeland Security was out there confiscating water bottles, women's beauty products and other dangerous stuff that could potentially take down a Boeing 757. What are you doing here interviewing me?"

"Well, certainly, Matt, securing our borders and ensuring our planes are safe for travel are part of the job. As we speak, there are teams out there doing just that. But Agent Harrison and I are responsible for gathering information that will enable us to stop terrorist activity before it gets here to American soil."

"Good to know. I feel safer already."

Neither man laughed.

"So, should I be asking to see some type of warrant? Should I have an attorney present?"

"We don't have a warrant, Matt," Rabin responded with a small shrug. "This meeting is completely voluntary. As to whether or not you should have an attorney, well, I guess that depends on whether you think you've done something wrong or have something to hide. Assuming you don't, we'd just like to ask you a few questions. Then we'll be on our way."

"I've got nothing to hide," Matt replied after a moment. "So why don't you guys just go ahead and ask your questions."

"Okay, then," Rabin said before nodding to Harrison.

The interview started out pretty mildly with Harrison inquiring about the dates Matt was in Iraq and Afghanistan, where he stayed and traveled and the names of other journalists with whom he'd come into contact while he was there. Rabin asked several general questions about the stories Matt had written and the research he had conducted. They seemed to be already familiar with the articles he had written, and Matt wasn't sure whether he should be flattered or alarmed that they had obviously spent some time researching him.

"So, other than the journalists and U.S. military personnel, who did you interview over there?" Harrison asked.

"I spoke with lots of the locals."

"Any tribal leaders? Or leaders within the rebel forces?"

Matt's body tensed and he didn't immediately respond. "Yes," he finally replied. "I spoke with leaders in the community and some military personnel."

"Taliban or al-Qaeda?"

Matt could feel Rabin watching him intently as he replied to Harrison's questions. "Both, but nobody high up."

"We'll need a list of all the people you spoke with."

"Not a chance," Matt snapped back without a pause.

There was silence from both men.

"Really," Harrison finally said, the word dragging out slowly. "And why is that?"

Matt waited a moment before answering. He had to control the anger rising within him.

"Journalism 101, gentlemen. If a journalist discloses his sources, nobody will ever talk to him again. Also, telling their names might get those folks in trouble. And they don't have any information that would be helpful to you guys."

"It's better if we judge what could be helpful and what's not," Rabin interrupted smoothly before Harrison could respond.

"Well, you're going to have to trust me on this because I'm not disclosing any names."

"You should worry more about protecting your own people, Matt," Harrison spat out. "The animals you're trying to protect aren't U.S. citizens. They're cold-blooded killers."

Matt shook his head. "No, Agent Harrison, they're not. They're people just trying to survive in a country that's being torn apart."

"Maybe you should explain that to the families of the soldiers that died over there," Harrison angrily continued. "They probably wouldn't see it quite that way."

Matt paused and considered his response carefully.

"I don't have any names that could be helpful to you guys," Matt finally replied. "And if word got out that I was providing those details, it would ruin my ability to get people to confide in me. I can't do my job if people don't trust me."

"How well would you be able to do your job if we made sure that every law enforcement officer in the State of Florida knew you weren't cooperating with us?" Harrison snapped. "Think people would trust you then?"

Matt felt his temper begin to rise up again, and again he attempted to quell it. With a few well-placed telephone calls, these guys could make sure no government official ever spoke to him again. They could make travel difficult for him. They could tie him up in red tape for years. In terms of his professional career, Matt was already on his seventh or eighth life. Making enemies with powerful men ~ with these men ~ could be a career-ending move.

"Listen, I appreciate what you guys do," Matt finally responded. "I really do. Believe me, if I had information that was important, I would tell you. But I simply don't know anything, or anyone, that would be helpful."

Harrison leaned toward Matt. He opened his mouth as if to say something, but before he could Rabin stopped him with a quick glance.

"Well, if you don't mind, Matt, we'll keep in touch," Rabin said. "You may think of something later. Something that might be important."

Rabin stood and nodded to Harrison. The younger man took his cue and stood up. At the door, Rabin handed over his card and asked Matt to contact him if he thought of something that might be helpful. Harrison didn't offer his hand or a card. He simply glowered at Matt from the front porch.

Just as Matt started to shut the door, Rabin turned back toward him. "Hey, Matt, one other thing. Whatever happened to that journalist that worked with you at *The Chronicle* years ago? I think he was also over in the Middle East at the same time you were."

When Matt didn't immediately respond, Rabin continued, "I can't remember his name, now, but you must know who I'm talking about. He went on to go write for some big paper in New York City."

"Stephen Cross?" Matt asked.

Rabin snapped his fingers. "Yeah, that's him. I sure liked his stuff. Where is he now?"

"As far as I know, he's back in New York," Matt replied.

"I'll have to check out the papers up there. I always enjoyed his articles."

Rabin turned and headed down the sidewalk toward his car, with Harrison following behind.

CHAPTER FIVE

"I'VE READ YOUR STUFF, Matt," Stuart Bellows began after introducing himself over the phone. "You're a very talented writer."

"Thanks, Stuart. I appreciate that," Matt said as he walked around the room with his phone pressed against his ear.

Matt recalled the gnome-like image of Bellows from *The Chronicle*, a guy in his mid-forties with a receding hairline and an extra fifty pounds that made him appear years older. The remaining hair he had was fair, his complexion ruddy and his stature portly.

"But you know, Matt. We get most of our material on the situation in the Middle East through our national office now. The embeds that were stationed in the Middle East at the beginning developed excellent relationships both with the troops on the ground running the military operations and now with the folks managing the security and rebuilding efforts. To the extent we still report on the activities going on over there, we use those guys. They've got the best information."

Matt's shoulders sagged and his pace around the room slowed.

Most people were surprised when Stuart Bellows was hired to turn around the advertising department of *The Chronicle*. He had never attained a four-year degree, despite attending several colleges over a period of time that would have made envious many callow fraternity guys not eager to enter the world of work and responsibility. After finally leaving college, he bounced around for several years, never holding a position for very long. He ultimately found success as a consultant, advising companies on how they could increase revenues through better marketing.

By all accounts he had been successful, but he wasn't without his professional detractors. His tactics were described by some former colleagues as Machiavellian at best, by others as completely unprofessional and by some as downright illegal. The staff at every organization where he had ever worked hated him. But the board of directors and shareholders loved him and the results he was able to achieve. With this in mind, the powers that be at *The Chronicle* determined that Bellows was more than qualified to run the most important division of the paper ~ the advertising division.

Matt wasn't quite sure why Bellows was now involved in the process of deciding which articles would be published, but at this point Matt didn't care. He wanted to get published, needed to get published, and if he had to go through Stuart Bellows to do it, then he would. Given the proper motivation, Matt could charm the beast as well as the next guy.

"But you have some great material," Stuart continued. The man seemed to enjoy the roller coaster ride he was putting Matt on. "I particularly like the piece on the Afghan people now, years after their liberation."

That article was the result of weeks spent interviewing the members of four families in Afghanistan. They had shared with Matt their personal experiences starting with Operation Enduring Freedom after September 11th, to the U.S. bombing of Afghanistan, the formation of the new government and finally ending with their thoughts on the rebuilding efforts. The adults in the families had heard about the billions of dollars that had been poured into the country but had seen little change in their own communities. Afghanistan still remained one of the poorest countries in the world. This was attributable, in part, to corruption among high-level politicians and the Taliban insurgency backed by Pakistan. The stories also described their resignation to a life of constant fighting and continued domination, either by the Taliban, the United States or the drug lords controlling the once-again robust poppy trade.

"The human interest story," Matt replied. "Great."

He picked a tennis ball up off the desk and began squeezing it as he settled into the chair in front of his desk.

"Yeah. I'd like to use that piece. I've tweaked it. You know, made it more timely, added some insight that we've gotten from our other sources."

"Hmmm. I see." Matt tossed the ball to the floor near the wall. It bounced on the floor, against the wall and then back toward him. He caught the ball easily.

"I'll email the article back to you," Stuart continued. "You can check out the changes and, assuming you're okay with them, I'll run the story on Sunday."

Matt tossed the ball again. "I'll have a look at your changes and let you know, but that sounds fine."

Another toss, another catch.

"Sounds good, Matt. Let me know as soon as possible."

"What about the one on the Predator drone strikes?" Matt asked. "Or the piece on the reconstruction efforts?"

"The drone article is good, Matt. Damn good. But we think it's probably better that we don't get out in front of that issue."

"Why not?" Matt asked sitting up.

"Well, the program has been highly successful..."

"You mean highly lethal," Matt interrupted.

The CIA had been flying unarmed drones over Afghanistan since 2000. CIA desk jockeys, working from an office in Northern Virginia, operated the joysticks that controlled the little aircraft. From their desks they were able to identify, track and conduct surveillance on terrorist suspects in the Middle East. Then, with a push of a button, they would launch a missile and watch as an explosion filled the screen and the target was eliminated. These covert operations had become an integral part of the U.S counterterrorism strategy. The authority given to those running the operation was the most sweeping since the founding of the CIA. Matt knew only too well the lethalness of these weapons as well as the potential for human error, resulting in the deaths of men, women and children who were not the primary target. They called it "collateral damage."

"I hear you, Matt. But the drone program is probably the most important component in the fight against terrorism today. The administration is going to be highly defensive of any negative comments we make."

Matt sighed. "And the other article?"

The other article was on the reconstruction efforts in Afghanistan or, more accurately, the lack thereof. Everywhere one looked in Afghanistan, construction projects were mired in incompetence, chaos and corruption. Projects were frequently abandoned when they were only a fraction complete. Billions of dollars had been paid to top-level Afghan leaders, including President Karzai, with no apparent results. The Afghan government was as inept as they were corrupt, but they weren't the only one in this game. Billions more had been paid to U.S. government contractors - many of whom had previously been suspended or debarred for misusing taxpayer funds and in some cases convicted of criminal fraud. They too had either dropped the ball on the work they were supposed to do or simply absconded with the money.

"We don't feel the reconstruction article is timely," Bellows responded. "Folks know how challenging the rebuilding efforts have been. We've reported on that ad nauseam and we don't think it would be of interest to our readers."

Matt couldn't imagine what could be more interesting than the billions lost in the Middle East. The federal deficit and the most recent election outcomes had resulted, in large part, from the money the U.S. government was paying into those operations. Politicians were currently debating which class ~ the rich or middle income ~ should absorb the cost of the massive deficit resulting in large part from government incompetence. In a rare moment for Matt, he kept his mouth shut for fear of antagonizing the man ~ and he needed his job.

The pregnant pause was apparently not lost on Stuart. "Matt, don't take this badly," the man finally said. "You're a talented writer."

Matt didn't respond. He lobbed the ball against the floor again. A half-hearted pitch. It went wild, but Matt caught it.

"Matt, you did a great job covering local politics when you were on staff before. Politics are still crazy here and no one can navigate those shark-infested waters better than you. Many of the players and the issues are still the same. If it's possible, we'd love to get you back to covering your old beat."

"I'd like to get back to reporting, Stuart. But I just got back from Afghanistan with some very important feature news. I'd like to write about that, and I even have some material that's timely and ready to go."

"Right, right, of course. I understand, but we can't do that right away. We need to bring you back slowly. See how the public responds to your return."

"You mean see how Commissioner Suarez responds."

"Well, yes, him too," Stuart conceded. "We'd like to start with this human interest article. Test the waters, if you will. And then we'll go from there."

It wasn't quite what Matt had wanted but it was a start.

After the men hung up, Matt checked Bellows' email message and began to read the revised version of the article that Stuart had sent him. *Tweaked it? The guy butchered it!* Matt had begun the article by describing the subjugation to which the Afghans had found themselves under the Taliban and al-Qaeda and then moved on to describe the indignities the Afghan people experienced under the coalition forces and the foreign firms now handling the reconstruction work. Bellows had taken it out. All of it. Gone. His article sought to compare the various "dictatorships" under which the Afghan people had found themselves over the years. "Imperialism is still imperialism even if the conqueror says the conquered will be better off." That was the general theme but apparently not an interesting one to Stuart Bellows, ad man turned censor.

Matt began to explore the websites of some other publications. In all, the articles on the Middle East seemed pretty superficial. A few reports touched on the issues Matt had identified and wanted to explore but even these were very general and without any significant details. No mainstream publications seemed to have any in-depth articles describing the more controversial aspects of the U.S. military operations in the Middle East. He searched the columns of some journalists that could normally be counted on for really good investigative reporting. For some, he was not able to locate recent articles about the Middle East. For others, he found articles that were relatively benign, boring actually.

"Sellouts," Matt muttered as he continued to navigate his way through the Internet.

He started looking at some of the less mainstream periodicals, the so-called liberal media. These outlets were considered more open-minded, more forward-thinking. The first one he tried was Mother Jones, a monthly that had been turning out hard-hitting investigative journalism from the far left for almost 40 years. He found and then clicked on the Mother Jones link from the drop-down list of his favorite websites.

He got an error message. He tried again and got the same response. Matt typed in "motherjones.com."

Internet Explorer cannot display the webpage.

He typed the domain name again, this time careful to check his spelling.

HTTP 404 - Not Found.

Frustrated, Matt went to his list of favorites and picked the link to The Nation.

Internet Explorer cannot display the webpage.

"Damn!" Matt muttered to an empty room. "What the..."

Matt knew that some of these independent sites had limited funding but couldn't imagine that in the relatively short amount of time he had been out of the country two of the largest ones had gone out of business.

Matt looked closely at the error message appearing on his screen. He had never seen this one before. "Web Site Blocked by Protegere Wall Filter" the message read. Matt didn't get it. He hadn't installed any new filters. He checked some other websites on his favorites list. He got through to most of them, but for others, he received error messages. Matt sighed heavily and ran his hand through his hair.

This sounded like a job for the Geek Squad, Matt thought.

Before logging out, he went back to his email messages. There was nothing from Stephen Cross. There was, however, another email from Alex Doren, again requesting an interview. Matt was impressed with the guy's persistence, but he still wasn't interested in opening that old wound and certainly not so someone else could exploit it. He had more important matters to attend to than helping a fellow journalist with his stories. He needed to get his own stories published, and at this rate it didn't look like an easy task.

CHAPTER SIX

THE NEXT MORNING Matt began tracking down some of his former colleagues. After his run-in with the commissioner, he had left the country rather abruptly without explaining what he was doing or even saying goodbye. It had been nearly impossible for him to keep in touch while he was in Afghanistan, but now he wanted to reach out to his fellow journalists who were connected to some of the most well-known publications in the country. He was counting on them for some suggestions about how to handle *The Chronicle* or find somewhere else that would appreciate what he had to offer.

His first call was to Yvonne Alfonso at *The Sentinel*. Yvonne was Cuban-American, born in the United States to parents of Cuban descent and a shining star in the growing Hispanic community. She was bright and articulate and, after only a couple of years of writing obituaries, had earned a top spot in *The Sentinel*. There, she began a regular feature dealing with issues important to first- and second-generation Cuban-Americans. She wrote about the latest developments with the Castro regime and explained the logistics of traveling or sending money to Cuba. Over the years, she had developed quite a loyal following of readers. Matt dialed her direct line and, after several rings, was connected to voice mail.

"You have reached the office of Rosa Perez ...," the message began.

Matt hung up and dialed again. When he got the same message, Matt assumed he had an old number for Yvonne and pressed "0." A receptionist picked up after several rings.

"Good afternoon. You have reached *The Sentinel,* your best source for news in the Sunshine State. How may I help you?"

"Hi. I'm trying to reach Yvonne Alfonso."

"There's no one working here by that name."

"Are you sure? She's been there for several years."

"I'm positive. I've been here for several weeks."

Matt sighed. "Okay, can you tell me where she's working now?"

"No, I can't," was the clipped response.

"Can you check your records, please? I'm an old friend and need to get in touch with her."

"One second," the receptionist huffed.

It felt more like several minutes before she came back on the line. "I don't have any information on Ms. Alfonso. I have no idea where she's working now."

"Thanks very much for all your help. Have a great day," he said cheerfully to a dead phone line.

Matt called Yvonne's cell phone, got voice mail and left a message.

Next, Matt tried Mo Al-Ahmed, a television journalist who worked for the local CBS news bureau. Over the years,

Mo had covered more wars, ethnic cleansings and national tragedies than any person Matt knew ~ including Stephen Cross. Lately, Mo had been spending most of his time in the Middle East. Born in the U.S. to Saudi-American parents, he spoke Arabic fluently. His culture and education made it possible for him to speak with major political figures and world business leaders. Mo explained better than anyone the Arab-Muslim perspective on the religious totalitarianism that gave rise to much of the conflict in the Middle East. His reporting had earned him tremendous respect not only in the United States but also abroad, where the U.S. journalism community didn't have the type of cachet it once had.

Not everyone, however, was crazy about how Mo covered the Middle East. Mo had been quick to praise the post-9/11 Administration for taking on Osama bin Laden and al-Qaeda, but he also criticized the Administration for using the tremendous upsurge in patriotism, bipartisanship and volunteerism to drive through a narrow right-wing agenda. He condemned the Muslim extremism that had become rooted in the educational systems and left much of the Muslim world in a backward state regarding technology and science. He also criticized religious leaders, pseudo intellectuals and educators in the Middle East who used their power, positions and oil wealth to spread an intolerant brand of Islam.

Matt's call to Mo's cell phone went straight to voice mail so he assumed that Mo was travelling. Since Matt was growing frustrated, not to mention hungry, he decided he would head over to Mo's parents' restaurant in Ft.

Lauderdale. He wasn't likely to catch his old friend there but he could get an update on his whereabouts not to mention a good meal. Matt grabbed his keys and headed out.

There were no customers in the restaurant when Matt arrived. Mo's little sister Mina was inside with her back to the entrance as she set the tables. Mo's father was standing in front of the cash register counting money. A bell chimed when Matt walked through the front door. Mina turned around to deliver a greeting to the new customer. Her father closed the register and looked up. Matt watched as the standard issue welcome for potential customers was replaced with looks of surprise, then happiness to see him and then something else.

"Oh, Matt," Mina cried dropping the silverware that was in her hands onto the table. She ran across the room and straight into his arms.

"Hey, Mina," Matt said down at the head pressed firmly against his chest. This was not a typical greeting from the painfully shy Mina. He tried to step back, but her arms were wound tightly around his waist, her face buried in the front of his shirt.

"What's going on, Mina? I haven't been gone that long," he joked weakly as he awkwardly patted her back. He couldn't see her face, but from behind the curtain of thick black hair it sounded like she was crying.

He looked up at Mr. Al-Ahmed. The sorrow in the man's eyes blindsided Matt, and he was suddenly overcome with dread.

Mr. Al-Ahmed put the "Closed" sign on the door as Mina led Matt to a table in the back corner. After getting him settled, Mina went to the kitchen. She soon returned with a pot of tea and four cups. After she was done pouring the hot tea, she sat down next to her father. As she settled in, her father reached over and covered her hand with his own. Mrs. Al-Ahmed came out from the back wiping her hands on the apron tied to her waist. She hugged Matt warmly and then sat down beside her husband.

"For the last several months, Mohammed has been traveling back and forth between Syria and Egypt," Mr. Al-Ahmed began.

He spoke slowly and with a slight accent. "We received word from him regularly ~ phone calls or email messages. Every day, we watched the newscasts of the violence over there and feared the worst. On those days when we hadn't heard from Mohammed, we worried he had been injured ~ or worse. But he always kept in touch."

He paused to catch his breath, and Mrs. Al-Ahmed reached out and touched her husband's hand.

"Last month," Mo's father continued, "he called to say he was returning to the States. This time, he was going to stay for a while."

"We were so happy," Mrs. Al-Ahmed quietly interrupted, looking over at her husband before she continued. "We hadn't seen him in so long."

"He was returning through Jordan," Mo's father continued. "He was going to stop there for a week or so to do some interviews. But then he was coming home to us."

The older man paused for a moment before continuing. "He called when he landed in Jordan. He knew his mother was worried about him. We missed the call, but he left a message."

Matt looked around the table. From the looks on their faces earlier, he had assumed the worst. Dread was giving way to shock and confusion.

"What happened?"

"We never heard from him again." Mr. Al-Ahmed responded as he used one of the table napkins to pat his eyes.

"Where is he? Is he still in Jordan? Did he go back to the Middle East?

"We don't know," Mrs. Al-Ahmed replied.

"We hired a private investigator," Mr. Al-Ahmed explained. "He went to Jordan and talked to everyone that came into contact with my son over the last few weeks. He was able to confirm that Mohammed was booked on a flight leaving Jordan, stopping in Frankfurt and then arriving in Miami. He went to the airport in Amman, but the officials there would not tell him anything. They wouldn't even confirm whether he got on the flight. But this investigator was able to confirm through the Frankfurt officials that he did not arrive there. Finally, someone working at the airport told the investigator that when Mohammed was trying to board the plane in Jordan, he was approached by three men." He hesitated. "There was ... an argument. A heated discussion. We don't know exactly. But Mohammed left with these men. He didn't get on the flight. This man, the man who saw Mohammed, said that it didn't look like my son left willingly and that the men he went with were dressed in uniforms like Jordanian military."

Mo's mother and sister were crying softly. Mr. Al-Ahmed leaned over and murmured something in his wife's ear.

"So was he arrested?" Matt finally asked.

Mr. Al-Ahmed turned back to Matt and shrugged his shoulders. "The private investigator was never able to find any records indicating that Mohammed had been arrested ~ by the Jordanian police or the military. Both deny they have him or even detained him."

"What about the U.S. government?" Matt asked. "Did you try to contact the U.S. Embassy in Jordan?"

"Of course. They said they would make some inquiries, but they haven't gotten back to us. We keep calling, but they say they don't know anything."

"What more can we do, Matt?" Mr. Al-Ahmed said urgently.

Mrs. Al-Ahmed reached past her husband and grabbed Matt's hand tightly. "You must help us, Matt." She looked at him with eyes filled with tears. "Please. We don't know what else to do."

CHAPTER SEVEN

THE NEXT MORNING Matt called Bob Sandberg, a war correspondent for the *Washington Post* whom he had met through Stephen. Bob was the veteran of the group, having spent time in Bosnia, Haiti and Iraq and having covered more wars than most career military officers. He was also the most cynical, no doubt after years of witnessing American soldiers at their best and the government agencies for which they served at their very worst. With his rapier wit, Bob was known for delivering narrative as deadly as rifle shots.

Bob arrived in Iraq before the war started and then traveled back and forth between Iraq and the United States for several years. Three years after President Bush declared the end of military operations, when it was clear that military operations were not at all over and wouldn't be any time soon, Bob found out that his bride, the fellow journalist he had married after many years as an avowed bachelor, was pregnant with twin boys. Almost overnight, his priorities had changed, and he returned to the States permanently.

Matt knew that since returning, Bob had been covering national politics for the *Post*. He still had to deal with warring factions and covert operations and the bad guy was harder to identify, but at least he didn't have to travel with armed guards and he wasn't ducking live bullets on a daily basis.

Matt called Bob's home in Bethesda, Maryland. A woman answered the phone on the third ring. Since Matt didn't recognize the voice, he identified himself and asked to speak with Bob.

Before the person answering the phone could respond, he heard a voice in the background asking "Who is it, Sandra?"

Although muffled, Matt could still hear. "Someone by the name of Matt Connelly. He's looking for Bob."

Matt heard shuffling and more voices in the background. Finally, a new voice came on the line. "Matt, it's Marie."

"Hey, Marie. Is Bob there? I just got back from Afghanistan and wanted to catch up."

There was silence on the other end of the line.

"Uh, if I've called at a bad time, I can call back later," Matt finally said.

"No, that's okay," Marie said. "Welcome back, Matt. I'm glad you're home safe."

"Thank you. It's good to be back. I was hoping to catch Bob," Matt reminded her.

Another long pause.

"Marie, are you still there?"

"Ummm... You don't know."

"Know what?"

"I don't know how to tell you this." Her voice sounded slightly off, distant but also slow and slurred, like she had been drinking.

"Tell me what, Marie? What's going on?"

"Bob died three weeks ago."

"Oh, my God," Matt exclaimed. He fumbled for the right words. "Marie, I had no idea. I'm so sorry." The words hung in the air awkwardly but they were all he had.

"How are you holding up?" Matt asked after a moment.

"I'm managing," she replied simply.

"What happened?"

He could hear the sound of a child fussing in the background and someone attempting to quiet the child.

"They say it was an accident," Marie began slowly before lowering her voice and continuing more quickly, "but, Matt, I know that's not right."

Before he could respond, he heard the woman in the background. "Marie ..."

"Matt, no one will listen to me, but I'm sure it wasn't an accident." The child's sobs grew louder.

"It's a bad time, Matt," Marie continued. "My sister's here. She's been helping me out."

"I'm sorry. I don't mean to bother you."

"It's no bother, Matt. I have to go now, but I would like to talk to you. Can you come visit me?"

"Of course, Marie."

"How soon can you come?" she said in a whisper.

Before he could respond, there was the sound of activity and then someone else was on the line.

"This is an extremely difficult time for us, Mr. Connelly," the new voice said. Marie's sister, Matt assumed.

"I understand," he stammered.

"Marie's quite upset right now. I have to hang up the phone."

"Okay," Matt said weakly.

Then for the second time in as many days, Matt was left listening to dead air.

Matt had debated his next call since first meeting with the Al-Ahmed family. He hated calling in favors and this one was particularly difficult, but Mo was in trouble and this was the only way Matt knew to help him.

He waited until after noon before doing it. Her assistant would be at lunch so she would answer the phone directly. It would be more difficult for her to dodge his call, if she was still so inclined.

She picked up on the second ring.

"Dana Fried," the familiar voice said in a clipped tone.

He hesitated briefly.

"Hello?" Dana jumped in impatiently.

"Hi, Dana," he began. "It's me ... Matt."

"Maaatt." She drew out the name, letting it linger in the air for several moments after she said it. "I heard you were back in town."

"Word travels fast."

"The power of the Internet."

Small talk and then a pregnant pause filled the distance between them.

"So, what can I do for you?" She was always to the point. "I assume this is not a social call."

"I need your help, Dana."

Again, that damn irritating pause.

"It's about Mo."

Matt knew that Dana liked Mo. After Matt had introduced the two of them, Mo had become one of her favorite people, and they kept in touch regularly by email. Matt also knew Dana would do whatever she could to help their mutual friend. She had already helped him professionally by introducing him to sources and contacts he had used for some of his investigations.

"What about Mo?" Dana asked.

"A few weeks ago, Mo was returning home from the Middle East. He was picked up in Jordan. He hasn't been seen or heard from since. Neither the Jordanian government nor the U.S. Embassy will say what happened, but witnesses say he was picked up by government officials."

Matt paused, and when Dana didn't say anything, he continued. "No one has heard from Mo. No one knows where he is or what's going on. His family is frantic."

"I had no idea," she replied softly with what sounded like genuine concern in her voice.

"How could this happen, Dana?" Matt asked.

"I don't know."

"Come on. You work for the government. What the hell's going on?"

"Matt, calm down," Dana said firmly. "I'm not responsible for this. I'm not the enemy. If you want my help, you need to understand that. Now, tell me what you know. And then I'll see what I can do."

"Okay," Matt said. He told her everything he had learned from the Al-Ahmed family. Dana asked several pointed questions, and he knew she was taking copious notes. It didn't take much for her legal training to kick in.

"Okay. This is helpful. I'll make a few phone calls," Dana said and then paused. "Matt, you know I'll do everything I can to help," she said after a few seconds.

"I know."

Matt looked at his watch and noticed that only ten minutes had passed since he started the call to Dana. It seemed like much longer.

"So ... uh ... Matt," Dana began, interrupting the silence. "How long have you been back in town?"

"Just a couple of days."

Another awkward pause. "How have you been?" Matt finally asked.

"I've been good. Busy but good. What with the war on terror and renewed focus on U.S. immigration policies, I've been keeping very busy. I can't complain, though. For me, insecurity is job security."

They both laughed weakly.

"I'm sure you're reveling in these new challenges, Dana," Matt finally said. "You've always been driven by more than just job security."

There was another awkward pause, and Matt wasn't sure he had it in him to keep this conversation going with more small talk. He suspected Dana felt the same way. They quickly ended the call rather than risk further engagement that might lead to topics they weren't prepared to discuss.

CHAPTER EIGHT

TWO DAYS LATER, Matt decided to go to New York City to check on his friend Stephen Cross. Afterwards, he planned to go to Bethesda to see Marie Sandberg. Matt still hadn't had any luck reaching his old friend but he wasn't worried. Stephen had been known to get wrapped up in a story and hibernate in his apartment until the story was done.

It was pouring rain, and his cab had barely come to a stop at Columbus and 78th when Matt leaned forward and pushed a few bills through the tiny opening in the Plexiglas separating passenger from driver. He jumped out of the backseat without waiting for change and raced up the stairs of the brownstone, even as the rain attempted to beat him back to the comfort of the car. He pressed the buzzer for Stephen's apartment and huddled under the meager overhang of the building waiting to be buzzed in. There was no response, so he pressed again and held the button down for several seconds. Still nothing. He leaned out past the overhang and looked up into the rain, squinting in the general direction of the window for Stephen's apartment then retreated back to the relative comfort of the stoop to give the buzzer one last try.

Matt was considering his options when the front door swung open and a man walked out with his dog on a leash. The man buried his face under the hood of his raincoat and started down the stairs without looking up. Matt caught the door as it started to close and walked into the vestibule of the building. He jogged up the four flights of stairs, still hopeful he might find Stephen buried in his laptop. An annoyed Stephen, irritated about being interrupted, would be a welcome reprieve from the interminable silence over the last several days.

Matt knocked on the door to his friend's apartment. He tried again when he didn't hear anything on the other side.

Matt looked up and down the hallway before he bent down in front of Stephen's door and lifted up the doormat. Nothing but dirt. Glancing around again, Matt reached up to the top corner of the door frame. He ran his fingers across the top. Nothing but smudged fingertips.

He was still there, contemplating his next move when a woman walked out of the apartment next door to Stephen's. Dressed in black pants and black sweater, she deftly juggled a coffee mug in one hand, her keys in the other and an umbrella wedged under one arm. She even had a large briefcase slung over one shoulder. She didn't notice Matt standing there as she balanced her formidable load while simultaneously locking her door. She turned away from the door and finally looked up as she started to walk down the hall. Her eyes widened when she noticed Matt standing there.

"Sorry ~ I didn't mean to startle you," he said quickly. "I'm Matt Connelly. A friend of Stephen's." He pointed to Stephen's door and then reflexively extended his hand before realizing that wasn't going to work.

"Hi, I'm Jill, Stephen's neighbor ~ obviously." She nodded her head back in the direction of the apartment before acknowledging Matt with a smile and tip of her coffee mug.

"Sorry to bother you. I can see you're on your way out."

"Yeah. On my way to work."

"Just real quickly before you go. Any idea if Stephen's around?"

She paused as she considered the question. "I haven't seen Stephen for a couple of weeks. I think he's out of town."

"On assignment somewhere?"

She put down her briefcase. "Well, at first I didn't think so because he usually lets me know before he goes out of town for work. I water his plants," she explained. "But I haven't seen him for a few weeks, so I guess he could be."

"Damn. I'm sorry to hear that," Matt continued. "I'm in town from Miami and I had hoped to catch him while I was here."

"You came all this way just to see Stephen?"

"Sort of. I'm on my way to visit a friend in Maryland so I thought I'd stop by. I'm catching a train at one o'clock."

"Well, that's a shame," she said as she reached down for her briefcase.

"Hey, listen," Matt began quickly, "you wouldn't happen to have a spare key to Stephen's apartment, would you?" She looked at him and didn't respond. "You mentioned you water his plants."

"Well, yeah, I do. We both travel a lot and gave each other copies, seeing as we don't have a super for the building and all."

"I know it's a lot to ask, but do you think maybe I could borrow it? I could hang out at Stephen's place until I have to leave to catch my train."

"I don't know," she replied slowly.

"I wouldn't be there for very long," Matt interrupted. "Just until I have to leave to catch my train."

"Ummm. I guess so," Jill said hesitantly.

"I'm sure Stephen wouldn't mind,"

"Okay. Let me get you the key."

"Thanks. I really appreciate this," Matt said as she walked back toward her apartment.

"Here you go," she said a moment later as she handed him the key. "Just make sure you leave it under my mat when you leave."

"Great. Thanks. I really appreciate this."

"Well, I have to run." Jill said as she leaned down and picked up her briefcase. "It was nice meeting you."

"Yeah, same here," Matt said and then watched appreciatively as she deftly maneuvered down the stairs.

Matt turned to Stephen's door, inserted the key and unlocked the deadbolt. He couldn't help but knock and call Stephen's name before slowly opening the door. He stepped hesitantly into the apartment and then stopped short.

"What the ..."

The place was trashed. Not work-at-home, bachelor-living trashed but torn-apart trashed, likely by burglars looking for anything of value.

From the front door of Stephen's apartment, Matt walked into a combination living/dining room, across from which were large windows looking out onto 78th Street. To the right, Matt could see a short hallway that led to the only bathroom and then a small bedroom. To the left was an even smaller kitchen.

In the corner of the living room sat a small desk from which Matt knew Stephen did most of his writing. The drawers of the desk had been pulled out and upended, leaving papers all over the surface of the desk and floor beneath it. On the opposite side of the room, Matt looked over at the large entertainment center in the center of the wall. The DVD player and stereo were gone. The large flat-screen television was still there but it was unplugged and pulled away from the wall. Perhaps the burglars had realized, after the fact, that they would look pretty silly walking down Central Park West carrying a flat-screen television. Or worse, they would get an honorable mention in the local paper's "Stupid Criminals" column.

Concerned that Stephen might have been there when the burglary happened and might still be there, Matt walked down the hallway toward the bedroom. He peeked briefly into the bathroom and saw that the contents of the medicine cabinet and the cabinet beneath the sink were strewn about the floor. The shower curtain had been ripped off the rod and lay half in and half out of the bathtub. But there was no sign of Stephen.

He continued on to the bedroom. The door was slightly ajar. Matt pushed the door the rest of the way open. The bed was in the center of the wall opposite the door. There was a nightstand on one side of the bed and a dresser on the other. Standing in the doorway, Matt could see that the books that had previously rested on the nightstand had been thrown on the floor. The dresser drawers had been emptied on the bed and then they too upended onto the floor. The contents of the closet were strewn about the room. Fortunately, there was no sign of Stephen.

Matt suddenly felt a breeze behind him. He turned back toward the hallway, just as a powerful blow caught him on the side of the face. His head whipped sideways, followed by his shoulders and then the rest of his body, sending him careening against the wall. He bounced off the wall, instinctively lunging back toward his attacker. Matt plowed forward and head-butted the taller man in the chest. He wrapped his arms around the man's waist and, as his rubber-soled shoes gained traction on the wood floor, pushed the man backward until they slammed against the wall in the hallway.

They both crashed to the floor. Matt was on top, but since he had never let go, his arms were pinned underneath his attacker. Matt scrambled to break free, to get up and get the hell out of there. Suddenly, a pain exploded in the back of Matt's head. His arms and legs ceased responding to any commands he gave them. His head became heavy, and the room went black.

When Matt finally came to, he was still lying on the floor of Stephen's living room. His right cheek felt slightly numb against the wood floor. Drool and blood had formed a puddle around his mouth. Without raising his head, he slowly reached into the pocket of his jeans and pulled out his cell phone. He thumbed the phone awake and drew it close to his face. It took a few seconds for the screen to come into focus and for him to make out the time. He saw that just over an hour had passed since the cab had pulled in front of Stephen's apartment.

He rose slowly, ignoring the screaming from his brain and rubbed the back of his head. There was no blood, but he knew he would have a good size lump the following morning. He staggered slowly into the living room and sat down on the edge of the coffee table, taking another close look around. A laptop bag sat open on the desk in the corner of the living room, but the laptop that would usually be found sitting in the center of the desk was gone. Clearly, Matt had interrupted a burglary in progress. But it was good that there was no sign of Stephen. Apparently, he hadn't been here when the burglary went down. Matt had been the one unlucky enough to walk in on it. Which still left the question *Where the hell was Stephen?*

Matt looked around the room carefully, picking up pieces of paper from the floor, going into the desk drawers, searching everywhere for some clue, something that Stephen might have been working on that would show where he'd gone or what he was doing.   He found nothing.

He looked down at his watch and squinted as the watch face came in to focus. He needed to leave soon if he wanted to catch that train to Maryland to see Marie Sandberg. Matt walked around the living room, surveying it one last time. He was debating whether to call the police and report a breaking and entering or, possibly, a missing person. But who had done the breaking and entering? Matt who coaxed a key out of a gullible neighbor to break into Stephen's apartment or some cranked-out crack head looking for anything of value that could be used to score their next high? Surely the latter but from the police's perspective, Matt was as guilty of trespassing as the burglars were of breaking and entering. Either way, it wouldn't matter. Stephen's place was still trashed, his valuables ~ to the extent he had any ~ were gone. Matt shrugged his shoulders in frustration.

He turned to Stephen's desk and grabbed a pen from the open drawer. He picked up a sheet of paper from the floor and wrote a quick note to his old friend. "Stephen, sorry about the mess. Obviously, not my doing. Just happened by at the wrong time. Call me! Matt." He threw the pen on to the desk and ran out the door to catch his train.

CHAPTER NINE

MATT WALKED UP the front path toward the white two-story house. A 50-foot oak tree extended its long limbs over the expansive front lawn. A toddler-sized double swing hung securely from one of the immense branches and swayed in the late afternoon breeze. Underneath the other side of the tree were two weather-worn Adirondack chairs that were currently catching leaves. The flowerbeds lining the walkway leading up to the front door were overgrown with brown stems and wayward weeds. The hunter green shutters framing the windows on the first and second floors could use a coat of paint. The flower boxes suspended below the windows on the first floor were empty.

A woman Matt assumed was Marie's sister answered the door.

"Hi," Matt said. "I'm Matt Connelly."

"What do you want?" Her greeting sent a chill through the air.

She couldn't have weighed more than one hundred pounds and stood only slightly more than five feet tall. Despite her size, she was a formidable looking woman with short silver hair, piercing eyes and a stern mouth.

"I'm a friend of the family. Marie asked me to come."

The woman didn't respond. She simply stood there seeming to consider turning Matt away.

"Tina?" Matt finally heard Marie call from somewhere inside the house. "I thought I heard ..."

Matt saw Marie turn the corner and stand behind her sister. She looked directly at Matt and he saw the recognition register in her eyes.

"Matt," Marie said smiling weakly. "It's so good to see you. Please come in."

When she saw the sentinel at the door was blocking his way, Marie reached awkwardly past her sister and took Matt's arm. The other woman glared at Matt as he squeezed past her and through the front door.

Marie led the way through the foyer and into the living room. As they walked, Matt looked over at Marie. She had aged considerably since he had last seen her. At forty, she was still attractive but her lips were drawn and serious. The lines around her mouth and eyes were new. Strange how they called them laugh lines, Matt thought. Marie looked like she hadn't laughed in quite some time.

They settled into the living room and Matt expressed his condolences, all the while silently cursing himself for doing a piss poor job. They made small talk. Marie looked away frequently, sometimes toward the room next door and other times down at her lap. She alternated between twisting her fingers into knots and picking imaginary objects from her slacks. She asked him questions about his travels and time in the Middle East but didn't appear to hear the responses. Watching Marie was pure torture for

Matt, but he let her go on, letting her create the aura of normalcy she seemed to need.

Ultimately, though, Matt grew weary of talking about himself and impatient with the meaningless small talk. He reached forward and clasped Marie's hands in his own, attempting to calm them. "Tell me what happened, Marie."

She hesitated before nodding. And then she began speaking slowly and softly.

"Bob went up to my family's summer home in the mountains. He was working on a project and wanted some time on his own to finish it. Since the boys were born, he'd done that a few times. He loved the boys and being with them," she explained. "But as you can imagine, it was impossible to get any work done here. I didn't think much of it when he told me he was going."

She paused and looked down at her lap again before continuing. "Bob had been gone only a couple of days when the police called."

The memory was apparently still new, the wound raw. Matt watched helplessly as the thin veneer of composure she struggled so hard to maintain began to crack. She started to cry softly. Matt applied a slight and hopefully reassuring pressure to her hands and shoulder. He waited patiently for her to continue.

"The police told me that Bob had been drinking and ..." Again, she hesitated and Matt waited while she regained her composure. "They said Bob had passed out or fallen asleep on the couch in the living room. They believe a spark from the fireplace hit the rug and started the fire. They said he probably never woke up. Never knew he was ..." Tears overcame her.

"Marie, I'm so sorry." Matt slid closer to her on the couch and took her in his arms. She was hunched over and crying softly into his chest.

After several moments, she pulled away slightly and looked up at him. "I just don't believe it, Matt."

She looked up and wiped the tears from her eyes. For the first time since he arrived, her eyes were bright and focused.

"You and I both know that Bob loved good food and good wine, both to excess. But when the boys were born, things changed. He still enjoyed an occasional glass of wine, but kids, midnight feedings and early morning wake up calls put an end to the debauchery of the old days. When he went up to the cabin, he was there to write. He wasn't there to drink."

"Marie, what are you saying?"

"Bob was murdered."

The words came out so strongly and quickly even Marie seemed surprised by them. They hung in the air between Matt and Marie as if savoring their impact.

"But, Marie, why would someone murder Bob?"

"I don't know." She shook her head before continuing. "But up until the day he died he was consumed with this project he was working on. I think his death may have had something to do with this, Matt."

"What project?"

"Well, see, that's just it. I don't know."

"You don't know what he was working on? How is that possible? I thought Bob discussed everything with you."

"Before, yes. But lately, he seemed to be ... withdrawn ... secretive even. Definitely not quite himself. He didn't talk to me about what he was working on. He had lots of meetings, some late at night. I probably should've taken more of an interest, but I was so busy with the boys. I just ..." Marie paused. "We just didn't have time to talk about things the way we did before."

"Did you tell the police any of this?"

"Yes," she said as she wiped the tears from her face. "But they didn't take me seriously. I think they assumed that we were having marital problems. They figured that's why he was staying somewhere else. But I know that's not true, Matt."

"I know that, Marie. Bob told me how happy he was, how thrilled he was about the boys. It's all he talked about."

"I think the story he was working on had something to do with what's going on in the Middle East."

"What makes you think that?"

"I don't know. It's just a feeling."

Matt mulled this over. He held instincts in very high regard. For journalists, a gut feeling or hunch was where a good story began. Marie was a former journalist and her instincts were better than most.

"But I may have something that could be helpful," she said interrupting his thoughts. "You know Bob always kept those notebooks where he would jot down things from meetings and telephone calls and stuff like that."

"Of course. I wish I was as organized with my notes."

"Well, Bob's most recent journals were with him at the summer house. They burned in the fire. But I found one under the seat in the car. I think Bob must have overlooked this one when he was unloading the car."

"And you think it could be helpful?"

"Maybe. I don't know," she admitted. "I've tried to go through it myself. It's full of names, numbers, a hundred different threads and unconnected ideas. But I've been so busy with the kids, I haven't had much time to go through it. I can't make any sense of what to focus on." Marie got up and walked to the desk on the other side of the room and retrieved a black and white notebook. "I was hoping you'd go through it."

"Marie, wait." Matt held up his hands, not touching the proffered book. "You should go to the police with this."

"The police won't do anything," she said as she pushed the notebook toward him. "They think this was an accident and that I'm just some inconsolable widow ~ which, of course, I am. But that doesn't make me any less right about what happened to Bob. What happened to my husband was no accident."

Marie stared down at him fiercely. Matt thought that for the first time since he arrived at her door, she resembled the woman he had met several years ago, the bright, ambitious and determined woman Bob had fallen in love with.

"I appreciate your confidence in me, Marie. But what do you want me to do with this?"

"You're a journalist, Matt. Do what you do best. Go through it. Figure out why my children will grow up without a father."

CHAPTER TEN

BOB SANDBERG'S JOURNAL was just like the wide-ruled composition pads that he had used to take exams in college. Black and white cardboard cover with a white space in the middle to put the course title. There, Bob had neatly printed in black block letters his name and telephone number and, underneath that, the year 2013, a dash and then the number 2.

Matt opened the book hesitantly at first. The pages, filled with Bob's thoughts and insights, were as intimidating now as the blank pages Matt had faced for each essay exam in college. He started to flip through the pages, slowly at first and then more quickly.

"Jesus," he said under this breath. *There was a ton of stuff here.*

The journal included notes taken during meetings and telephone conversations, lists of things to do and Bob's observations about life in general. Matt laughed out loud at Bob's diatribes against big government, observations about various politicians and random musings about his daily life. Bob had been an extremely talented writer, full of energy, with more than his fair share of moments of brilliance and, always, a large dose of sarcasm. The journal showed how nimbly he moved between the different worlds he occupied ~ family man to a loving wife and two young boys and antagonist to some of the most powerful men in Washington.

Bob had been working on several different story lines. There were notes on the worsening situation in the Middle East, the positions of powerful politicians on certain issues and the primary sources of funding for various campaigns. There were several references to specific private military corporations and their annual revenues.

The notes regarding Afghanistan included interviews with representatives of the United Nations, Afghan nationals and former members of the Taliban. There were paragraphs about the U.S. presence in the Middle East and suggestions for extricating the U.S. military forces from the beleaguered region. The observations were from different points of view, coming from academic, diplomatic and journalistic pundits. The notes about politicians included some intriguing speculation about the relationships among various politicos and certain high-powered lobbyists. There was even some speculation of a more salacious nature about the sex lives of certain officeholders.

Matt didn't know which was the more insidious. The powerful elected officials who used their power to exploit the young men and women desperate to make it ahead in Washington or the corporate lobbyists who filled the politicians' campaign coffers in exchange for earmarks and political favors. It was hard to say. But it was ultimately the lobbyists to whom most politicians seemed to owe their allegiances, not their constituents, their families or even their lovers. These relationships were so corrupt it was conceivable that Bob had stumbled across something that could have gotten him killed, but it would take a flow chart to map that out.

There were several comments in the journal regarding private military companies, or PMCs ~ commercial outfits to which the government outsourced things like communications, logistics and security. Most people knew about the use of PMCs for logistics like housing and feeding American soldiers in some of the most remote and dangerous regions on the planet. But most of the public didn't know that PMCs represented the newest addition to the modern battlefield and that their role in contemporary warfare was becoming increasingly significant.

"A study from the Office of the Director of National Intelligence," Bob wrote, "notes that in 2008, private contractors made up 29 percent of the United States Intelligence Community, and cost the equivalent of 49 percent of their personnel budgets."

"*Unbelievable*," Matt thought. That meant the amount of money involved was staggering.

From Bob's notes, Matt was able to glean that over the years, the U.S. government had used PMCs in regional and ethnic conflicts in places like Colombia, Haiti and Bosnia. PMCs worked with the State Department and foreign governments to train soldiers and reorganize militaries. The PMC's provided armed bodyguards at first and then whole teams of retired special ops men who worked all over the world.

Mercenaries, Matt thought.

After September 11th, a new Pentagon policy had developed emphasizing high-technology combat systems, sophisticated weaponry, small, nimble ground forces and, perhaps most important, greater reliance on private contractors. It was the brainchild of former U.S. Secretary of Defense Donald Rumsfeld and was known as the Rumsfeld Doctrine.

The Middle East was considered the wild west of U.S. contracting as a result of the unbridled flow of U.S. taxpayer dollars into the area with little to no oversight. There, the use of contractors was so murky the U.S. government itself couldn't figure out how much each of the different government agencies was paying subsidiaries and affiliates of the different PMC conglomerates, let alone how many millions of dollars were lost in each step of the process. The Pentagon had a long history of failing to oversee the businesses they hired on the government dime. Even the seemingly simple question of how much total federal spending goes to foreign subcontractors annually had no clear answer because of the complex chain of contractors involved in each project.

There were several references in the journal to a company called Information Management Services. Other than an address in Florida, there didn't seem to be much information about it. Matt noted that Bob had written over the name several times and the initials IMS were in several places in the journal.

In the margin of one page Matt noticed a name written in Bob's scrawl. *Alex Doren.*

That name again.

He flipped through the journal again quickly. He noticed the initials "AD" appeared in several places throughout the pages. Matt studied the entries where AD's initials appeared. There didn't seem to be any particular common theme, but "AD" figured prominently in Bob's thoughts. Alex Doren had evidently been in touch with Bob even before he had sent Matt several emails requesting an interview since his return. Matt had no idea whether there was any connection between Alex Doren and Bob's death. But coincidence or not, Alex Doren was finally going to get that interview.

By the time Matt pulled up to his house, it was almost midnight and he was exhausted. His meeting with Marie had drained him, mentally and emotionally. His head still throbbed from the unfortunate encounter at Stephen's apartment. On top of all this, he continued to be plagued with worry about Mo and Stephen. The assignment he had accepted from Marie was exactly the type of thing he would typically talk through with both men, but they were currently missing in action.

As Matt walked up the driveway toward his darkened house, he heard a voice behind him.

"Connelly. Matt Connelly."

He turned back to see a heavyset man standing in the middle of the street. The light coming from the streetlamp behind him prevented Matt from identifying the guy. Matt stepped forward and squinted in the dark as the man stepped out of the shadows.

"Commissioner," Matt finally said, acknowledging the man walking slowly toward him.

As the commissioner approached, Matt noticed an unfamiliar black Mercedes parked across the street and another man standing next to the driver's side door. The man's arms were crossed in front of his chest.

"I heard you were back in town, Matt," Commissioner Suarez said casually. He was dressed in typical Miami business casual attire. Tan linen slacks and a white guayabera shirt. His black hair was slicked back and curled loosely around his neck. A gold watch and a diamond pinky ring glinted in the dim light.

"You heard right."

"Welcome back," the politician said as he took a step forward. He stepped into the driveway but stopped some distance away from Matt.

"Thank you, Commissioner."

"I also heard you're still in the news business."

"Of course," Matt shot back. "I love it. You know, educating the public. Championing the underdog." Matt paused. "Exposing corrupt politicians."

Matt could barely make out the other man's features in the shadows but could swear he saw the right corner of the commissioner's mouth begin to twitch.

Suarez was running for re-election in his district despite the corruption charges still pending against him. The challenger was a competent and, by all accounts, honest local attorney. But he was woefully underfunded, a newcomer to the high-stakes game of South Florida politics and, perhaps worst of all, naïve enough to think that he could win without making promises to the large corporations in South Florida willing to pay big bucks in cash and in-kind donations to those elected officials that, once elected, were willing to invite the corporate executives to the party.

Commissioner Suarez, on the other hand, had amassed quite a war chest from his loyal constituents and the executives of the local companies that would no doubt benefit from his being in office. Matt knew Suarez viewed his job as commissioner as nothing more than a high-stakes poker game where, as dealer, he was able to facilitate the passing of money from one player to another. He was willing to make sure the corporations that supported him had a seat at the high-rollers' table. He had a proven track record of doing so. The sitting commissioner was projected to win by a landslide.

"Listen, Matt," Suarez finally said. "I came here tonight to give you a little friendly advice, to extend to you a little professional courtesy between us public servants."

The commissioner raised himself up an inch and took a step toward Matt, although still maintaining a healthy distance. The commissioner's driver or bodyguard had also moved closer to the two men.

"Stay out of my way, Matt." Suarez continued. "Do not mess with me, my family or my business." He leaned forward. "It didn't work so well for you the last time. It will be even worse this time."

"Ah, it wasn't so bad, Commissioner," Matt said. "You needn't worry about me. I had a wonderful time in Afghanistan ~ practically a vacation." Matt stepped closer to the commissioner. "As a matter of fact, I hear you're facing the prospect of your own extended vacation."

The commissioner stiffened but didn't respond.

"How is that investigation going, by the way? It must be a bit of a distraction from your campaign."

"*Mierda*," the commissioner spat.

He took two steps forward before he stopped himself. From this distance, the twitching in the right corner of the commissioner's mouth was unmistakable. The man standing by the Mercedes also started to move and was walking quickly toward them. Without turning his back to Matt, Suarez raised his hand and stopped the man in his tracks.

"Consider yourself warned, Matt," Commissioner Suarez said, his face now within a few feet of Matt's and his finger now pointed at him. "You don't want to fuck with me."

Before Matt could respond, Commissioner Suarez turned on his heel and slithered back into the shadows.

CHAPTER ELEVEN

FIRST THING THE NEXT MORNING, Matt started to go through his emails, searching for the one he had opened from Alex Doren a few days before. Having deleted it, he was forced to go dumpster diving in the cyber trashcan containing advertisements, spam and deleted emails. Eventually he found the email.

"Sorry for the delay. I'm ready to talk," Matt typed before asking if he was still interested in an interview.

He knew Doren would be and Doren didn't disappoint, responding almost immediately and inviting Matt to meet for lunch that afternoon in Coconut Grove.

The restaurant was only a couple of blocks away from his house and parking could be challenging, so Matt left the Jeep and walked down to the center of the small community. What used to be a village populated by longhaired artists high on life and "Mary Jane" was now a favorite destination for the teenagers of Miami's elite high on their parent's money and prescription drugs. Streets once lined with head shops, art galleries and health-food restaurants were now lined with fashionable shops filled with overpriced items and trendy restaurants serving mediocre food.

The only remnants of the old Grove were the occasional offbeat festivals, including the totally irreverent King Mango Strut Parade, which poked fun at local and national politics. This parade, which Matt tried not to miss, was now conducted with significantly less enthusiasm than in prior years and even less tolerance from the local politicians who were frequently the butt of the fun. Despite the diminished public support, a small group of local eccentrics and ex-hippies continued to support the parade ~ but who knew for how much longer.

As agreed, Matt waited by the tall clock in the center of CocoWalk, the open-air pedestrian mall in Coconut Grove. He scanned the tourists for someone resembling an extremely persistent journalist. Unfortunately, in his haste to schedule a meeting, he had forgotten to get Doren's description. And he had no idea whether Alex Doren knew what he looked like.

Doing a slow sweep, Matt sensed a presence behind him. He turned around and almost drowned in a deep pool of hazel green sprinkled with flecks of gold. The surprise prompted a quick step back. In black shoes, well-fitting blue jeans and a pressed, white button-down shirt, the vision stood practically as tall as Matt. The young woman's shirt was unbuttoned enough to reveal the slope of her breasts above a white tank top underneath. Black sunglasses were slipped into the low neckline of the tank top. Her dark brown hair was pulled back into a long ponytail.

"Hi," Matt said delivering his most winning smile.

"Hello," the stranger replied politely.

She made no move to leave, and Matt began to feel optimistic. "What brings you here?"

"I'm just waiting for someone. I thought you might be him."

"I could be," Matt replied. "Depends on who you're waiting for."

Matt continued when she only responded with a small smile. "Someone with boyish good looks and a self-deprecating sense of humor? Someone capable of maintaining an intelligent conversation?" Matt silently prayed Alex Doren would stand him up.

Her laugh was throaty and deep, trailing off to a mischievous smile as she extended her hand. "I'm Alex Doren, Matt."

He just stared.

"This is awkward," she said after a moment, still holding her hand out.

"For you?" Matt responded as he took her hand. "Imagine my side of this moment."

So Alex Doren was a female. It had been his experience that female journalists looked more like the Margot Kidder Lois Lane than the Terri Hatcher or Kate Bosworth Lois Lane. But Alex Doren was more Lois Lane meets Julia Roberts. *Hello, trouble!* Matt thought.

"I thought we might go to Green Street Café," Alex said, interrupting his thoughts.

"Sounds great."

Matt gestured for her to lead the way and then watched appreciatively as she moved easily through the crowd.

Green Street Café Lounge and Restaurant was located in the center of Coconut Grove and was the premier "seen and be seen" restaurant in the area. A favorite meeting place any time of day or night, it was frequented by politicians, athletes, artists and locals from The Grove and the surrounding areas.

Matt had no intention of allowing Alex to turn this into an interview. Immediately after they were seated in the outdoor terrace, he went straight to the point. "I think we have a mutual friend. Bob Sandberg? Or had a mutual friend," Matt said correcting himself.

"Yes. I knew Bob. But only briefly," Alex said, putting down the menu and looking at him. "I was so sorry to hear about what happened. What a tragedy." She paused for a moment. "Were you two close?"

"Yeah, we were. I was just with his wife Marie. She's torn up about his death."

"I can't even imagine what she's going through, especially with those little kids." Alex paused a moment, shook her head and turned her attention back to her menu.

After they placed their order, Alex reached into her backpack and took out a pad of paper and pen. Before she could ask the first question, Matt fired off one. "So, how did you know Bob? He never mentioned you to me."

"I met him through a friend of a friend," she said opening her pad and clicking her pen. "I only met him a couple of times. As I said, I didn't know him that well."

"Really? I got the impression that you were better acquainted. Maybe working on some project together ..."

"He was helping me with a project I was working on."

"What kind of project?"

"Nothing interesting," she replied slowly, apparently not comfortable with being on the receiving end of the questions. "It's kind of stalled right now."

"What was it about? Maybe I can help."

"Matt, what's with all the questions?" Alex said smiling tightly. "I thought I was doing the interview."

Matt decided to get right to the point. He leaned in. "Bob Sandberg's wife believes his death was no accident. She believes he was killed." Her eyes widened. "And killed because of some story he was working on."

"Wow," Alex said. "But what has this got to do with me?"

"That's what I'd like to find out."

Matt decided to come clean and explained the journal that Marie had entrusted him with. "I saw your name and initials in the journal."

"Jeez," Alex said taking a drink. "I don't know what to say."

"You can start by telling me about this story Bob was helping you with."

"I doubt my pet project had anything to do with this."

"It's a place to start."

"Okay," Alex began slowly. "For the last several months, I've been researching how the media has been covering the Middle East. I have been comparing the coverage of the first Iraq War under President George H.W.

Bush, to the coverage of the War on Terror under his son George W. Bush and finally to the coverage of Operation Enduring Freedom under President Obama. I wanted to show how technology and social media in particular have affected news coverage generally and, more specifically, major media events like the conflict in the Middle East."

"I would imagine things like the Internet, blogs and alternative news sources have also had a significant impact."

"Yes, exactly," Alex said nodding. "The Internet - with help from social media - has definitely had an impact on the amount of information that people have access to and this in turn had an effect on public awareness and public opinion. For one thing, the public is much more informed about what's going in the Middle East than it has ever been before."

"The American population is informed? Are we talking about the same population?"

Alex ignored his snarky comment. "Prior to 9/11, many people hadn't heard of Iraq or Afghanistan. Most couldn't have identified them on a map. And they certainly had never heard of al-Qaeda. After 9/11, people were suddenly more aware and interested in what was going on there."

"Largely because we were sending their sons, daughters and spouses there," Matt interrupted.

"True," Alex conceded.

Their meals arrived. After they both sampled a few bites, Matt encouraged Alex to continue.

"Whatever the reasons, the general public is more knowledgeable than ever before about foreign affairs, countries that have nuclear weapons capabilities and our relationship with those countries. They are also more engaged, more vocal and passionate about their positions."

Alex took a small bite before continuing. "Today, people have strong opinions about whether the war was a good idea or not and whether we should continue to have a significant presence in the Middle East. They care about what's going on in Syria and our relationships with North Korea and Iran."

"The events of 9/11 were quite a wake-up call."

"That's right," Alex agreed. "And as horrible as 9/11 was, one positive thing that came out of all of it is that we're more informed and aware of what's going on outside our borders."

She paused. "Or at least that's my conclusion."

"Sounds like an interesting project," Matt said.

"I think so," Alex replied.

"Where did Bob fit into all this?"

"Well, Bob heard about my research through some mutual friends. My friends said he thought it was interesting, so I called him. I knew that, because of his experiences, I could get some great information from him. I was thrilled when he agreed to meet with me and help me."

"Help how?"

"Well, he was primarily a sounding board. We bounced ideas back and forth. We would talk for hours. Because of his prior experience with other conflicts, he knew the difference in the coverage between this conflict and earlier ones."

"And ..."

"And we just talked."

"So, what happened?"

"Nothing." Alex shrugged her shoulders. "I didn't hear from Bob for about two weeks and then I heard about the accident ... uh ... fire, whatever it was."

She paused for a moment. "I still find it hard to believe that his death could have been anything other than an accident. I can't imagine anyone would want to kill Bob."

Matt resumed his eating as he absorbed everything Alex had told him.

"I guess you like this place," Matt said eyeing the empty plate in front of her. "Either that, or you just haven't eaten in some time."

Alex gave him a thumbs-up as she washed down the last of the meal with a swallow of water.

"Listen, Matt," Alex finally said. "I can't believe that Bob was murdered. But even if he was, I can't imagine that anything Bob and I talked about contributed to his death. Really. I think you're barking up the wrong tree with me."

"But I do thank you for the meal," she said, smiling brightly as the waitress put the check down in front of him.

"You're welcome," Matt said as he pulled out his wallet.

"But, wait," Alex said. "What about my interview? I have a lot of questions about your experiences in Afghanistan."

Matt tossed bills on top of the check.

"I know. But now is not a good time."

"Wait, Matt. I just need –"

He started to rise. "Sorry, Alex, I have to go."

"Matt, at least take my cell phone number. Call me. Anytime. Please, I have so many questions."

"Alright, Alex," Matt said as he pulled out his cell phone. "Give it to me."

As she recited the numbers, Matt input them into his cell phone. While Matt still wasn't sold on the interview idea, he felt good about having gotten her telephone number.

CHAPTER TWELVE

THE DOWNTOWN MIAMI Public Library was unlike most government buildings. It was sunny and cheerful, with a central plaza where people met, read and ate. Beginning in college and even while he was working for *The Chronicle*, Matt preferred doing his research and writing here, usually in the back, sitting at his favorite cubicle.

Although he had access to most information through his computer and *The Chronicle* archives, libraries had librarians. They bore a comforting resemblance to elementary school teachers, and were always eager to help. Each visitor was a pupil to be educated on the secrets the library held within its walls and each query a challenge to their investigative skills. It was like having a team of free research assistants at your fingertips, assistants that smelled like his mom and offered the occasional figurative pat on the head.

Matt had stayed up late into the night poring over the journal again. He felt compelled to find some basis for the theory advanced by Marie or at least to know he had exhausted every possible avenue exploring the idea. Without doing that, he felt he was letting Marie down. If there was ever a person who shouldn't be let down especially right now, it was Marie.

He had a good grasp of the points Bob was working on and wanted to do some additional research to see if there was anything there. Bob's observations on the Middle East were interesting but not timely. The stories had been told before. To quote the words of Dave Kagan, these stories were "old news." The notes regarding politicians merely identified a few of the schemes that our public servants, once having achieved office, used to pilfer from the government coffers for their own personal enrichment. The notes bemoaned the fact that every boon a municipality conferred upon its citizens was at once exploited by these same politicians or lobbyists. The so-called tax cuts for the working class which largely benefitted those in the upper income brackets were just one example. Another was the no-bid contracts allegedly awarded to support the troops and make our country more secure that ultimately benefitted the politicians' biggest donors.

There was one topic referenced in Bob's journals with which Matt had some general knowledge but wasn't deeply familiar. They were PMCs - or private military companies - so Matt began by focusing on them. The fact that the wars in Iraq and Afghanistan were the most privatized in American military history was not breaking news. But the numbers Bob had cited were staggering. According to the website of the Center for Public Integrity, since 1994 the United States Defense Department had entered into 3,061 contracts valued at more than $300 billion with twelve

United States-based PMCs. Since the war in Afghanistan, these contracts had increased significantly.

Bob described how contractors - in addition to raking in the cash supporting the U.S. military - have provided the Administration with political cover. Using PMCs allowed the government to deploy private forces in a war zone free of public scrutiny, with the deaths, injuries and crimes of those forces shrouded in secrecy in exchange for the Administration's shielding the contractors from accountability, oversight and legal constraints.

Bob listed the names of the different companies and the figures opposite their names. The amounts paid to these corporations were staggering. Matt started with the first name on the list and worked his way down, not really sure what he was looking for. For each, he did a Google search, browsed the company website and then looked through the public filings of the companies that were public. There was nothing he could immediately identify as unusual.

Flipping through the journal, Matt saw several references to a public relations firm called Information Management Services. A Google search revealed nothing. Searches using several other search engines yielded no hits for the company. An extremely eager and diligent librarian couldn't find anything either. The company had no website and apparently wasn't doing a good job promoting itself.

Matt stepped outside for a break and decided to call Alex. She picked up on the second ring.

"Hey, Matt. Ready for that interview?"

"Not yet, Alex. But, I was hoping to get your help."

"Sure, what's up?"

"I'm trying to find information on a company called Information Management Services. There was a reference to the company in Bob's journal. Based on his notes, it looks like it's a public relations firm. Ever heard of it?"

"Actually, yes," she responded immediately. "But I don't know much about them. It's a very private public relations firm."

"Sounds like an oxymoron."

"No kidding," she laughed. "But they are good at what they do."

"What's that?"

"Crisis management ~ providing damage control to companies in serious trouble. You know, corporate theft, executive officers misbehaving, that kind of stuff."

"Being involved in such high-profile cases you'd think they'd do a better job promoting themselves."

"You'd think so, but for whatever reason, they don't. Even though you may not have heard of the company, I'm sure you're familiar with some of their work."

"Like?"

"Remember that oil company that owned the tanker that spilled millions of tons of oil off the coast of Spain?" Alex asked.

"Sure. What a mess. I can still see the pictures of environmentalists suited up in their hazard gear cleaning off wildlife covered in oil."

"That was them. They hired IMS, and then, a year later, the U.S. government gave the company a permit to drill for oil in Alaska - this despite leaving the government in Spain on the hook for millions in environmental cleanup."

"Interesting," Matt responded.

"It gets better," Alex continued. "When Moammar Gadhafi was still in power, he was spending millions of dollars a year on a PR campaign to burnish his global image as a statesman and a reformer."

"A campaign led by IMS."

"You got it. Rumor has it that the President of Syria paid this firm big bucks to try and portray him as a transformative leader instead of the oppressive dictator he is."

"Okay, I'm impressed."

"Where are you going with this?" Alex asked after a short pause. "What does this have to do with Bob?"

"I'm not sure," Matt conceded. "I'm just sifting through the information in his journal."

"Okay," she said. "But, Matt, promise me you'll call me if you need anything else. I'd like to help."

Hanging up with Alex, Matt tried to figure out how this new information could tie into Bob's death. It was Matt's experience that PR firms were zealous advocates for their clients - in many cases, overzealous to the point of annoying, but definitely not murderers.

As Matt was leaving the library, he was assaulted by the aroma of one of Miami's well-known population segments. The homeless. In light of its warm climate, Miami had always had a large homeless population. That had only increased since the unemployment rate had skyrocketed, the real estate boom several years ago had eaten up all the affordable housing, and public assistance had been reduced to negligible levels. At night the homeless slept in shelters and encampments scattered throughout downtown. During the day, they wandered the streets of Miami, swathed in every piece of clothing they owned. Unbathed homeless people wrapped in layers of unwashed clothing, baking in the Miami heat was not a winning combination.

During business hours on the weekdays, the homeless regularly frequented the local public libraries, taking advantage of the free admission and air-conditioning. It was difficult for municipalities to balance protecting the rights of the homeless who had no place else to go and the rights of the general population to enjoy public places unmolested. The City of Miami had fought that battle and lost. The homeless were permitted to enjoy the cool indoors and free literature, and the others just had to accept it.

As he walked through the crowd, several people reached out to him asking for spare change. Matt averted his eyes and kept walking. A long-haired man was particularly aggressive and stepped in his path. Matt brushed past him. He glanced around, avoiding any form of eye contact. Yet, the man's tattered T-shirt caught his eye. "Fuck your fascist concept of beauty," it screamed. Matt couldn't resist a small smile as he shifted his gaze back to the ground and continued walking.

The homeless guy kept pace and extended his hand. A universally understood gesture.

"No, sorry," Matt said without breaking stride. Undeterred, the man followed, that insistent hand still hanging out there.

"I'm in a hurry," Matt said veering off toward the stairs on the opposite side of the plaza leading down to street level.

From a brief glance the man looked vaguely familiar but many of the homeless had been living on the streets and hanging out at the same locations for several years. Matt was a regular fixture at the library when he was working downtown. He had probably seen this guy before, possibly given him some spare change.

So Matt did the only thing that worked in these situations. He reached into his pocket. Still avoiding the man's eyes, he proffered everything he dug up - a crumpled dollar bill, several coins and some lint. Much to Matt's surprise, however, the guy wouldn't take it. He must be one of the many mentally unstable people that lived on the streets, Matt thought. He gave up, shoved the contents back into his pocket and pushed past.

The man kept pace and tried to place a piece of paper in Matt's hand. Now Matt was back on familiar territory. A flyer from a local business.

"No, thanks, but here." Matt again attempted to hand over the contents of his pocket.

"Please, take this. It's the word of the Lord." His shadow spoke for the first time.

"I'm not interested," Matt replied firmly.

He couldn't imagine what words the Lord would have for him at this point in his life, but they couldn't be good.

"Matt, take it." The shadow spoke urgently.

The familiarity shocked Matt. He stopped in his tracks.

"What? How did you . . ." He whirled around to face the stranger.

Matt struggled to make out the features from underneath a baseball cap pulled down low. Unshaven and with long greasy hair, sunburned and with parched lips, the man looked like every other homeless person Matt had sought to avoid. Then, the man lifted his head and looked directly at Matt from underneath the brim of his cap. His blue eyes pierced through Matt before they darted around the courtyard.

"Oh my God," Matt exclaimed. "What the hell . ."

"Matt, just take this." The man shoved the piece of paper into Matt's hand and closed his fingers around it, his eyes still scanning the courtyard.

"But~" Before Matt could get anything else out, the shadow shuffled away and disappeared into the crowd.

Matt looked down at the scrap of paper in his hand. The word of the Lord instructed him to be at Jimbo's at five o' clock the next afternoon. The Lord's messenger also told him to be careful as he was probably being followed.

By the time Matt looked up, Stephen Cross was gone.

CHAPTER THIRTEEN

LATE THE NEXT AFTERNOON, Matt once again headed over toward Scotty's Landing. This time, he didn't stop at the bar. Instead, he headed for the Grove Harbour Marina adjacent to the restaurant. The Marina had 90 boat slips and 260 dry dock storage spaces. Carlos, the dock master, was an old friend. After exchanging pleasantries and $200, Matt was behind the wheel of a 25-foot, center console-open fisherman boat.

Matt pushed off the pier and stepped back behind the wheel. The boat was old, but the twin 250 Yamahas were relatively new and in great condition. Matt nudged the throttle and easily navigated the boat out of the slip. Standing behind the wheel, resting against the leaning bench, Matt headed down the channel of the harbor. He maneuvered easily around the boats anchored and coming in and out while he scanned the bay for slow lumbering manatee.

As soon as he left the no-wake zone, Matt pressed down on the throttle. The engines immediately responded, and the boat raced toward open waters. He started to relax when the marina faded from view. Once completely out of sight to anyone on the shore, he changed direction and headed toward Key Biscayne. Matt was no expert at subterfuge and couldn't really imagine that he was being followed. But he thought, in an abundance of caution, this might work. The $200 Matt paid Carlos also ensured that no one else would be able to borrow or rent a boat at the last minute as Matt had done.

Twenty minutes later he arrived at Jimbo's Shrimp Shack on Virginia Key, the lesser known of the two barrier islands separating Miami from the Atlantic Ocean. Key Biscayne, the more commonly known of the two, had been developed as a luxury residential property. Virginia Key, on the other hand, was relatively untouched and offered the most privacy. Jimbo's was a local watering hole located on the northeastern end of the island and tough to find unless you were local and had been there before.

As he approached the landing, Matt navigated around decrepit-looking houseboats that, if not abandoned, most definitely should have been. After shutting down the engines, Matt jumped off the boat and tied off the lines to the dilapidated pier. As he walked toward Jimbo's, Matt looked back toward the ocean. There were no boats careening down the inlet spraying salt water in their wake. No cars blowing clouds of dust as they came barreling down the lone dirt road leading to Jimbo's. Matt's first attempt at subterfuge may have been successful, or perhaps Stephen's paranoid delusions had been unfounded.

Jimbo's was a throwback from simpler times. A ramshackle fish smokehouse that started as a gathering spot for fishermen had became the quintessential South Florida watering hole for characters ranging from crusty old sea

dogs to City of Miami politicos. The roof of the main
structure was leaning in, the house jam-packed with lobster
traps and old fishing gear. As a result, patrons sat outside in
lawn chairs and even a few La-Z-Boy recliners that had
found their way there. When the weather was cold, patrons
huddled around bonfires created in old steel drums filled
with whatever had washed ashore that couldn't be salvaged.
The trees shading Jimbo's were lit up with outdoor
Christmas lights, illuminating the tree branches the year
around. From fishing lines tied to the branches hung beer
cans, empty bottles of alcohol, plastic cups and deflated
beach balls and inner tubes. This completed the look of the
strangest all-season holiday tree.

Matt walked slowly around the main structure and to
the booths located on the other side of the house. On the
way, Matt checked out the bocce ball court and
surrounding tables for any sign of Stephen. The only
patrons were two old guys sitting in aluminum lawn chairs
in front of the bonfire and four other people playing a game
of bocce ball. One of the players was the bartender. He
looked up briefly to acknowledge Matt with a nod before
tossing the ball high in the air. It fell in the sand with a
muted thud before rolling into his opponent's ball, pushing
it out of the way. Matt grabbed a Bud Light from the cooler
and placed two dollars under the rock on the table next to
the cooler. He settled into a lawn chair some distance away
from the bocce ball players.

Thirty minutes later he was still waiting. Matt had just
begun to worry that he had lost Stephen again when a

shadow whispered behind him and a man slipped into the empty chair next to him.

"Hello, Matt," Stephen said as he settled into the seat.

"Man, am I glad to see you," Matt said urgently as he leaned toward Stephen and clapped him on the shoulder. Stephen returned the greeting.

As Stephen opened his own beer, Matt surveyed his old friend. Stephen's usually neat blond hair hung slick and stringy to his shoulders. His face hadn't seen the sharp end of a razor in quite some time. His clothes hung loosely on his frame, and yesterday's T-shirt was another day riper.

"I've been trying to reach you since I got back," Matt began.

"Sorry about that, Matt, but I've been off the grid."

"I can see that. But I've been really worried about you."

"Why's that?"

"Well, when I couldn't get hold of you, I went to your place~"

"You were at my apartment?"

"Yeah. When you didn't return my messages, I decided to check on you in New York. And, well ... after, seeing your place, I only got more concerned." Matt hesitated when he saw the look on Stephen's face. "I hate to be the one to tell you this, man, but it was trashed."

When Matt was finished giving him the details, Stephen shook his head. "I'm not surprised. I've pissed off a few people."

"What's going on, Stephen?"

For several seconds, Stephen didn't say anything. He simply stared out at the water in front of them.

"Since you've been back," he began slowly. "I'm sure you've noticed the media's take on the situation in the Middle East. The coverage has been a little weak, to say the least."

"Sure, anyone who's been to the Middle East couldn't help but notice that the media has done a piss-poor job on their coverage of what's going on over there. But what the hell does that have to do with anything? With all this secrecy, your apartment, you," Matt gestured at Stephen.

"Actually, I believe it has everything to do with what happened to my apartment and so much more."

"You'd better fill me in then, Stephen, because I'm not sure I understand."

"Listen, Matt, you don't want to get involved in this. That's actually the reason I wanted to meet with you ~ to warn you." Stephen leaned in toward Matt. "You need to walk away from this."

"Walk away from what, Stephen?" Matt replied. "What the hell's going on?"

"You don't want to know."

Matt grabbed Stephen's arm. "Yes, I do," he insisted. "If you're in trouble, I want to help."

The men looked at each other for several seconds. Stephen was the first to break away. He got up and walked toward the shack. Just as Matt began to wonder whether Stephen had disappeared again, his old friend returned holding two beers. He passed one to Matt before settling back into his chair.

"When I got back from the Middle East, I noticed there was a lot of misinformation about what was going on over there," Stephen began. "At first, I thought it presented a great opportunity for me. I had real-time information that I thought would be highly marketable. But as I continued my research, I realized there was something more going on."

Matt nodded his head in agreement. "I know what you're talking about. For me, since I've gotten back, the only thing more astounding than the information gap was the general indifference about that gap among members of the news media and the editors."

"Exactly. It seemed that even the so-called liberal media outlets weren't interested in the facts. At first, I was shocked, then I was intrigued. It was around this time that I got in touch with Bob. He and I began to discuss the idea of media manipulation."

"Bob Sandberg was involved in this?" Matt asked, a black hole starting to open in his gut.

"Yeah," Stephen confirmed. "I needed his help, his connections."

Bob had significant contacts. Matt recalled that he had used his relationships in Washington to get himself admitted into the embed program when it was originally instituted during the Bush Administration. From there, he had a bird's-eye view of the war on terror, literally and figuratively. Stephen and Matt got a good laugh every time they caught a flash of Bob in a brand-new flight jacket reporting live while perched on top of an M-88 tank recovery vehicle in a convoy flying toward Baghdad. When the attention turned to Afghanistan, Bob had been able to use those same contacts to get strategically placed there as well. Meanwhile, Stephen and Matt ~ who decided to take the moral high ground and not join the embed program ~ were left wandering around on their own scavenging for whatever news scraps they could find.

"With Bob's help, I figured out that the news about the events in the Middle East wasn't merely the result of sloppy reporting or the failure of the media to combat the spin-doctors in the White House. Unfortunately," Stephen continued,"we also discovered just how serious the group behind this is about keeping their not-so-little secret."

"Stephen," Matt interrupted, "start at the beginning. Just what did you and Bob figure out."

"Well, I don't need to remind you about the fake accounts of what was happening over there in the beginning."

"Of course not," Matt said. "I know that from the beginning of the War on Terror, the media was all too happy to pass along the government's description of the events without question. In some cases, they simply regurgitated what the government spat out. But we learned from that. The media's not falling for that crap anymore."

"Oh, I think we learned from it alright, but I don't think everyone learned the same lesson. Some of us ~ like you and me ~ learned to be a little bit more skeptical. But, others ... well, others figured that there were opportunities to use the media to influence the public."

"What do you mean?"

"Bob found out that a small public relations firm is behind most of the press coming out about what's going on in the Middle East and that the firm is intentionally providing misinformation."

"Let me guess," interrupted Matt. "Information Management Services."

"How did you know?" Stephen asked.

"You and Bob aren't the only ones who know how to do a little digging," Matt replied.

"Yeah. Bob and his digging ..." Stephen said as he shook his head sadly. "We met several times and talked about these things. He got me the identity of the PR firm and the group that's behind it. From there, I was able to use another contact to get more information. But, there's no way I could have figured this all out without Bob."

Matt leaned in close. "What happened, Stephen?"

"Those assholes killed him," Stephen spat out. "That's what happened."

Matt was stunned. Despite Marie's earlier insistence that Bob's death was no accident and Stephen's declaration, Matt struggled with accepting that Bob had been murdered.

"Are you sure about this, Stephen?" Matt finally asked.

"No doubt in my mind, Matt," Stephen replied. "Bob discovered that IMS was hired by someone ~ we don't know who ~ to manage a public relations campaign in the United States."

"To do what?"

"As far as we can tell, they are working hard to promote a very specific picture of what's going on in the Middle East," Stephen responded. "They have been the driving force behind some documentaries on the progress that has been made over there. They've also been behind several articles touting the new governments in Iraq and Afghanistan and the great job they're supposedly doing bringing democracy to the region. This firm is also the money behind a not-for-profit organization that has written several research papers about the benefits of fossil fuels over alternative energy sources. This PR firm is being paid to create news that is specifically intended to put a positive spin on what's going on in the Middle East. "

"That's what PR firms do." Matt interrupted.

"That's true," Stephen conceded. "But we know from our own experiences over in the Middle East that what they're reporting isn't true. And these guys do more than just spit out positive press releases that people know came from a public relations firm and can interpret the information through that lens and as they deem appropriate. They spread their spin in such a way that it looks like an unbiased report. We were able to track the language from their press releases and link it to several hard news articles ~ with the exact same language. They're able to get legitimate news organizations to take their reports ~ that are factually incorrect – and publish them as news."

Matt thought about this for a minute. He had to admit that he could see the value of an effective PR campaign. The City of Miami had to do something similar after several tourists became victims of a series of carjackings that occurred over a period of several months. A number of cars with out-of-state license plates that had ended up lost in the wrong part of town were stopped by groups of very organized street thugs waiting for just this opportunity. The occupants were robbed and terrorized at gunpoint and, in a few cases, someone had been shot. When news of this specific form of attack had gone public, there was a significant drop in tourism, Miami's primary source of income.

So the City Commission authorized the placement of better signage pointing out-of-towners in the direction of the airport, hotels and tourist attractions. But the city didn't stop there. They also authorized the spending of millions of dollars on PR firms that coordinated a massive marketing campaign designed to assure the public that the city was safe, highlight all of the fun and exciting activities the city had to offer and downplay the escalating poverty and crime that plagued many pockets of the city. The campaign was a huge success. It didn't take long for the tourists to forget about the history of violence. Once they did, the land of sandy beaches, turquoise water and pink flamingos became popular again.

"I get it, Stephen. But, how does a PR firm have the power to influence the press to that extent?" Matt asked.

"It's easier than you think," answered Stephen. "All it takes is one lazy paper to pick up a self-serving press release, not vet it properly and publish it verbatim as news. Then voila! a puff piece becomes fact. If that story is picked up and repeated enough times, nobody remembers where it came from, certainly not whether it came from a legitimate news source."

"The echo effect," Matt said. An information source will make a claim, which people will then repeat over and over again. Like the game of telephone, the message will become distorted, frequently exaggerated. But in the end, most people will assume that the story ~ or some variation of the story ~ is true.

"That's right," Stephen confirmed. "And if you've got a PR firm that can put out enough press releases, documentaries and white papers, you can create the illusion that the message is coming from different sources and that it must be true."

"A PR firm really has that much influence?" Matt asked.

Stephen nodded. "In case you hadn't noticed, Matt, in the struggle between quality unbiased content generated by paid professional journalists and self-serving material generated from other sources, quality content is getting its ass kicked."

"And you really think this information ~ or misinformation campaign ~ somehow got Bob killed?"

"Yeah. I think it did."

"A man was killed over spin?" Matt said shaking his head in disbelief.

"There's a lot at stake," Stephen said interrupting Matt's thoughts. "Billions of dollars. Lives. Reputations. World standing. Enough to kill for."

"Assuming you're right, Stephen, how did they find found out about Bob and what you guys were doing?"

"Initially, Bob and I didn't hide what we were working on. We thought we didn't need to. We met on several occasions in public places and it was pretty well known in our circles what we were doing. Bob even went to his paper to pitch a series of articles on the topic. He described our preliminary findings to his editor and folks at a couple of other media outlets. We were hoping to generate interest in hopes of a broad distribution when we were ready to go with the story. Shortly after that, Bob was dead. I don't think that was a coincidence."

"And this is why you're living ... like this?" Matt asked, gesturing at Stephen and their current surroundings.

"As soon as I heard about Bob's death, I considered that it might be related to the story, although I didn't know for sure. I haven't been back home since. I didn't even know my apartment was trashed until you mentioned it ~ although I'm not surprised ~ and I think it only confirms my fears."

Not to mention Matt's fears. He had felt from the outset that it was no ordinary burglary.

"Does anyone else know about this?" Matt asked.

"Yeah, one other guy. Another source Bob and I were using. I got in touch with him immediately after I heard about what happened to Bob. I explained to him that we needed to shut down our investigation ... at least until we figured out our next move."

"Who's this guy?"

"I can't tell you. He's nervous, very nervous. I swore to protect his identity so he trusts me. But he's not a journalist, and he's getting pretty squirrely."

"So what's your next move?" Matt asked.

"I don't have a next move, Matt," Stephen admitted. "Even if I did, you don't want to get involved in this. I only told you in the hopes that it'd knock some sense into you. Walk away from this. I'm telling you. Walk away now."

"Listen, Stephen, I am involved. I made a promise to Bob's widow."

Matt explained his meeting with Marie, the conversation they had and her insistence that he figure out what happened to her husband. "Even if I hadn't promised Marie, Stephen," Matt continued. "I still wouldn't walk away. I'm not going to let you deal with this by yourself."

Stephen shook his head. "You don't owe me anything. And this is way too dangerous."

"I'm going to help ~ whether you like it or not," Matt replied. "If it makes you feel any better about accepting my help, consider this: I'm certainly not going to let go of such a potentially great story. Now you can let me go off half-cocked and try to investigate this on my own, which you know I have a tendency to do, or you can tell me what I can do to help."

Stephen stared at Matt intently for several seconds. "Alright, Matt," Stephen finally replied raising his hands in surrender. "You win."

Matt grinned, but he wasn't quite sure he should feel like a winner.

"So, what's the next step?"

Stephen sighed deeply and shook his head. "I told you, I haven't figured that out yet."

"If what you're suggesting about Bob is true, shouldn't we go to the police?" Matt asked.

Stephen got up and began pacing in front of the chairs as he considered this. "No," he finally said. "We can't go to them yet. I don't have enough information. I don't have any real proof."

"So, what do we do?"

"I don't know." He ran his hands through his hair. "But I'm working on it. I have some ideas but I need some time." He collapsed back into his seat with a sigh.

A long silence followed. The only sound came from the click of the bocce balls in the background and an occasional hoot from the table of old timers exchanging stories.

"It's late," Stephen finally said slapping his thighs and sitting up. "You've got a lot of information to absorb ~ and I still have some additional information I need to get. I think maybe we should call it a night."

"Okay. But, Stephen, come back with me tonight," Matt said. "You can stay at my place."

"No, that's not necessary," Stephen shook his head. "I'm good. I have a place to stay ~ it's not the Ritz but I'm okay."

"Come on, man," Matt said. "I don't like the idea of you out on the streets on your own ~ especially after everything you've told me."

"Matt, I appreciate your concern. I really do. But, I think it's better for you ~ and me ~ if we aren't seen in public together. Whoever got to Bob hasn't found me yet, although not from lack of trying judging from what you tell me about my apartment. I'd like to keep it that way."

"But ~"

"No, Matt," Stephen responded. "I can't put you in any more danger than I already have. I've got some things I have to do. I need to figure out our next step. I can't do that if I'm worried about you."

Matt argued with Stephen for several minutes longer, but his old friend was adamant that he would not go home with Matt and Matt was not going to change his mind. He knew Stephen was probably right about keeping a distance, but that didn't make Matt feel any better about leaving his friend out on his own, especially if things were as bad as he had suggested. The last thing Matt wanted was to have to pay any visits to Stephen's parents, like the one to Bob's wife.

CHAPTER FOURTEEN

FROM THE MOMENT Matt dropped off Stephen at a spot on the mainland in Downtown Miami, Matt began watching the time more closely. The more he worried about Stephen, the slower the hours seemed to drag. So Matt kept busy as best he could. He continued researching story lines, spending time with Pierre and renewing other acquaintances. He also called Dana to find out whether she had heard anything about Mo's situation. When Dana called him back, she asked him to meet her at Perricone's Marketplace & Cafe, a popular restaurant near downtown.

Perricone's was built out of lumber from a well-preserved wooden barn built in the 1700s in Vermont. The restaurant's owner had the barn taken apart piece by piece, transported to Miami and carefully reconstructed on the property. The hand-hewn beams, walls and flooring beautifully complemented the old banyan trees surrounding the structure. The restaurant is a hidden oasis amid massive hammock trees and towering skyscrapers.

The place was starting to fill up with a lunchtime crowd. Matt asked the hostess to seat him because he knew he was in for a wait. Dana could generally be counted on to be late, frequently very late. Dana didn't mean to be rude. She just had a tendency to over commit herself and to get lost in whatever she was working on. He was seated in the outside patio at a corner table overlooking the rest of the restaurant. From there he watched the lunch crowd cut deals, settle cases and get to know each other on safe first dates.

Dana finally made her entrance. She breezed past the hostess stand and stood in the middle of the dining room. Matt watched her scan the room. She spotted him and strode toward the table. On the way, she stopped at two different tables to exchange greetings with people she recognized. When she finally arrived at the table, Matt rose and they exchanged a brief hug.

"Sorry for being late," she said as she settled into the chair across from him. "I got dragged into a meeting at the office."

She began looking over a menu he suspected she knew by heart. Her brown eyes shone brightly behind her very stylish black-rimmed glasses. Her normally olive complexion was deeply tanned. She was wearing a cream-colored sleeveless dress. It fit snugly against her trim figure. The black sweater that fell loosely around her shoulders and was tied in front only served to accentuate her shapely arms and the swell of her breasts.

Matt waited for Dana to put down her menu before speaking. He asked about her and her parents. She inquired politely about his travels and his friends. They stuck to the superficial, Matt knowing it was safer that way and Dana likely feeling the same way.

The waitress arrived and took their order.

"Were you able to find anything out about Mo?" Matt asked as soon as the waitress was out of earshot.

"Yes. But it wasn't easy."

She went on to explain how the establishment of the Department of Homeland Security was supposed to make the exchange of information among the different agencies easier. Instead, after the purported consolidation of the agencies under one umbrella, turf battles between the famously competitive agencies ~ the FBI, CIA and Secret Service ~ erupted. And interagency communication became more difficult. Over the last couple of years, communication and information sharing among the intelligence agencies had started to get better, but the former INS, which was generally considered the red-headed stepchild of the DHS, wasn't in that communication loop.

"I appreciate everything you had to do," he finally interrupted. "I know it couldn't have been easy. But what about Mo?"

"He's being questioned by the Department of Justice," Dana replied matter of factly.

"About what? What interest could the DOJ possibly have in Mo?"

"They want to know more about what he was doing in the Middle East," she paused. "And his relationship with a terrorist cell located near the Afghan-Pakistan border."

"What relationship with a terrorist cell? Mo has no relationship with terrorists!"

"The Justice Department isn't so sure," Dana responded, still maintaining a face that gave nothing away.

"They have found some possible links between Mo, the Taliban and this terrorist network. So they picked Mo up when he returned from the Middle East to ask him about his trip and this group."

Matt was shocked. He wasn't sure what he found more disturbing ~ the fact that the U.S. government had picked Mo up for no reason or that Dana was sitting here so calmly attempting to justify the government's actions.

"Dana, first of all, this whole thing is absurd." Matt leaned in to deliver the words, his voice low and hard. "Second, how can the DOJ just arrest Mo and hold him for several weeks without letting him make a phone call. To his family? To an attorney? That's completely illegal."

"Matt, you're being dramatic," Dana said dismissively as she turned her attention to the salad the waitress put in front of her.

Matt ignored the steak placed in front of him.

"Mo hasn't been arrested," she said in between bites. "He's merely being questioned. The government has the authority to detain people while they're being questioned."

"I thought only enemy combatants could be detained by the military."

"Even American citizens can be detained in the interest of national security."

Matt was shocked and dumbstruck for several seconds as he processed this information.

"How long can they hold him, Dana?" He finally asked. "I heard he's been missing for weeks."

"They can hold American citizens indefinitely. Particularly when they're considered enemy combatants."

"An enemy combatant!" Matt slammed his fork down on the table, drawing glances from the folks at the neighboring tables. "Are you kidding me? This is ridiculous. Mo is not an enemy combatant!"

"I know that, Matt," Dana continued after looking at the tables around them, smiling tightly and then leaning in. "But the Justice Department believes that in some cases certain actions, which would otherwise be considered extreme, are necessary to protect national security. As a result certain people can be held indefinitely." She looked at him earnestly before she continued. "They just need to get some information from Mo, confirm he is what he says he is and then they will release him."

"What kind of information? How many questions could they possibly have?"

"Well, that's just it. I've heard that Mo hasn't been cooperating. He's refusing to answer their questions."

"Well, I'm sure if he's refusing to answer questions, he has a very good reason."

"That's exactly what the government is afraid of. They're concerned it means he's hiding something ~ or is actually involved with these groups."

"Well, that's a Catch-22. If he doesn't confess to anything because he has nothing to hide, then the government assumes he has something to hide!" Matt could barely control his anger. "Dana, Mo is not involved with these groups. He's not a traitor, and he definitely isn't an enemy combatant. You know that," he said urgently.

"You know Mo," he insisted when Dana didn't respond.

Dana signaled Matt to lower his voice as she looked around the room. "I shouldn't be telling you this, Matt." She leaned in closer. "But we know that over the last year Mo has traveled extensively throughout the Middle East. Mo has met with several high-ranking officials of the Taliban. And more recently, he has been spending time in Syria."

"Come on, Dana. He's a reporter. He meets with people for a living. He gets interviews no one else can get. That doesn't make him a traitor. That makes him a damn good journalist." Matt continued before Dana could interrupt. "If he's not speaking with the people at the Department of Justice or the Department of Homeland Security or whatever, it's probably because he's trying to protect his sources. That actually makes him a journalist with integrity."

"I'm not an idiot, Matt. I don't need the speech," she said tightly. "I care about Mo just as much as you do and, for the record, I don't think he's a terrorist. But he has met with some important people and the Justice Department has every reason to believe that he has information that could be helpful." She leaned in again and continued in hushed tones. "He could know locations of hideouts, information regarding terrorist cells."

"Even if Mo does know anything, and I have no idea if he does, the government can't force him to disclose that information. So they can't hold him until he does. Right?"

"I'm familiar with the concept of freedom of speech, Matt. Journalists generally can't be forced to divulge their sources. But this is different, Matt. We're at war."

"Oh, jeez," Matt exclaimed. The smack of his hand against the table made the salt and pepper shakers jump. "If I hear that again, I'm going to ..."

The waitress rushed over to see if they needed anything else. Or, more likely, she was eager to get them out of there. At this point, Matt was eager to get the hell out of there too. He signaled that she could take away his plate ~ even though he'd barely touched his meal. This meeting had only served to infuriate him.

But he needed Dana. She was the only person he knew who had connections with the people who were holding Mo. She also knew Mo and had to know he wasn't involved in anything illegal and she could make that case to the people that mattered.

"Dana," Matt began, this time trying a softer, more conciliatory tone. "I visited with his family ~ his mother, father and younger sister. They are completely distraught. They have no idea what's happened to him and what they can do to help."

Dana was staring at him without expression but Matt thought he noticed a softening around her jaw.

"You know Mo, Dana. You know his character, and you know he's not involved with terrorists. He's a friend and he needs our help ~ your help. Isn't there anything you can do?"

Dana sighed heavily. She looked down at her plate for several seconds then finally looked back up at Matt. "I have some connections with the Justice Department. I'll see what I can do."

"Dana, that would be great," Matt said quickly. "I can't wait to tell Mo's fam~"

"Don't," Dana interrupted. "I'm not making any promises. Do me a favor and don't say anything about this."

"Okay, I understand." Matt said quickly. "But, Dana, I really do appreciate this."

"Yeah, whatever," Dana said. "In the interim, Matt, I suggest that you keep a low profile."

"Me? Why? What are you talking about? Am I at risk of being picked up as well?" Matt felt the indignation began to rise in his throat again.

"That's not what I'm talking about, Matt. I heard from one of my friends at the commissioner's office. Suarez knows you're back in town, and he's not real happy about it."

"I know. He's already paid me a visit."

Dana's eyes widened. "He has? What happened?"

Matt gave Dana an abbreviated version of his earlier run-in with the commissioner on the street outside his home. "I knew he'd eventually get wind of my return, although I didn't anticipate the personal visit to welcome me back," Matt said. "But you know what? Commissioner Suarez's insecurities are not my problem."

"Unfortunately, Matt, Commissioner Suarez's insecurities are everyone's problem." She scanned the room quickly. "You know better than anyone else what a vindictive bastard he can be. If anything, he's gotten worse since you left."

"Why's he still fixated on me? I hear he's on track to win his bid for re-election. He should be satisfied."

"Suarez is never satisfied. He's already strategizing on how he's going to get back some of the leadership positions and political clout he lost during the investigation. He's got an ambitious agenda planned for his term and then it's on to the Senate for him. You know he and his brother have always figured they'd take both seats of the Senate."

"They're not still planning that, are they?"

"Oh, yeah."

"That would be a pretty ballsy move to go after that seat so soon."

"He's always been aggressive, and now he's fixated. He's not someone you want to cross."

"I hear ya, Dana, and I appreciate the advice. I'll steer clear of him." Even as he said it, Matt knew he wasn't sure how long he could avoid the temptation of a good target like Commissioner Suarez.

After they gestured for the check, Dana turned the conversation to their mutual friends.

"How's Stephen Cross doing?" Dana asked.

The question took him aback, especially when a picture of Stephen as he had appeared the night before flashed in his head. But he shouldn't have been surprised. When Matt and Dana were dating, Dana had gotten to know Stephen fairly well.

"He's fine, as far as I know. I haven't seen him since I've come back from the Middle East."

Matt felt bad about lying to her but figured the less she knew, the fewer the complications for both of them. In any event, he needed her attention firmly focused on Mo.

Matt struggled to fill the void in conversation while they waited for the bill. They had exhausted all topics except one.

"So, are you dating anyone?" Matt finally asked.

Dana smiled. "Yes, I am."

"Great," he responded with as much warmth, sincerity and interest as he could muster. "Anyone I know?"

"I don't think so. His name is Jeffrey Rosen. He's a doctor, a psychiatrist, actually. A long-time friend of the family."

"Is it serious?"

"We're engaged." She smiled as she extended her hand toward him and wiggled her fingers. On her left index finger was a rock, a very big rock, surrounded by two other slightly smaller rocks. Only a man would have missed this very substantial and extremely tangible proof of undying love. Matt didn't know a damn thing about diamonds, but he was impressed.

"We're getting married in six months."

She began to talk about her fiancé, his successful private practice providing therapy to the Miami Beach crowd, his family here in South Florida and the life that he and Dana had started to build together. It sounded like everything Dana had ever wanted.

The waitress finally returned with the bill. Matt quickly paid, gesturing Dana away when she attempted to contribute.

They said their good-byes, as they waited for the valet attendants to bring their cars.

"Listen, Matt," Dana said as she got into her Mercedes SL Class convertible. "I'll do everything I can for Mo. You know that, right?"

"I do, Dana," Matt replied as another valet attendant pulled up behind her car in his Jeep. "And I really appreciate it."

Matt knew she meant it but he wasn't sure how much she could do. Whatever it was, he hoped it was enough.

CHAPTER FIFTEEN

ALEX DORAN HAD continued to call and email Matt since the day they had lunch in Coconut Grove. Her emails and calls were friendly and in some cases flirtatious but each time they ended with a reminder that he had said he would let her interview him. At first, he had taken the calls and responded to the emails but avoided making any firm commitment about the interview. At the same time, he picked her brain about what she learned from Bob. She didn't appear to know much more than what she had originally told him.

After a few of these phone calls, he decided he couldn't keep stringing her along. He decided to tell her what was going on. He hated being dishonest and he thought her research skills might be helpful. After he told her about his conversion with Stephen, he shouldn't have been surprised when she asked if she could join Matt the day he was supposed to meet up with Stephen again. There was something about her that still made him cautious ~ he wasn't sure whether it was fear of sharing the story with someone or something else ~ but he ultimately agreed.

Alex arrived at Matt's house one hour before the appointed time. She was wearing a fitted blue button down shirt and khaki pants that hugged her body and stopped just above brown flat shoes. She had a brown messenger bag slung across her torso and resting on her right hip. They left in Matt's Jeep.

They traveled up and down several back roads of Coconut Grove, back tracking and retracing their steps, with Matt checking frequently in the rear view mirror. An amateur in evasion tactics, Matt had no idea whether they were really being followed or not. After twenty minutes of this, he pulled up in the parking lot of the Coconut Grove community center, very close to where they had actually started off.

"Let's go," he said, jumping out.

Instead of heading toward the building, Matt walked quickly to the back of the parking lot. He looked around before veering off to the right toward a path at the end of the asphalt, with Alex following closely. He had traveled this route regularly when he took the train to *The Chronicle* offices downtown. Ahead, he could see the stairway to the bridge that crossed above US-1 and led to the Metrorail Station for Miami's heavy rail rapid transit system. Matt heard a train approaching and turned to see that it was a northbound train.

"Come on," Matt shouted as he began to take the stairs two at a time.

He looked back and saw that Alex was keeping up with him easily. They raced across the bridge. Once on the other side, Matt pressed some tokens into the machine. They pushed their way through the turnstile and jogged along the platform, stopping as the train pulled in and ready to board the train when the doors of the incoming train slid open. Matt urged Alex in ahead of him.

Once on the train, Matt turned to the window. He saw two stocky men race across the bridge they had just crossed. Matt thought he recognized one of the guys as the man that had been standing under the street lamp on the night he had the visit from Commissioner Suarez, but he couldn't be certain. They could be just regular guys trying to catch a ride on a form of transport commonly used by many Downtown commuters. The train began to move and the men faded from sight.

When Alex and Matt got off the train, they were still a few blocks from their destination. Matt guided Alex past an empty parking lot that served as a campground for the homeless and toward Bayside Marketplace, an open-air complex sitting along the water's edge. With more than 140 shops, restaurants and bars, it was a destination spot for the thousands of tourists coming through Miami every day. Next to the American Airlines Arena, home of the Miami Heat, it also attracted people attending a home game.

They wandered through the crowd, pretending to admire the wares of the local cart operators as they made small talk. A cruise ship was in port so the marketplace was packed. Matt checked his watch frequently and scanned the crowd looking for Stephen. Five minutes before their appointed meeting time with Stephen, Matt and Alex headed to the middle of the main courtyard. Matt noticed two seats next to each other and gestured toward them. They sat together for a few minutes, as kids ran around them, chasing each other and squealing with laughter. Parents watched absently while enjoying the live band and colorful frozen drinks.

Matt finally decided to make use of the time to find out more about Alex.

"So tell me about yourself."

Alex looked at him quizzically.

Matt shrugged. "It looks like we may have some time to kill."

"Well," she began slowly. "My dad was in the military so we traveled around when I was little. We ended up in Tampa when he was transferred to MacDill Air Force Base. I was about 10 and grew up there."

"Ahh." Matt nodded his head. "An Air Force brat. That explains a lot."

"Also, the youngest of four and the only girl."

"That explains even more. A real tomboy, I'll bet." Matt smiled as he put his hands in a defensive gesture. "Remind me not to pick a fight with you."

"Actually, it gets better. I'm ex-military myself."

"Really?" Matt was shocked. "I never would have guessed."

"Yeah," she chuckled softly. "My short-lived military career started with the smooth seduction of a four-year ROTC scholarship. I majored in computer technology at the University of South Florida."

"Interesting. And now you're a writer. What made you decide to go from the exciting world of combat and foreign travel to the calm ~ not to mention solitude ~ of writing?"

"That part was easy," she smiled. "Writing was always my passion. Unfortunately, our government doesn't place a high value on that particular profession, which is why I majored in computers."

"Ah, practicality and love of country prevails. How'd you make the transition to writer?"

"Well, I haven't yet. For now, writing is just a hobby. I don't actually make a living at it. After I completed my commitment to the government, I took some time off to try and break into the world of writing. Unfortunately, though, no one would hire me without some background in journalism or without having been published. So I decided to write the book. Hopefully, I can parlay it into a full-time career."

"Sounds like a plan," Matt said encouragingly. "I'm sure it'll pay off."

"It better pay off soon, because out-of-work computer techs are a dime a dozen since the technology bust."

"Well, I hate to tell you this but writers aren't worth much more."

Matt checked his watch again. Stephen was thirty minutes late. He canvassed the faces of the passersby one final time. The family of tourists was still there, but the kids were starting to tire and were whining to their parents that it was time to go. A trio of suits were walking unsteadily by and headed toward the parking lot. An unkempt homeless man was picking through the large trash can next to Matt.

The man stopped when he noticed Matt staring at him. He snarled in their direction and Matt quickly looked away.

"Damn!" Matt said suddenly. "I'm an idiot!"

"What?"

"I know where to find Stephen." He stood up and grabbed her hand. "Let's go!"

"But ... where?" Alex stammered as she followed him.

Matt didn't reply. Outside, he strode back the way they had come and to the large city parking lot across the street from Bayside. He continued through the lot, weaving his way through parked cars.

Matt noticed a crowd had gathered at the back of the lot, the dark and shadowy part under the I-95 overpass. No man's land. The area was covered with large cardboard boxes cobbled together as shelters as well shopping carts and black plastic bags used to transport personal effects. Here, the homeless had established a camp, a city-sanctioned place to loiter and sleep without being accosted. The police were not allowed to harass or arrest them.

The wind strengthened and there was a chill in the air that felt heavy with moisture, redolent of approaching rain. Matt picked up the pace. A few grizzled faces squinted out from the shelter of boxes in various shapes, some apprehensive, most angry at the intrusion on their personal space.

Matt noticed a crowd of people had gathered up ahead, some in dirty layers of clothing, others in Tommy Bahama shirts, Bermuda shorts and flip-flops. Not the usual cast of characters hanging around the homeless camp. Matt headed in that direction, with Alex still following closely behind. He passed the army of rags and then wove his way through a crowd of homeless men and women along with a few outsiders that had also found their way to the action.

Matt and Alex pushed their way to the very front where a police officer was talking to a homeless man who appeared to be in his late thirties. His long, matted hair hadn't seen a comb in a very long time. Matt could see foreign objects in the thick long mustache and beard. He was holding court, talking loudly to an enthralled crowd. He seemed thrilled to have an audience and was telling a story with great dramatic flair.

"I already told you, officer," Matt heard when they were within earshot.

"I know," the patrolman said, "but tell me slowly this time."

The man sighed heavily before continuing.

"I was just sittin' in my crib mindin' my own bizness when this big guy comes walkin' down the sidewalk. Actin' like he owned the damn place. He bumped up against my house and knocked it down." The man gestured to a large refrigerator box laying crumpled next to him. "He had no cause to do that. The man didn't even stop to apologize."

"Then what happened?" The officer asked patiently.

Matt noted that, with his boyish good looks and bright blue pressed uniform, the police officer couldn't have been on the job for more than a few months. Those were the ones typically assigned to watch over the homeless lots, where the most heinous crimes were petty theft, fighting among the homeless or an occasional homeless beating by bored teenagers weaned on violent video games.

"He walked over to my friend King and just started whalin' on him. Bam! Bam! Bam!" The man shouted as he gestured wildly, punching an imaginary foe. "He had no cause to do that. None at all. King ain't done nothin' to him. This is what you call an unprovoked attack."

The police officer held up his hand. "Slow down, sir. What exactly happened? I need all the details. Where was your friend?"

"King was sittin' over there on that bench." He pointed to a place off to the side where two police officers were pushing the crowd back as they tied a yellow tape around the scene. Matt couldn't make out what exactly the officers were trying to protect with their yellow tape.

"He wasn't doing nothin', officer. Nothin'. He was just mindin' his own business, writin' in his book. King never bothered no one. He always kept to himself. The big guy just goes over to King and picks a fight with him. I hear them carryin' on, arguin' and such."

"What was the fight about?"

"I don't know. I couldn't hear what they were sayin'. I was tryin' to put my house back in order."

The crowd was entranced. One tourist even took a picture. When the homeless man noticed the flash, he stopped to pose for another.

The police officer glared at the tourist taking the picture and gestured for the woman to put the camera down. "And what happened after that, sir?"

"King didn't say nothin'. He just bent down to pick up his book. And, then, just as he leans down ..." The homeless man leaned down as if to pick an object off the floor. "BAM!" His fist flew through the air pounding toward the ground. "King fell down. Then while King was down, this guy picks a bottle up off the ground and whacks King over the head with it." The man picked an imaginary object off the ground and struck the air violently with it.

"I wanted to help but there weren't nothin' I could do," he explained to the crowd. "When King got up, the Big Man just smiled. King's standin' there, barely, with blood running down the back of his head and this damn fool is smiling at him. I'm telling you, this was one sick motherfucker." He then quickly turned and smiled apologetically at a middle-aged woman standing in front of the crowd with two teenage kids. She smiled back tentatively.

"Big Man then throws down the bottle and punches King. One time and then another time. King goes down again. This guy just starts kickin' him over and over again." The man pulled his leg back and violently kicked the air. "And stomping on him like he was a damn bug. I ain't never seen anything like it. It was ugly. He kept at it until King wasn't moving."

"What did this man look like?"

"I told you, man." He scowled at the police officer. "He was a big white man. A big badass white man with a big badass temper."

The police officer sighed. "Anything else you can tell us?"

"Yeah, this guy is one fucked-up motherfucker, and you better get him off the streets," he shouted as he wagged his finger at the cop. A few people in the crowd nodded in agreement.

"We'll do that. In the interim, we have to track down your friend's next of kin. This guy King." The officer referred to his notes. "What was his first name?"

"Nah, man," the homeless man replied scowling and shaking his head in apparent disgust. "King weren't his real name. We called him that because he was always writin'. You know, like that scary writer dude. You know who I'm talking about." He said pointing his finger at the officer. "He wrote *Carrie* and shit. Stephen King. My man's first name was Stephen."

Matt had heard enough. He extricated himself from the crowd and made his way over to where another group had congregated, apparently near the area where the attack had taken place. Two police officers stood ground while a small group of onlookers watched the crime scene investigators sift through the area. He inched as close to the scene as the yellow tape would allow.

The body had already been bagged and taken away. Shards of green bottle glass covered with blood were scattered over the ground in a thick pool of a dark liquid. Lying nearby he saw a large clear plastic bag, marked John Doe with an identification number. A wallet. A watch. And a book. The shape of the book and the bright red cover looked familiar. Matt leaned closer. One of the officers noticed him and instructed him to step back.

He turned around and took Alex by the hand, leading her out of the crowd and back to the Metrorail Station where they had been dropped off. A few minutes later they were back on the train heading south.

"I know what you're thinking," Alex said as soon as they sat down in a Southbound train. "But we don't know that was your Stephen."

"It was Stephen," Matt said as he looked straight ahead.

"You don't know that," she said grabbing his arm hard. "That couldn't have been him. He wouldn't have been living on the streets."

"He was, and it was."

She paused and then finally asked, "How can you be so sure?"

"I saw the bag of personal effects of this 'homeless man'."

"There was a book," he continued slowly. "A book called 'The Media Monopoly'." She didn't say a word, so Matt continued. "How many homeless people do you know read about the chilling effects of media consolidation?"

Alex made no reply.

"And then there was what the witness said about the victim. He said his name was Stephen," Matt reminded her. "Like the writer."

When they finally arrived at Matt's house, Alex followed Matt up the walkway and through the front door. He hadn't invited her in, but he was thankful for the company. She sat down on the sofa as Matt walked to the kitchen. He soon returned with two glasses of amber liquid. He handed one to Alex who took it without comment. The scotch burned slightly as it went down. Macallan. The good stuff. The stuff he pulled out to celebrate a brilliant and well-received article, a Miami Dolphins' win against the New England Patriots or, these days, a Dolphins' win against anyone. Tonight, though, the drink would serve a different purpose. The welcome sensation finally penetrated the numbness.

Matt was the first to speak.

"I met Stephen in New York after September 11th. By then, Stephen had already covered many conflicts ~ all over the world. But I was only 22, and this was my first major assignment. Stephen was a reporter at *The New York Times* and had won a Pulitzer Prize for his coverage of the war in Bosnia. He was flying high. Yet, for some reason, he took me under his wing and spent a lot of time showing me the ropes."

He looked over and saw that she was watching him, so he continued.

"For Stephen, it wasn't about scooping other journalists. It was all about educating people ~ himself and his readers. He was a great mentor ~ the best."

The sun had set, and the only light in the house came from the street lamp in front and the back porch light. Matt made no move to turn on any lights inside.

"So, what do we do now?" Alex finally asked the question weighing heavily on Matt's mind.

"I'm not sure, Alex," he started slowly. "But I think I have an idea."

She must have noticed the hesitation in his voice. She was watching him intently.

"Stephen said he and Bob were working with someone," Matt continued. "Someone who was helping them gather information. Someone that seemed to have an inside track on what's going on. I need to speak to that person. Talk to him. Find out everything he knows and exactly what's going on."

"How do you find him?"

"I can find him," Matt replied firmly.

He could tell by the look on her face that she was doubtful. Fortunately for him, she didn't ask any questions. If she had, she would have realized there was little basis for his certitude.

"And the police?" Alex asked. "Do you think you should we get them involved?"

Matt thought about this for a few moments. "And tell them what?" he finally said. "Tell them about the whacked-out conspiracy theories of an overmedicated, grieving widow and a journalist who was last seen living in shantytown with the homeless and is now dead." Matt shook his head. "No. I don't have any proof. At this point, all I know is that Stephen's apartment was burglarized and he was killed in an attack at a homeless camp where he was hiding out. I need to get more information."

"What can I do to help?"

"Nothing," Matt replied firmly. He put his glass down on the table and turned toward Alex. "Stephen warned me about getting involved. He said it would be dangerous and that I'd be better off staying out of it. Apparently he was right. And I made a mistake getting you involved. I need to go it alone from here on out."

"No, Matt."

"Listen to me," he said. "This is what I do."

"I can help. I can do research," she continued quickly. "Remember I'm the one that got you that information about IMS."

"I know, Alex. But this could be very dangerous and I don't want you to get hurt."

"I'm not letting you do this alone, Matt. This is more than just a story to me. A man ~ two men ~ may have been killed."

Her mouth was set. Her eyes determined. Her shoulders were back and her hands were clenched in fists, as if waiting for a fight. She wasn't giving in and Matt wasn't up for fighting tonight.

"Okay," he finally conceded. "I just hope you know what you're getting yourself into."

CHAPTER SIXTEEN

THE NEXT AFTERNOON Matt returned from a five-mile run, his head no clearer than when he had started. Once again, the so-called runner's high had eluded him. He had indeed exercised strenuously. His labored breathing was a testament to that, but he wasn't feeling euphoric or even particularly happy. The events of the last few days weighed too heavily on him.

As Matt walked into the house, he checked the telephone log and found several missed calls from a blocked number. He also had one voice mail message from Cole Harrison, who said he needed to see Matt urgently and requested a call back immediately. This was Harrison's third message in as many days. With each call, the degree of annoyance evident in Harrison's tone had increased exponentially. In this latest message, the man sounded downright pissed off. Matt paused before muttering, "Screw you." He deleted the message as he had done all the rest before heading to the bathroom.

Fifteen minutes later, his hair still dripping from a quick shower, Matt threw on a pair of well-worn jeans and a faded green pullover. He stepped into the shoes set on the floor just inside the back door and walked outside. Matt paused to take a look around the playground of his childhood. The backyard wasn't small but the corpulent banyan tree squatting in the center of the yard took up most of the space. High, thick shrubs running around the back and sides of the yard created the impression of a tropical oasis, notwithstanding the gentrification that had been going on in the neighborhood for the last several years. Over the years, it had been a jungle where he had slain imaginary dragons. A nature preserve where his mom and dad had taught him about the many tropical plants and local wildlife that laid claim to the property.

Matt's parents had bought the house in 1970, shortly after they were married, and had lived there until their deaths in 2008. Matt was working at *The Chronicle* and living in an apartment nearby when his father was diagnosed with cancer in early 2007. The cancer was caught too late and spread quickly. His father died within less than a year of the diagnosis. His mother had been heartbroken after the loss of the love of her life and died within six months. As the only child, Matt inherited the house and the modest savings account his father accumulated over his years as a college professor. With so many good memories occupying the walls of his childhood home, he hadn't had the heart to sell it.

Matt descended the three steps to ground level and walked over to the grill parked close to the wall of the house. He rolled it out from under the eaves and to the far corner of the patio. After turning it on, Matt moved easily between the kitchen inside and the grill outside as he prepared the steaks, potatoes and vegetables. He marinated the meat, rubbing in a homemade mixture of spices, olive oil and Worcestershire sauce. He pricked the potatoes several times with a fork, rubbed them with oil, wrapped them in tinfoil and then placed them on the grill. Matt cut the vegetables and then stacked the pieces on metal skewers, drizzled them with their own marinade and then put them to the side for later. The prep work and cooking were easy. Mindless. A good time to organize his thoughts.

Alex should be over shortly. He was anxious to tell her about the results of the research he had done earlier in the day. Matt heard someone open the gate on the side of the house.

"Back here," Matt shouted. Several moments later, he looked up to see Alex walk around the corner of the house, carrying a six-pack of beer.

"I thought we could use some of these," she said gesturing with the contents of her hands.

Matt needed no introduction to his old friend Sam Adams. "Good call."

"Do you want me to put these in the refrigerator?" Alex asked, noticing his occupied hands.

"No, you can just put them there," Matt said nodding toward the cooler against the wall and in the shade. Earlier he had dragged it out from the garage, cleaned it and loaded it with ice.

He put down the tongs he was holding and walked toward her. He opened the cooler, took the beers out of her hands and began to bury them in the ice. Alex took the bottle Matt offered and waved away the frosty glass he had pulled out of the cooler.

She looked around, surveying the setup Matt had established outside on the patio. She looked toward the house and then nodded. "I get it, Matt. You're now taking Stephen's warnings seriously."

He didn't respond.

"Well, it's a gorgeous afternoon anyway," Alex continued. "Too nice to be inside."

The table was large enough for six but they sat at one end, Matt at the head and Alex to his left. Small tea candles in mismatched glass vases littered the table. The lights created flickers across their faces and just barely illuminated the stag horns and orchids hanging from the muscular limbs of the banyan tree.

"So ..." Alex began after Matt finished putting the grilled steaks, potatoes and vegetables on the table. "What did you find out?"

"Well, I started with what we know," Matt replied as he sat down. "And what we know is that this IMS seems to be behind some big conspiracy to manipulate the media and public opinion."

"Everything does seem to point in that direction," Alex confirmed.

Matt began slowly. "I can see why a public relations firm would be hired to spin the bad news. It's not good for anyone to think that the Middle East is out of control, that all Middle Easterners hate Americans or that the U.S. is at risk of another attack like September 11th. It creates insecurity here and abroad. That's not good for the economy. It also suggests that the billions of dollars we have spent in nation building have been wasted. I get it."

"But this PR firm isn't telling the truth," Alex said. "They're peddling what their clients' want the general public to believe is the truth."

"PR firms aren't generally known for their objectivity. They're hired to promote a particular position. At *The Chronicle,* we had to deal with that all the time. Every day, we'd get press releases from PR firms wanting us to tell stories that were helpful to their clients. Sometimes, if we had time, we'd try to see behind the puffery into the real story, but most of the time, we simply didn't have time or we really didn't care. If we needed a story and theirs worked, we'd use it ~ sometimes verbatim."

"But based on what Stephen told us, this company's doing a little more than just putting out favorable press releases and hoping it sticks. What they're doing borders on propaganda."

"You're right," Matt agreed. "And that's the part I don't get. The fact that they are putting something out there that is completely false ~ and the fact that the media is buying it. Slow media day or not, a news publication isn't going to let you do that, if for no other reason than the fact that a competitor is going to point out the truth and you're going to end up with egg on your face. Or worse, you will have lost credibility ~ and credibility is essential for a news organization."

"If the stories they're peddling are completely fabricated," Matt continued, "how could no one have noticed or said anything? How could one company have that much influence over the media?"

"Well, that part may not be as hard as you think," Alex said as they both began eating. "Over the last several years, media companies have been fighting for relaxation ~ or, better yet, elimination ~ of the media ownership rules. It's reached the point where, right now, about seven companies control ninety percent of what ordinary people read and watch on television ~ seven. These companies own stock in each other and cooperate with each other in media joint ventures. The fact that the media is in the hands of so few and that those companies are working together makes it much easier for them to manipulate information to their advantage."

Matt nodded. "I've experienced that media consolidation directly. *The Chronicle* went from an independent, family-owned business to a subsidiary of Armstrong Media Corporation, a large media conglomerate. Around that same time, my boss Dave Kagan went from a champion of take-no-prisoners investigative journalism, to a reluctant censor careful to print only feel-good news. He seems to have become too worried about stepping on toes, afraid of the advertising sales department and his bean-counter corporate bosses."

"But what about the Internet?" Matt asked. "You can find anything on the Internet. Stuff you don't even want to know about. There doesn't seem to be any type of filter there."

"Sure," Alex responded. "That was the idea. And, yeah, you can still find the outlier website arguing that the earth is flat, showing how the space program is a hoax to cheat us out of tax dollars, or describing how to make a pressure-cooker bomb, but most of the news on the Internet is still being generated by the same conglomerates that control the newspapers, television networks and radio stations. These seven companies control all forms of media -- newspapers, television, radio, cable, satellite and the Internet."

"Hold on," she said, taking a last bite of her vegetables and pushing her plate to the other end of the table to make room in front of her. "Let me show you something,"

She reached down to the messenger bag she had arrived with. She pulled out a stack of papers and began shuffling through them.

"Look at these charts," she said as shoved the papers in front of Matt and pointed. "AOL Time Warner owns HBO and CNN. It also owns Netscape and several publishing companies. Viacom owns CBS, several radio networks, TV stations and a publishing company. Rupert Murdoch's News Corporation owns a television empire in broadcasting, cable and satellite, along with some Internet websites, and dozens of newspapers like *The New York Post* — even *The Wall Street Journal* — plus a handful of book companies. The same seven multinational media companies control what you read in the paper, just about everything you watch on television, read on the Internet and see in the movies."

"This is pretty scary stuff," Matt said as he scanned the papers.

"I'll say."

Matt stood and began to pace the length of the deck.

It may or may not be difficult to tell the population what to think, but it certainly wasn't hard to tell the public what to think about. It is only after the media emphasizes or exposes a particular topic that the public starts to care about it. And, it is only then ~ after the public catches on and creates a public outcry ~ that the politicians focus on the subject.

"What do you think, Matt?"

He could feel her watching him as he continued to pace. He sat back down and placed the papers down on the table.

"Actually, I think you might be on to something," he said.

"Well, it's still speculation, but I thought it would be helpful," Alex said modestly.

"I'm not sure how it all fits together, but it is helpful."

"Okay," Alex said after a moment. "So, what's next? What do we do with this helpful information?"

"We talk to Stephen's contact. Hopefully, he'll be able to confirm some of our suspicions and lead us to the next step."

"And how do we find out who Stephen's contact is?"

"Well, based on what Stephen told me, this guy obviously trusted Stephen, so I would bet Stephen had used him as a source before and protected his identity."

"It still doesn't seem like a lot to go on."

"You're right, but I think it might be enough. I've been digging up Stephen's old articles, and I found a series of articles Stephen had written about the recovery efforts in New Orleans and the surrounding areas post-Hurricane Katrina. One was an exposé on a national contractor that had been awarded major contracts for the clean-up and rebuilding efforts in New Orleans. They were able to successfully bid on these contracts despite having a terrible track record of poor work and over-billing. They did this by creating several shell companies and subsidiaries. No one knew that all of these entities were related to each other."

"How does that help?"

"I remembered asking Stephen how he was able to uncover the scandal. I mean, the government accounting office isn't exactly known for its ability to identify incompetence and corruption. And the company reaping the benefits of the government's lack of adequate oversight certainly isn't going to disclose what's really going on. I asked Stephen how he was able to figure it out, how he was able to uncover the scam."

"And?"

"Stephen mentioned someone who did work for the contractor and had the computer skills to track down the common officers and/or owners of the many different shell companies that were awarded the contracts. He was able to use that information to connect back to the one contractor."

"And?" Alex urged. "That's the guy you think was Stephen's contact? What was his name? How do we get to him?"

"Hold on, Alex," Matt said holding up his hand. "I don't know for sure that this is the guy. Being a good journalist, Stephen never confirmed that was his source. But I think it could be."

"Okay ..."

" I think I might have a good idea who it is."

"That's great! But, how...?"

"I think I actually know him ~ I think I may have introduced the two of them. If it's the guy I think it is, his name is Patrick ~ a computer genius who has done complex programming work for some of the largest companies in the world. He's kind of . . . eccentric, I guess you could say. A very nice guy and really smart."

"This is great, Matt," Alex said. "I just can't believe he'd be willing to talk to us after all that's happened. And based on what we know, I can't say I blame him."

"Well, that's just it." Matt shifted in the chair. "He hasn't exactly agreed to meet with us." He paused. "I haven't spoken to him yet."

Alex looked at him, her brow furrowed. "Then how do you know he'll meet with us tomorrow?"

"Simple. Tomorrow is Saturday. The Heat are playing." Matt continued as Alex looked at him quizzically. "And I know just where this guy will be watching the game."

CHAPTER SEVENTEEN

THE BAR AT KEG SOUTH is smaller than 1,000 square feet but set up to allow for maximum occupancy. There was a long L-shaped bar surrounded by bar stools. Four picnic tables ran parallel to the long side of the bar with a row of high-top tables running along the wall on the same side. A pool table, jukebox and two video games took up the rest of the small space. Two large flat-screen televisions at either end of the bar and several smaller strategically placed televisions ensured that you could spend hours here and never miss a major, minor or quasi sporting event. The windows were blacked out and the only natural light came when someone opened the heavy steel door to enter or exit. The bar had a limited menu but the beers were ice cold and the Keg Burgers grilled to perfection.

Dan, the bartender, had worked at The Keg almost as long as Matt had been coming and Matt received a warm greeting when he walked in the next afternoon.

"Matt, we've missed you," Dan said as he placed a beer in front of Matt. "You were gone a long time."

"I've been doing a little travelling, Dan," Matt said with a grin.

"So I heard," Dan replied. "Actually, I heard that you were over in Afghanistan. And that you got blown up."

"Naahhh," Matt responded. "Any reports of my death were greatly exaggerated."

Not long after Matt introduced Alex and Dan, the two were talking like old friends. To Matt's surprise, Alex was holding her own in a conversation about the top performers in the NBA regular season and her prognostications for the playoff games. Matt was left nursing the beer Dan had placed in front of him while the two discussed the Miami Heat's chances in the conference finals.

It was Saturday afternoon and the place was packed with the usual suspects. Patrons ranged from college kids whooping it up with their friends to middle-aged men throwing back a few while their kids monopolized the pool table and video games, to old-timers nursing their beers and telling the same old stories.

"Interesting taste in art," Alex commented after Dan left to go attend to some regulars sitting in front of empty glasses and giving him the stink-eye.

Matt followed her gaze across the bar to a picture of a girl with her naked chest painted like the face of two cats. Solid black noses and whiskers obstructed the view of the most intimate parts of her breasts. It was likely a souvenir from someone's crazy weekend at Fantasy Fest in Key West.

The wall had started as a locker room of sorts when the bartenders began putting up pictures of their girlfriends, wives and, later, children. It had evolved into a shrine to the history of The Keg and its regular clientele, including pictures of customers with their catches from Keg South-sponsored fishing tournaments, girls in bikinis or various other stages of undress and even a few baby pictures, which seemed out of place. Juxtaposed one on top of the other, the pictures covered every inch of the wall and overlapped some items that had likely been there for twenty years.

"This place is an institution, Alex," Matt responded looking across the room. "I had my first legal beer here." He pointed to a high-top table in the corner. "I interviewed the Mayor of Miami at that very table."

"Relax, Matt," Alex said smiling. "I actually like the place. Although the decorating could use a woman's touch."

Matt snorted. He doubted the owner Butch would be very receptive to the idea.

Matt gave Alex his recommendations and, when she deferred to his judgment on the house specialties, he placed their order. Fish dip and an order of wings to start, then Keg Burgers for each and an order of fresh-cut French fries to share.

Several regulars came over to say hello and welcome Matt back. He introduced Alex to the guys. All eyes scanned her up and down and then registered approval. Alex smiled graciously in return and Matt sat a little taller.

"So what time are we expecting this guy?" Alex asked when the commotion had died down and the fish dip had arrived.

Matt looked at his watch. "The Heat game starts in thirty minutes. He should be here soon."

Alex took this opportunity to turn her attention to the food in front of her.

After taking a few bites, Matt continued. "Last year, during basketball season, football season and even baseball season ~ just about every time I came in here ~ Patrick would be here. He's a regular. A real friendly guy. An Irishman who loves to drink and have a good time."

"Imagine that," Alex replied stuffing her mouth with a cracker full of dip.

"Anyway, one day I'm here with Stephen and Patrick shows up. We all started talking and he mentions he's a computer technician. Stephen was a bit of a computer buff so he was really into it."

Alex nodded as she proceeded to dig into the Keg Burger that had just arrived.

"So, we start talking about computers, technology and the work Patrick does. By this time, we've all had a few drinks but Patrick proceeds to blow us away with talk about the stuff he's working on. Computer security. Firewalls. Cookies that, once planted on your hard drive, would track user activity and then transmit that information back to the mother ship ~ or wherever."

"Patrick definitely knew his stuff. And, unlike me, Stephen understood most of what he was talking about." He picked up a chicken wing out of the basket between them. "I recall they exchanged contact information and knowing Stephen's ability to foster good contacts, sources and experts, I'm sure Stephen kept in touch."

"This all sounds promising but why do I get the impression there's something you're not telling me about this guy?" Alex asked as her eyes narrowed. "Last night, you said something about his being eccentric."

"Well, yeah." Matt considered his response as he wiped some blue cheese dressing off his chin. "Patrick was always coming up with these wacky conspiracy theories. Kind of like CIA involvement in the Kennedy assassination but crazier. Like, get this." Matt took another bite of his burger, washed it down with some beer and wiped his hands clean. "Remember, shortly after 9/11, there was a rumor that Osama bin Ladin had placed a number of stock trade orders before 9/11 that enabled him to profit from the attacks?"

"Sure," Alex said nodding. "Supposedly, he went short on stocks like some of the airlines that were impacted ~ betting the stock would fall ~ and bought significant interests in defense contractors ~ betting the stocks would rise. The rumor was that he made millions of dollars off those trades."

"That's right. But that rumor just kind of went away. There was never any confirmation of whether it was true, even though tracking the rumor would have enabled the United States government to determine information about the al-Qaeda money network. Right?"

"Well, I'm not sure I ever really bought into all that, but, yeah, I'll go along ..."

"Patrick's theory was that it was in fact investigated but the results were never released because they discovered that al-Qaeda wasn't the only one that placed those kind of trades." Matt paused. "The CIA did the same thing."

"What?" Alex didn't bother to hide the skepticism on her face.

"I know. Crazy," Matt conceded. "Patrick tried to convince me one day that the CIA knew about al-Qaeda's plans but they couldn't stop the attacks because the CIA didn't know the exact details. They found out about the investments al-Qaeda made because they had been tracking that money for years. Someone high up decided that if they couldn't stop the attacks, the United States government could at least make some money. So the CIA matched the trades."

She shook her head firmly. "I don't buy it."

Matt shrugged his shoulders. "I don't either. But he made some pretty convincing arguments."

After a moment, Matt continued. "Patrick also believes that the federal government uses hidden computer cookies -- very sophisticated cookies ~ to track not only browser activity but everything that ordinary citizens are doing on their computers. Things like which websites they're visiting and what they're doing there, the books they're buying, where they're traveling ~ everything. All of that information is run through a big computer server in the sky and filtered through a computer program that identifies certain patterns. And there are people monitoring all this information."

"This Patrick guys sounds completely paranoid," Alex said.

"Yeah, you could say that," Matt responded. "Patrick is brilliant but definitely a little nutty."

Alex wiped her mouth with a paper towel and dropped it into her empty basket. "So, this guy believes that the government is monitoring everything we do. And say, for example, if a kid is writing a paper on al-Qaeda for a school project, mom is exchanging Internet chat with someone in the Middle East and dad is ordering fertilizer online from Home Depot, the government may come breaking down the door because a software program tells them there's a possible terrorist in that household."

"Exactly."

"I see," Alex continued. "And it is the guy who is plagued with these paranoid delusions that we're relying on to help us understand what's going on?"

"Pretty much," Matt conceded.

CHAPTER EIGHTEEN

MATT AND ALEX LOOKED toward the door when cheers rang through the crowd of regulars. Patrick had arrived. The Irishman was a large man. Matt guessed he stood over six feet tall and weighed more than two hundred pounds. He had a ruddy complexion behind a thick mustache. In blue jeans and a flannel shirt, he looked more like a construction worker than a computer expert. Patrick started at the front of the bar, greeting the regulars with a hearty hello in a deep baritone voice and a clap on the shoulder. It took a few minutes for him to finish making the rounds and find his way to Matt and Alex at the opposite end of the bar.

"Matt, my man, it's about time you came back to visit us little folks," he said swallowing up Matt with a big bear hug.

"And who's this beautiful lass?"

"This is Alex Doren, Patrick."

Patrick took her hand and put it to his lips for a quick gentle brush of a kiss.

"It's my great pleasure to meet you, Alex."

Patrick settled his large frame into the stool next to Matt as Dan slid a beer down in front of him.

"Cheers," Patrick said, raising his mug. He had a mischievous twinkle in his intelligent eyes that Matt could see even behind his thick glasses. "To you, luv," he said to Alex. "May any misfortune that follows you never catch up."

They all clinked glasses.

Matt sat back and watched as Patrick chipped away at any reservations Alex may have had about him with the charm that was his birthright.

"How the hell have you been, lad?" Patrick finally asked, turning his attention to Matt, even as he stole a quick glance at the television screen. "It's been a long time."

"I've been better," Matt replied.

"Well, that doesn't sound good. And, here you are in the company of such a beautiful lass and good friends on such a fine day. What could possibly be better?"

Matt waited until after the tip-off that signaled the start of the game before saying anything. "Patrick, we need to talk to you about Stephen," he finally said.

"Yeah? Where is the bugger?" Patrick said, taking a sip of his beer and then looking at Matt. "Why has he not come with you? I heard he was in town."

Matt and Alex shared a quick glance.

"Stephen's dead, Patrick," Matt said.

Patrick's jaw dropped and his eyebrows came together in a dark scowl. "What the bloody hell are you talking about, man? I just saw him ..." He looked from Matt to

Alex. "Is this some kind of joke?" Creases etched deep across his forehead as he continued to look at both of them. "Bleedin' Jesus, you're serious," he said when neither responded. He pounded his fist against the bar. "*Shite.*"

"I'm sorry to have to be the one to tell you. I know you guys were close."

Several more seconds passed before Patrick spoke. "What happened?"

"Stephen was killed at a homeless camp under the overpass on Biscayne Boulevard."

"A homeless camp, you say?"

Matt nodded. "Apparently, Stephen had been living there for at least a few days."

Patrick didn't say anything. Matt noticed that Patrick avoided looking in Matt's direction. Patrick took a paper towel from the roll on the bar and mopped his brow, never looking in Matt's direction.

"Some guy beat heat him to death," Matt said. He noticed that Patrick seemed saddened but not terribly surprised. "I don't know why someone would do that," Matt continued.

"Truth be known, Matt, you don't know about a lot of things," Patrick intoned as he looked in the direction of the television.

"I know what happened to Stephen had something to do with what the two of you were working on," Matt said, watching closely for Patrick's reaction.

Patrick looked up and scanned Matt's face intently. Matt returned the gaze steadily.

"Pisser, Matt," he finally said. "This is not good. Not good at all." He shook his head.

"Patrick, you need to tell me what's going on."

"*Aye.*" He paused and looked over at Alex. He looked back at Matt as he jerked his thumb toward her. "You sure you want the lass involved in this?"

"She's okay, Patrick," Matt said nodding in Alex's general direction. "You can trust her. Now, tell me. What the hell's going on?"

Patrick didn't respond.

"Patrick, when was the last time you spoke with Stephen?" Matt pressed.

Patrick sighed heavily and then finally spoke. "About a week ago."

"What did you guys talk about?"

"He was working on some big story. He called me to talk about it and get some technical information."

"What was the story about?"

"He was investigating a public relations firm."

Matt and Alex exchanged a look as Patrick continued.

"This PR firm was using some sophisticated programming for information management, so he called for my help."

"What kind of help?'

"He wanted me to check them out, see what they were doing and then explain it to him."

"What did you find out?" Matt asked.

"What I found out scared the bloody hell out of me." Patrick said looking around. "You see, Stephen believed that this firm was manipulating information on the

Internet. He thought they were tracking articles, blogs, even emails. They were also blocking access to certain material."

"What kind of material?"

"Material that was not consistent with the messaging this PR was putting out."

"But how could they do that?" Matt asked. "How is that possible?"

"Well, lad, that took some figuring out, but it seems that someone has developed some state-of-the-art malware."

"Malware?"

"Malware is short for malicious software. That's a general term used to mean a variety of forms of hostile, intrusive or annoying software or program code. You know, lad, things like viruses and worms designed to get around your security, break into your system and then either gather information about you or disrupt your computer operation."

"Got it. Go on."

"So this computer program monitors activity over the Internet," Patrick continued. "Everything. Websites. Message boards. Blogs and even emails. When certain key words or phrases are identified, alarms go off. Then, depending on what it finds, a course of action is taken. Say, for example, some offending material or website is identified, the program may simply monitor the activity or block access to the material or website. If that doesn't work, the program sends in a "worm" to destroy the files or to corrupt the file system. These worms are able to shut down the entire site."

Matt must have looked skeptical.

"I didn't believe it at first, Matt," Patrick said looking at them with wide eyes. "But Stephen and I tested it. The program is brilliant. Fucking brilliant."

"How did you guys figure this out?"

"To test Stephen's theory, he created some articles with words, phrases or concepts that he figured would get picked up. I posted them on some obscure message boards. Then, I sat back and watched the program go. It was a bloody work of art the way it found the articles ~ within minutes ~ and deleted them. It was as if they never existed ~ and that's not easy to do on the Internet."

Patrick sat up taller and his eyes shone brighter as he spoke. Alex and Matt both watched him intently.

"I developed a dummy website and we posted a bunch of the articles. I installed some very complex firewalls, some of my best stuff. It didn't take long for the program to find the articles. But we'd figured on that. Then the program got through my firewalls and destroyed the articles. It eventually infected the website and shut it down."

"But it sounds like you saw this happening. Wouldn't someone else know that their computer was being tampered with?" Matt asked.

"No," Patrick said shaking his head. "This program is completely transparent. It's disguised in something innocuous or even desirable ~ like a complementary antivirus scan or an appealing advertisement. We call that a Trojan horse. It's fairly common."

"But, certainly, the webmaster for the website would figure it out when the material disappeared or the site went down."

Patrick shook his head. "To the average webmaster, it would appear as if there was a programming error or the file server was down. They would assume the website was infected with some random virus."

Matt looked over at Alex. She appeared engrossed, no longer the skeptic she had been when he first mentioned talking to Patrick.

"She's a beauty." The admiration in Patrick's voice was obvious. Matt and Alex both knew he wasn't talking about Alex.

Alex then chimed in and spent several minutes asking Patrick details about the program. They could have been speaking a different language for all Matt knew. Matt sat back and contemplated what they had just learned, connecting the dots in his mind.

"Wait," said Matt interrupting Patrick and Alex's discussion. "How can you be so sure that the PR firm is behind this program?"

"That's a good question," Patrick conceded. "The only reason I know ~ or speculate ~ about who's behind this is because there's a wee small component of the program that I recognize." Patrick paused. "It had a signature on it."

"A signature?" Matt asked.

"That's the online equivalent of the tagging that graffiti artists do. In the world of computer programming, a programmer includes his alias or affinity group in the software programming."

"Okay, but how did that lead you to the PR firm?" Matt asked.

"It was my signature."

"What!?" Alex and Matt said simultaneously.

"You created this thing?" Matt asked.

"Wait, hold on there." Patrick said holding up his hand. "I didn't create the entire program. I was involved in the development of one part, and I had no idea what the end product would do."

"How is that possible?" Matt asked.

"This firm hired me and several other programmers to do some high-level work," Patrick explained. "The company had all of us working on different parts of the project. That's not so unusual, but what was unusual was the incredibly tight security. No one person in the group knew what the entire program, completely integrated, would do. We worked independently and we weren't supposed to know who else was working on the project. I worked on a security piece of this software. It was pretty sophisticated and unique, and I can see my signature in those elements of this program. So that's how I know which company is behind this."

"Why didn't you or Stephen go to the authorities with this?" Matt asked.

"And tell them what, Matt? A story about some rogue computer program?" Patrick shook his head. "Other than speculation, we can't tie the bleedin' program to the PR firm. I haven't been able to get that close to the program, let alone inside it, since I did my initial work on it. Also, I signed a non-disclosure agreement. If I reveal anything about my work for this company, I'll lose the money I earned plus I'll have to pay some very serious penalties. I can't afford to do that."

He then leaned in closer toward Matt and lowered his voice. Matt could barely hear him over the cheers from the crowd at Keg South.

"What's more important, Matt, is I'm not willing to cross these people ~ not after what happened to Stephen." Patrick shook his head as he sat back. "Bloody hell! I have a family. I can't end up the way Stephen did."

Matt understood. He didn't have a family and he still didn't want to end up like Stephen.

"So, what was Stephen's big plan?" Matt finally asked. "Last time I saw him, it sounded like he was working on one."

"Well, sort of," Patrick admitted reluctantly. "He figured he'd expose the whole thing in a big way. This would force them to stop what they're doing."

"And just how was he going to do this?"

"I spent a couple of weeks developing a program that would get into their system, through the firewalls I was responsible for developing. This was my own bit of malware," Patrick said smiling proudly. "It would do a couple of things. First, a virus would shut down their program. It would practically paralyze their entire system. Once that was done, the program would access all of their contacts and release some content Stephen had written describing the program and those behind it in great detail."

"That sounds great," said Matt somewhat encouraged.

"Well, hold the applause, mate," Patrick cautioned. "There were a couple of challenges. First, my virus would shut down their program only temporarily, just long enough to allow my program to release the articles Stephen had written. Once their program figured out what was going on and went on the offensive, it would destroy my virus and go back to work and search and destroy all the files we'd have released. However, we expected that it would take some time for it to do that, and by then it would be too late. The secret would be exposed. And, once that happened, Stephen figured they would be forced to shut down the system themselves."

"Okay, so what were you guys waiting for?" Matt asked. "Why didn't you just load the virus and shut down the system?"

"Well, that's the other challenge. Because I had built some really great firewalls for this company, the program would have to be loaded from the server. The firewalls would block anything foreign coming from the outside."

"Okay, so what's the problem? Where's the server?" Matt asked impatiently.

"The servers that store all of this company's technology and data are located at the headquarters of this company's parent company."

"Okay," Matt said slowly, still not understanding the challenge.

"Matt, the PR company is owned by Protegere."

Matt groaned.

Protegere was one of the largest defense contractors in the world. They had developed the type of sophisticated technology and weaponry that had enabled the United States military to be the finest and most advanced in the world. The defense contractor also had as one of its subsidiaries the most powerful private military company in the world. Its professionals were trained to guard diplomats all over the world. They also trained foreign militaries on how to fight wars and entire police forces on how to maintain the peace. Their state-of-the-art weaponry combined with highly skilled mercenaries was a deadly combination.

Using their government connections, Protegere was able to build a military compound in a remote location in the Florida Everglades over the objections of several environmental groups. There, the company operated a military training camp, where the company's operatives trained members of the U.S. special forces. Several environmental groups also said the company tested military-grade weapons on the Everglades wetlands. There were occasional complaints from people living in Everglades City of strange noises and lights late at night coming from the general vicinity of the compound. But no one had been able to confirm that and the local authorities were not sympathetic.

"Jeez," Matt said looking down and shaking his head. "What the hell was Stephen going to do? "How was he going to get in to load the program?"

"You know Stephen." Patrick chuckled. "He had balls larger than anyone I know. He was going to break into the compound."

"And you were going to help him?" asked Alex.

"Oh, no," Patrick said shaking his head firmly. "I couldn't help him, even if I wanted to. The security system there is the best. I could get him into the computer system but I couldn't get him into the facility."

"How was Stephen going to get into the facility?" Matt asked.

"I don't know," Patrick said as he finished off his beer. "He took the disk with the virus I created, the one I couldn't even guarantee would work, and he said he'd 'take care of it.'"

Informed now about what they were up against and without a game plan or even a leader, Matt was out of questions. Alex, too, was very quiet. She excused herself to go to the restroom while Matt paid the check. After counting out a generous tip for Dan, Matt turned toward the big Irishman.   He sat there quietly now, neither watching the game nor drinking beer any more.

"Patrick, about that program you developed for Stephen," Matt began. "Did you by any chance keep a copy for yourself?"

"Sure, it's a compilation of some of my best work. I have the program at home."

"Can I get a copy of your greatest hits?" Matt asked. "Unsigned, of course."

"Aye. I could make you another copy of the disk," he responded slowly as his eyes narrowed. "But, Matt, what are you going to do with it?"

"I have no idea, my friend. No freakin' idea."

CHAPTER NINETEEN

BEFORE MATT AND ALEX could work through their next steps, there was something Matt had to do, a place he needed to go. Unfortunately, it was not a place or event Matt went to easily. On the contrary, it was the most difficult thing Matt had ever done. He needed to attend a memorial service for his college friend Yvonne Alfonso, a woman his own age and whose life had been cut tragically short in a white-water rafting accident in North Carolina.

Yvonne was Cuban-American, born in the United States to parents of Cuban descent. In Miami, Cuban Americans represented more than a third of the local population. They were a strong force in the community, largely responsible for transforming Miami from a beach retirement town to a modern city with a distinct Caribbean flavor. Yvonne was a shining star in the growing Hispanic community. She was bright and articulate and, after only a couple of years of writing obituaries for another paper, had earned a top spot at *The Sentinel*. There, she began a regular feature dealing with issues important to first- and second-generation Cuban Americans. Over the years, she had developed quite a loyal following of readers.

Matt and Yvonne had been close friends during their
time at the University of Miami. Both sports enthusiasts,
they had started a fantasy football league on campus. While
the league became quite successful and the prize for first
place substantial, neither one of them really cared about the
money. The league was just an excuse to trash talk each
other's players and team performance through the long
football season and to give themselves a reason to get
together periodically to watch a good game.

Matt hated funerals, memorial services and any other
reminders of lives tragically cut short. Yet here he was,
driving back from Yvonne Alfonso's wake. He hadn't been
looking forward to it, but when he had found out about
Yvonne's accident and called her parents to express his
condolences, he had promised Yvonne's mom he would be
there. He and Alex talked about it before and, according to
plan, had stayed just long enough to allow Matt to pay his
respects. Now they were on their way back to meet Patrick
at The Keg before it closed.

Just as he was pulling out of the funeral home, Matt's
cell phone rang. He saw it was Dana and answered it
quickly, hoping for some good news.

"Matt, we need to talk," she said without saying hello.

"We're talking," Matt snapped back.

"In person, Matt."

"I can't right now, Dana. What's going on?"

"I got a call from Commissioner Suarez," she said
after a moment. "He asked me what you are doing back in
Miami and what you are working on."

While Matt and Dana were dating and before Matt had made himself a pariah in the Miami social scene as a result of his encounter with Commissioner Suarez, Dana and Matt had run into the commissioner at many political fundraisers and charity events. Commissioner Suarez had always been kind to Dana, a fellow public servant, as the commissioner liked to say. Matt suspected his kindness had more to do with the fact that her parents were extremely large contributors to his campaigns.

"What did you tell him?" Matt asked.

"The truth. As far as I knew you were just getting settled back into town."

"So, what's the problem?"

"He didn't buy it. He thinks you're up to something."

"We need to talk about this," Dana persisted when Matt didn't respond. "Where are you?"

"I'm on my way back from Yvonne Alfonso's memorial service."

"Oh, yeah. I heard about her accident. Matt, I'm sorry." She paused before continuing. "Where was it held?"

"In Marco Island. I'm just leaving there now," Matt replied quickly changing subjects. "Did you find something out about Mo?"

"I really don't want to do this over the phone, Matt. Can't we meet when you get back?"

"Just tell me what you found out." Matt looked over and saw Alex watching him. The phone conversation was hard to ignore in the confines of his Jeep.

Dana didn't respond.

"Dana, in about five minutes I'm going to be going through the Everglades and cell phone service will be sketchy. Can you just tell me what you found out? Please."

She sighed deeply before beginning. "I heard it from a confidential source that Mo has been sent to Mogadishu for questioning."

Matt's mouth dropped open and for several seconds he couldn't find any words.

"Dana, are you saying Mo was picked and shipped off as part of the extraordinary renditioning program?" He finally said.

"Yes, Matt, that's what I'm saying."

Matt's stomach clenched. Since 9/11, potential terror suspects were regularly picked up and taken in for interrogation ~ without any type of trial or legal proceeding and usually to a place that had a higher tolerance for extreme interrogation techniques. Mogadishu, the capital city of Somalia, was one such example. The CIA had a huge operation there, with its own building, hangar and planes. They used the basement as a secret prison to get information out of suspected terrorists they had snatched up from all over the world.

Taking them off U.S. soil and denying any activities of this kind left the agency free to use "extraordinary rendition," otherwise known as torture, to get information out of the prisoners. Some said it was great way to get valuable information. Others noted that people would confess to just about anything to stop torture. Either way, President Obama had promised to shut down all the CIA "black sites," but many of them were still open and running.

"Dana, you've got to stop this."

"Are you kidding? I have no idea how to get him out of there ~ I'm not even supposed to know he's there."

"We need to meet, Matt," Dana continued when Matt didn't respond. "We need to figure out how we're going to handle this."

Matt paused and thought about his plans to meet Patrick at the Keg later than evening. "I have something I need to do first. I'll call you afterwards."

"What do you have to do, Matt? What could possibly be more important than helping Mo?" Dana said harshly.

"I'll call you back and we'll figure this out."

"Matt-"

Matt punched the disconnect button and tossed the phone onto the center console. He looked over and saw Alex staring at him, eyebrows raised. Matt didn't say anything as he turned his eyes back to the road. But his mind was whirring. He couldn't help but think about Mo. And renditioning. And torture.

Matt left Marco Island and headed back toward Miami. Marco Island is a large barrier island located off the coast of southwest Florida. In order to get back to Miami, which was almost directly due East, Matt needed to travel across the state of Florida through the Everglades, the subtropical wetlands that covers much of the southern portion of the Florida peninsula. Over the years, the boundary between the protected wetlands and the Miami suburbs had become blurred and Tamiàmi Trail, the road running through the Florida Everglades, was one example of that. Although the highway linked two major cities, the drive was about as rural as you could get. Nothing to see for miles but grassy wetlands and the alligators that frequented the waterways beside the road and often sunned themselves on the road.

Running along Tamiami Trail and throughout the Everglades were canals constructed in the early part of the twentieth century to prevent flooding in low-lying areas, especially during the summer months of heavy rain and tropical storms. The system was working overtime this week. The canals were swollen from two days of heavy rain and the black-top was slick from the torrent which continued to beat down on it.

Matt looked down at his watch and noticed they would need to hurry to catch Patrick. Fortunately, at this time of night and on this particularly lonely stretch of highway, the only other car on the street was the one behind them. Matt still didn't know Patrick's last name or telephone number and had no idea how he would reach him if he missed him at the bar. He pressed on the accelerator. The old Jeep responded immediately.

"How are you holding up, Matt?" Alex asked.

"I'm fine," Matt said looking over. She was staring at him skeptically. So he gave her a tight smile. "Really," Matt confirmed.

Matt could feel Alex watching him, as if waiting for him to say something else. He continued to focus on the road ahead. After a few moments, she pulled out her cell phone and began thumbing away.

Matt checked the rear-view mirror. The car behind them hadn't fallen back when he'd accelerated and was very close behind ~ too damn close. Judging from the position of the headlights, it was an SUV. He hated tailgaters, especially when it was raining. He shot another glance at the rear-view mirror and noticed what looked like two male figures in the front seats. If the roads hadn't been so wet, he would have tapped on the brakes to send a message.

A moment later he had to slow down as they approached a sharp curve in the road, but he saw that the SUV didn't follow suit. He looked away when high beams filled his rearview mirror.

"Idiots," he muttered.

Just then, the SUV struck the car from behind. The impact pushed them against their shoulder restraints, but Matt held the wheel steady.

"What the hell?" Alex said turning to look back.

"Dammit!" Matt said as he slowed down, intending to pull over onto the muddy right shoulder of the road. "We don't have time for this."

He briefly checked the rearview mirror and then did a double take as he saw the SUV right on his tail. They were not slowing down.

"Oh, shit!" He braced himself just as the vehicle slammed into the back of the Jeep again.

Alex screamed.

"Alex, hang on!" He slammed the gearshift into second and stomped on the gas pedal. The Jeep slid on the slick shoulder. The tires spun uselessly as they failed to gain traction. Then finally, the tires connected with the pavement and the Jeep leapt forward. Back on the road, Matt struggled with the steering wheel, the Jeep slewing dangerously on the wet pavement.

"What's going on?" Alex shouted.

Matt pulled away from the car behind them and raced around a curve.

"Apparently the idiot behind us is not very happy with us," Matt responded. He narrowed his eyes, alternating between the piss-poor view of the road ahead and the black monster behind them. Rain pelted the windshield as the wipers struggled to keep up.

Matt braced himself as he saw the vehicle move in again. This time, he was prepared for the impact but he caught a glimpse of Alex being roughly thrown forward before the seatbelt jerked her back to the seat.

A yellow sign indicated they were approaching another curve in the road. There was no slowing down. The SUV was right on his ass. *Damn*, Matt thought. *We're approaching too fast.* He glanced over at Alex. With the fingers of one hand gripping the dashboard and the other clenched tightly around her seatbelt, she was staring straight ahead. As they took another hit and Alex flew forward again, Matt realized the Jeep wasn't going to make the turn.

He slammed on the brakes, felt pressure for a moment and then nothing. They were riding a swell of water along the slick asphalt. He downshifted and started pumping the brake pedal, but it was too late and there wasn't enough road. The Jeep slid off the road, planed across the wet grass and crashed through the steel guardrail, continuing its wild ride through some high saw grass and down a slight embankment. Finally, the Jeep crashed into the canal. A thick stream of water sprayed over the windshield. The lights went out and they were plunged into darkness just as the driver's side air bag exploded in Matt's face, pushing his head back against the headrest and taking his breath away.

The seat belt held him in a vise grip, constricting tightly against his chest. Matt struggled to see past the air bag. The Jeep was stuck at a sharp angle so its hood was almost completely submerged, while the back of the Jeep was high above the water, the rear tires apparently maintaining some traction with the embankment. Water soaked Matt's shoes and continued to rise quickly up his pant legs. Breathing became easier as the seat belt slowly released its grip.

Matt reached around the air bag and found the steering wheel, then the column and finally the ignition. He pulled the keys out and fumbled for his Swiss army knife key chain. It was one of the smaller, cheaper versions. Not too many options. A corkscrew, a bottle opener and a knife. He found the knife on the first try. He plunged the knife into the air bag. It didn't penetrate. He pressed the bag against the steering wheel, making the plastic taunt, and struck again. He punctured the bag and it began to deflate.

Matt looked over to Alex and saw that she was unconscious.

"Alex," Matt said as he leaned over and shook her shoulder. "Alex, wake up."

She didn't move. He cupped her chin and turned her face toward him. She had an ugly welt on the right side of her face.

The front of the Jeep sank farther. The water was now at Matt's lap and rising quickly. He heard a roar from behind. He turned to see the SUV backing up, apparently getting ready to finish the job. Matt reached over and began shaking Alex, harder this time. As Matt had leaned toward Alex, he had taken his foot from the brake. With nothing stopping it, the back tires lost their hold on the embankment and the Jeep slipped headlong into the black canal.

More water poured in, filling the vehicle.

The SUV's final hit from behind plunged the Jeep into the canal, but it had also liberated Matt from his seatbelt. He floated around the front of the Jeep. He fumbled in the darkness but had no idea where he was and in what direction he was facing. Floating up, Matt found a pocket of air beneath the roof of the Jeep. He gulped it in. He felt around and scanned his new surroundings. He was in the back of the Jeep. It was pointed nose down with the back still slightly elevated but sinking quickly.

Alex.

Matt took a deep breath and plunged back into the water. He felt his way forward and down. He found the space between the front seats. Grabbing the front seats, he pulled himself forward and then reached to the right. He touched Alex's shoulder. She was conscious now and struggling against her seatbelt. Her eyes were wide with panic. Seeing him, she relaxed slightly, allowing him to reach down and unlock the seat belt. Grabbing the front of her shirt, he pulled her to the back of the Jeep, guiding her between the two front seats and up to the air pocket.

Air. Sweet mother of God, we need air.

They finally reached the back of the Jeep, both gasping. Matt noticed that the space had decreased significantly. There was only enough room for their faces as they pressed them upward, their lips brushing the roof of the Jeep as they inhaled the last remaining oxygen. They didn't have much time.

Matt could make out lights flitting across the canal. The men were still out there. But the air was running out. Matt looked over at Alex. He could see in her eyes that she knew it. They had no time left. They had to go back into the water.

"Wait here," he sputtered.

Matt plunged back into the water. He had driven the Jeep since he was nineteen. He knew every inch of it. He pulled himself to the front and turned himself around so that he was on his back. He was curled into a ball, his legs pointed in the direction of the driver's side window. He kicked the window. The impact reverberated through his legs and lower back. The force pushed him against the passenger side window. He reached up and used his hands to brace himself against the passenger side window, curled his legs up and, again, kicked hard against the driver's side window. Again and again. He heard the window crack and finally break. With his shoes he swept away the glass remaining around the window frame.

He quickly made his way back to Alex. The air space was even smaller. Her eyes were wide with panic.

"Okay," he sputtered as he took in some air, grabbing her hand at the same time. "Let's go." She nodded.

They both took a deep breath and plunged into the water. Matt led her through the two seats and out the driver's side window. Once outside, he kicked hard, pushing them fast and far. His legs pulled Alex with him, his heart pounding in his ears. His lungs began to burn. He felt grass pressing against his face as they finally reached the other side of the canal. Still, he didn't rise to the surface.

Matt pushed deeper into the weeds. He pulled Alex close to him before starting a painfully slow arc to the surface. When he finally broke through, he tried to breathe calmly and quietly from behind the weeds. Alex quickly followed. He put his hand over her mouth lightly as she gasped for air. With his other hand, he put one finger to his lips and motioned with his head to the other side of the canal.

They were still not safe.

They watched the lights in the distance, flickering across the canal. They sat there in the water, shivering as the rain cut through them. Dark clouds now covered the moon. And still they waited. Large heavy drops of rain continued to pelt their bodies. Finally, the flashlight beams were extinguished and the SUV pulled away.

CHAPTER TWENTY

CATCHING A RIDE hadn't been easy after dark on the nearly desolate street but the storm and their thoroughly soggy appearance had helped elicit some sympathy from a trucker on his way down to Key West. Keg South was on the man's way and he was happy for the company, although he was probably disappointed that Matt and Alex weren't such good company.

Matt didn't expect to find anyone still at the Keg when they arrived but thought they needed to try. Alex and Matt exchanged looks as they pulled into the parking lot and saw two cars parked in the back. Matt recognized one as Dan's truck. Perhaps Patrick had waited after all.

They thanked the trucker and headed to the entrance of The Keg, their clothing beginning to dry. Matt pulled on the door handle, expecting it to be locked and was surprised when it opened easily. He walked through the doorway and stopped just inside. It took a few seconds for his eyes to adjust to the cave-like darkness. He felt Alex close behind him.

"Dan?" Matt called into the dark room.

"Patrick?" He tried again when there was no answer.

The bar was quiet. No music. No sound of pool balls colliding into each other before falling into pockets. There was the smell of stale beer and fryer grease but something else as well. Something Matt couldn't immediately identify. He turned the corner of the bar, instinctively looking toward the register where Dan should be closing out. He stopped short. Alex bumped into him from behind. He heard her sharp intake of breath.

The area at the back of the bar above the register was covered with something. Splattered across the pictures of the loyal Keg customers that had earned a spot on the wall was something dark. Red. Blood. And something else. A robbery, Matt thought. Dan must be on the floor behind the bar.

Matt started to take a step forward, but Alex grabbed his arm and stopped him. He turned to look at her and saw she was staring down. He followed her gaze to the floor in front of them and saw a small trail of a thick dark liquid. Blood. His eyes tracked the blood across the floor as the trail grew wider.

It ended under a tall stool in the far corner of the small bar. The stool was placed behind a high-top table. Again, it took a few seconds for his eyes to adjust to the even deeper and darker recesses, but he could just make out the silhouette of a man. A large man. It took him a few minutes to make out his features. A moment more to realize that there, propped up against the wall, was Patrick Mullarky.

Patrick's mouth was open as if in a silent scream, a wad of paper towels filling the void. His eyelids were open but his eyes were unseeing. There were two dark holes where his eyes should be. Blood ran down both sides of his head. Matt's eyes traveled downward. A rope was tied tightly across Patrick's chest and around his upper body but disappeared behind him. His hands rested on the table in front of him. There was a stab wound in the middle of the back of each hand and several fingers missing from both. Matt looked down and saw the missing fingers scattered on the floor around the small table.

Matt felt himself begin to gag and immediately looked away. He placed his hand across his mouth. He turned away and pushed Alex as he did so, turning her around roughly so she wouldn't see what was behind him.

"Get back. Don't look at this."

She didn't resist and moved away with him until they were back near the entrance of the bar.

Matt's eyes went to the wall of infamy. He ignored the splattering on the wall and the many familiar faces as he searched the wall. He was looking for something in particular. A picture. A picture of Patrick, Stephen and Dan. He knew it was up there. Matt had taken it himself with Dan's camera. Dan had proudly pointed it out the next time Matt had come in. The picture had occupied a place of prominence ever since.

He recalled the afternoon. The big event was Super Bowl XLI. The Indianapolis Colts were playing the Chicago Bears. In the end, Colts coach Tony Dungy became the first African-American head coach to win a Super Bowl in a game that featured the first two black coaches in Super Bowl history. But that wasn't the reason that Matt, Stephen and Patrick had ended up at Keg South to watch the big game. The game was memorable for another reason. The game was played at Miami's Dolphin Stadium. The last Super Bowl played at the stadium. Matt had failed to get tickets so they had come here to watch the game.

His eyes searched urgently for the picture, desperate to find something that remotely resembled normalcy. There it was. He made out their smiling faces and somewhat glassy-eyed looks, the result of several pitchers of beer. The picture was slightly obscured by a manila envelope pinned to the bottom half. He squinted in the dim light and barely noticed his name in tiny letters on the bottom right hand corner of the envelope.

Matt approached the bar tentatively. Standing on the chair rail affixed to the bottom of the bar, he leaned over the counter and across the aisle behind the bar. He grabbed the photo and the envelope. As he started to bend back upright and step off the rail, he briefly looked down. He closed his eyes when he caught a glimpse of Dan's body behind the bar, but he couldn't avoid the unmistakable stench of fresh blood.

He quickly stepped back and hurried toward the exit. He threw the door open and rushed out of the bar. He raced to the farthest corner of the parking lot. He bent from the waist and grabbed the chain-link fence for support as he prepared to expel the contents of his stomach. But he hadn't eaten since the morning. The dry heaves continued for several seconds.

"Are you okay?" Alex asked, resting her hand gently on his back.

"I'm okay."

"So what did you get?" she asked after a moment. He stared at her blankly. She gestured to the items in his hand and he looked down.

"I'm not sure," he said as he opened the manila envelope and flipped it over. A flash drive slid out.

"Something Patrick left for me," he said. This time it was her turn to look at him blankly. "And I don't think it's a compilation of U2's greatest hits."

"Should we call the police, Matt?" Alex asked as they walked a few blocks to a nearby college bar that was still open. From there, they planned to ask the bouncers to call them a cab.

Matt didn't say anything for a while. He looked at the ragged old photo that he continued to hold.

"This is big, Alex," Matt said finally looking up. "I know it's all part of the same thing, but I just can't connect the dots right now."

"I'm certain you're right." She paused a moment before continuing. "Should we go to the police with what we know?"

"No," Matt replied firmly. "We have to find out more and be totally sure who's behind this before we go to the police."

He half expected Alex to fight him on this, but she surprised him by agreeing with him.

Neither Matt nor Alex said a word on the cab ride to the Brickell apartment where Alex was staying. Matt paid the driver with soggy bills from his wallet.

"It's my friend Christina's apartment," Alex said as they rode up in the elevator together. "No one knows I'm staying there," she continued. "So, even if those guys somehow figure out who I am, they can't trace us back to the apartment."

"Sounds good, Alex," Matt said as he watched her retrieve a key hidden underneath a fire extinguisher in the hallway outside the apartment.

"My friend works for a public accounting firm," Alex said as they walked through the front door. "She travels several months out of the year, particularly this time of year."

Matt walked to the middle of the room. It was an open floor plan. From where he stood, he could see the entire apartment, including into the bedroom on the other side of the living room. The apartment was conservatively furnished. It was also kind of sterile, Matt thought as he looked around, without any personal touches like art on the walls, photos or books. As a result, the apartment revealed little about the woman who lived there.

The sliding glass door leading to the balcony was open. A soft warm breeze was picking up the sheer drapes causing them to stir and float into the living room. Matt walked out to the balcony. Outside, he took in the gorgeous view of Biscayne Bay and Rickenbacker Causeway, which linked the mainland to Key Biscayne. It was raining, but the overhang of the balcony was deep enough that Matt could sit on the balcony without getting wet despite the storm that continued to hang over the city. Laughter, loud voices and the sounds of K.C. and the Sunshine Band interrupted the quiet of the night. Matt heard before he saw one of the many booze cruise party boats floating by in the water down below. *Baby, give it up. Give it up. Baby, give it up.*

Alex came out bearing two glasses full of a light amber liquid. Wordlessly, she handed one to Matt and sat down in the chair next to him. Both faced the water, neither looking at the other or saying a word. They hadn't bothered to turn on the lights in the living room, and the only light on the balcony came from the full moon cascading across and then bouncing off Biscayne Bay. Matt watched the palm trees running along the bay whip about from the wind and rain. Occasionally, lightning in the distance flashed against the dark sky and the crack of thunder rolled over them.

Alex was the first to speak.

"What happened in Afghanistan, Matt?" she asked. She said it so softly the words seemed to float in the breeze. A caress almost, but for Matt the words carried a powerful punch.

So much had happened in Afghanistan, so much he could tell. But he knew exactly what she was asking about, what she wanted to know. And he sensed that this was not the time to be evasive. Still, he hesitated. The story had waited a long time to be told and the words did not come easily.

"After the bombing in Kandahar~" he looked over at her to confirm he was starting at the right point, that she had read the papers and knew at least the story that had been published. She nodded.

"When I was being held captive, the Taliban who'd found me wanted to keep me alive. So they sent for a doctor to look after me. His name was Aamir. We quickly became friends ~ despite the circumstances or maybe because of the circumstances. I'm not sure which ~ probably both." He was stumbling around, the words trying to find their footing.

"One night Aamir came for one of his regular visits. When the guards were out of earshot, he told me I was in danger. He said I needed to get out of there immediately."

She didn't say anything but urged him with her eyes to continue.

"The Taliban were going to move, he told me. The coalition forces were closing in, so my captors wanted to relocate somewhere where their group had a stronger foothold. They were debating whether to kill me as a statement before they left or to take me as additional insurance. Either option would have been bad news for me. Best-case scenario, I would be going on a very dangerous road trip with some very bad people. I needed to get the hell out of there."

"And ... What did you do?"

"Aamir told me we were relatively close to the Pakistani border so we decided to make a run for Chanan in Pakistan."

"Pakistan?" Alex interrupted. "You were making a run for Pakistan?"

The irony of leaving Afghanistan for the "safety" of Pakistan was not lost on Matt. Pakistan's Interservice Intelligence agency supports and, in some cases, directly assists the Taliban and Al-Qaeda insurgents. As a result, the

Taliban continues to operate in Western Pakistan, fighting the elected government, its army and NATO security forces.

"I know what you mean, but Pakistan was and is a major ally of the United States in the war on the Taliban, and there was a U.S. command post in Pakistan not too far away. I wanted to try to make it there. I didn't have a good plan, but Aamir was willing to try. We thought that we could use the chaos that was going on around the city at the time to get out undetected. Once we got near the U.S. camp, I could use my status to talk our way in. Admittedly, it wasn't a great plan, but it was all we had."

"And Aamir? Why was he going with you?"

"Not just Aamir ~ his wife and kids too. I never could have gotten out of Kandahar alone, and once the extremists figured out who had helped me, Aamir and his family would be in jeopardy. I guess Aamir saw this as his shot to get out as well."

"So what happened?"

"The next night Aamir came to check on me. But this time he came bearing gifts for the guards he had gotten to know and who would soon be leaving. Alcohol. Three bottles of some rotgut he'd bought somewhere."

"That was a big deal," Matt explained. "During the Taliban rule, alcohol was banned in the country. In the wake of the Taliban, the ban was lifted but it was lifted only for non-Muslims and foreigners. Even then it was very hard for Afghan people to drink alcohol without being subjected to scrutiny from the 'morality police.' The men holding me were not Muslim fundamentalists, so they were all too happy to partake."

Matt looked over at Alex. The moon was bright and he could easily make out her features. She was watching him. The rain had increased in intensity. The palm trees were really whipping about now. On the balcony, Matt and Alex remained dry.

"They drank for hours," Matt continued. "Fortunately for us, these guys had little tolerance for alcohol. By midnight, they were piss drunk. That's when Aamir came back and got me and we got into a car parked out front. That part was surprisingly easy. His wife and two kids were there waiting for us. I remember Aamir's five-year-old son was awake when we got to the car." Matt smiled at the memory of Masud, the young boy's eyes bright with excitement. "He thought this was some big adventure and was really excited." Matt shook his head at the memory. "Can you imagine?"

"Sure," Alex said. "He was a kid."

"Aamir drove. His wife sat in the front seat with their daughter on her lap. The little girl was about two or three. Masud and I sat in the back. We did pretty well going through the city. It was late and the streets were quiet. Aamir drove quickly. By the time we got to the checkpoint leaving the city, we were nervous as hell. I was wearing the traditional garb and headgear worn by Middle Eastern men. Since I had been held captive for some time, I had even grown a pretty good-size beard. So, we thought I might be able to pass for Middle Eastern, as long as I didn't have to open my mouth."

"At the checkpoint, everything seemed to be okay. I couldn't understand what Aamir was saying but he told me before that he was going to tell them some story about going to stay with his wife's family outside the city. I saw Aamir slip some money to the guy at the gate. That's how everything was done there."

Matt paused. "But just as the guy started to let us through, we heard gunfire behind us."

He stood up and began to pace the balcony.

"'Go, go, go' was running through my head. Some of the men watching the checkpoint, farther away from the car, got up. They started looking around, trying to figure out what was going on. Aamir was still working on his new best friend. The guy even walked toward the gate and started to lift it. He was just about to wave us through when someone, some guy that appeared to be in charge, started heading toward us. He was yelling and gesturing wildly."

Matt ran his hands through his hair, still pacing.

"Aamir didn't wait. He slammed the gas and we barreled through the wooden barricade. I looked back and saw a vehicle turning the corner. It was a truck full of men, three in the front seat and about four of them in the back."

Matt stopped. He turned to face the water. No party boats out there now. The rain was now relentless. Even the tourists weren't willing to go out in this weather.

"They followed us through the gate and out of the city. As Aamir drove, I watched some men from the checkpoint get into another car. Others ran to their weapons and started turning machine guns in our direction. Ahead, I could just barely make out the lights from the American camp. It seemed so damn far away.

Matt ran his fingers through his hair.

"Suddenly, the men started firing at us from behind. We continued racing along. But, then, as if things couldn't get any worse, the Americans started firing at us too. Those days, no one knew who the real enemy was and everyone was trigger happy."

"Jeez, Matt."

He could feel Alex's eyes boring into him. He was standing now, facing the water. He didn't turn around.

"When we got within range of the Americans, the guards from the checkpoint that were chasing us turned around. But the men that were in the truck continued to fire at us. Aamir shouted something to his wife. I didn't understand what he said. But she reached for a bag that was on the floor. She pulled out a string of American flags and ran them outside the window. But the Americans didn't stop. It was dark. Perhaps they couldn't make out the flags. Perhaps they had fallen victim to this trick before. I don't know."

"Aamir's little girl woke up and was screaming. His son wanted no more of this big adventure and began to cry. The two kids were frightened out of their minds. Hell, we were all scared shitless."

"As we drew closer to the camp, Aamir was honking the horn and flashing the lights. By now, we were within machine-gun range. And, unfortunately for us, the Americans were much better shots then the men behind us. Bullets began striking the car. The headlights shattered first. Then the windshield. I covered Aamir's son with my arms and body. I heard Aamir screaming. I looked up into the front seat and over at Aamir's wife. I could see blood on the front of her blouse. Her eyes were open but she was already gone. As long as I live, I will never forget that sight or the sound of Aamir's screams."

"Matt ..."

She was standing now and put her hand on his back.

He finally turned to face her. He had to finish. Other than the authorities, he had never told anyone this story.

"Aamir kept driving. But at the same time, he was reaching over to his wife. Shaking her and, I think, pleading for her to wake up."

Tears were streaming down Alex's face. She didn't make any move to wipe them away. Matt couldn't stop, even if he wanted to.

"Before I could do anything, or even think of what to do, a huge blast ripped into the car. I don't remember much after that. Just flying through the air and then nothing."

"And that's it," he said softly after a moment. "When I woke up I was in a tent in the U.S. Army camp. I was fine. Banged up but fine. But Aamir" ~ the words caught in his throat ~ "Aamir, his wife and daughter were dead. And Aamir's son is just another war orphan in the Middle East."

CHAPTER TWENTY-ONE

THE NEXT MORNING, Matt and Alex found coffee, liquid egg whites and stale bread in Christina's kitchen and made a quick breakfast. They huddled together around the kitchen table. Slowly, and then more quickly, they agreed on a plan. The plan required going straight in to the lion's den with Patrick's flash drive. It was reckless. It was very risky. But it was the best idea they could come up with.

Alex dug up the keys to Christina's vehicle and they took the elevator to the condo garage. Matt got behind the wheel of the green Land Rover and they headed out. The first stop was a local wireless store for replacement cell phones. Matt and Alex paid cash for prepaid phones with no annual contract and only minimal records of their purchase. Next stop was a local Target for some clothes for Matt. He didn't want to risk going back to his house.

They headed down I- 95. After they passed downtown and left behind the interminable delays caused by the never-ending construction on Miami roads, Matt picked up his cell phone and dialed the number for Protegere. It took him several minutes to navigate through the computer phone system and then several highly protective executive assistants, but he finally got through to the right person.

"Hello, Mrs. Davis. This is Matt Connelly from *The Chronicle*. I'm doing a story on Protegere and wanted a tour of your facilities. I understand you're the person I need to speak with."

"Certainly, Mr. Connelly," the woman replied. "I can schedule a meeting with Sandra Parker, our VP of Corporate Communications. She would be happy to provide you with information about our company and give you a tour of the campus."

Matt listened to her tap away on her computer. "How does Wednesday of next week look to you?"

"Unfortunately, that won't work," Matt replied. "I'm on a deadline for a story that's going to run on Monday. It has to be today or tomorrow at the latest."

"I'm sorry, Mr. Connelly, but our offices are closed over the weekend ~ and Ms. Parker is based in our North Carolina office. She would need to fly down for the meeting. The earliest date I could schedule something would be next week."

Matt knew that Monday would be too late and he thought the weekend would be perfect. He hoped that over the weekend the company's corporate campus would be less crowded and security less tight.

"Well, that would be a shame," Matt said after a moment. "Because I'm working on an article about private military companies and their role in the torture and abuse of prisoners in military prisons run by the private military companies." There was silence on the other line. "It's shaping up to be an interesting article," Matt continued, "but I wanted to get perspective from a well-respected defense contractor with a private military contractor division."

Another brief pause before Mrs. Davis finally replied. "Mr. Connelly, I can assure you that a conversation with Ms. Parker and a tour of our facility would be most insightful and would add tremendous value to your article. May I ask if it would be possible to reschedule your story for later in the week ~ after you've had a chance to meet with Ms. Parker?"

"Unfortunately, no. My editor has already allocated the space for my article in Monday's paper ~ beginning on the front page. We'd have a tough time filling that space at this late date. I have most of the article written. I just need to get the PMC angle and to write the conclusion."

There was a heavy sigh before the woman responded. "Let me see what I can do. I'll call you back."

"That would be great," Matt said. He gave the woman his new cell phone number before ending the call.

"So this is why I needed to bring this old thing," Alex said gesturing to the practically antique 33-millimeter Nikon laying at her feet.

"Yeah," he said, looking over at her quickly and then turning his attention back to the crowded six-lane highway.

"This is your master plan," she continued. "You're impersonating a journalist."

"Some might say I've been doing that for most of my professional life," Matt replied.

Attempting to execute Stephen's plan was dangerous, perhaps impossible. But Matt didn't see any other option. After Patrick's death, it became clear that whoever they were up against was serious about protecting their secrets. Deadly serious. Yet Matt didn't have any idea what those secrets were, who was trying to protect them and why.

Could Protegere, the largest private military company in the United States, possibly the world, really be behind this? Stephen and Patrick certainly seemed to believe it was. Protegere was a powerful military force regularly retained to fight wars the government couldn't fight or couldn't publicly admit to fighting. Matt had encountered enough private military contractors in the Middle East to know that they had the skills to be able to carry out the kind of intimidation Patrick and Stephen had suggested. They certainly had the manpower to engage in a war against the media.

Then there was the technology angle. Did Protegere have the technology that would enable them to monitor Internet activity to the extent Patrick had suggested?

Matt recalled some research he had done many years ago on the Information Awareness Office established after 9/11 by an agency of the Department of Defense. It was created to apply surveillance and information technology to track and monitor terrorist activity and other threats to national security. The Department of Defense wanted to achieve what it cryptically called Total Information Awareness. The department believed this would be achieved by creating enormous computer databases to gather and store the personal information of everyone in the United States, including personal emails, social networks, credit card records, phone calls, medical records and other such information, without any requirement for a search warrant. The information would then be analyzed to look for suspicious activities, connections between individuals and potential "threats." The program also included funding for biometric surveillance technologies that could identify and track individuals using surveillance cameras and other methods.

The program had never gotten off the ground. Approximately a year after the office was established, Congress cut off funding and disbanded the office after several groups raised concerns about the privacy issues and publicly criticized the program. There was public criticism that the development and deployment of this technology could potentially lead to a mass surveillance system.

Several recent exposes into government surveillance activities suggested that big brother was in fact listening, tracking, and watching. So, who's to say the private sector, with significantly more resources and less oversight couldn't be doing the same, Matt thought.

Mrs. Davis called back less than an hour later.

"Mr. Connelly, I was able to schedule an appointment for 11 a.m. tomorrow morning."

Matt looked over at Alex and gave her a quick nod. "I can do that," he said into the phone.

"You'll get a tour of the campus," Mrs. Davis continued. "But Ms. Parker will not be able to be there herself, so the person conducting the tour isn't authorized to speak on behalf of the company. Tomorrow afternoon at 4 p.m. we have arranged for a conference call between you and Ms. Parker to discuss our company and answer any questions you may have. You must agree not to use any information you obtain from the tour until you have spoken with Ms. Parker."

"Agreed," Matt said quickly. "Anything else?"

"Yes. You must arrive at least 30 minutes before the appointment to allow enough time to clear security."

"Understood," Matt confirmed. He explained that he was bringing a colleague, a photographer to take pictures of the corporate campus.

The assistant took down Alex's information, confirmed that Matt knew how to get to the campus and agreed to email Matt the details for the conference call. Matt anticipated that the conference call with the Protegere communications officer, if it ever occurred, would be very interesting.

CHAPTER TWENTY-TWO

THEY SEARCHED FOR a small motel reasonably close to the Protegere campus, one less likely to ask for a credit-card deposit. They were now taking quite seriously Stephen's warning that their actions were being monitored. If Protegere, through its PR firm subsidiary, could mine computer data on articles, blogs and web postings, some of which were protected by sophisticated computer firewalls, they could certainly monitor his credit-card activity.

Once checked in, they dropped their overnight bags on the floor and surveyed the room. There were two double beds, both with faded covers, the patterns no longer discernible. The carpet was threadbare and of an indeterminate color. Even the smell of industrial cleaner couldn't mask the odor of stale cigarettes and mildew. Alex quickly suggested they go out to get something to eat before calling it an early night.

A small rustic café in the middle of Everglades National Park suited their purposes. They stuck with small talk while they waited for their food. For thirty minutes they exchanged relatively benign stories about their childhoods and college years as they devoured the mediocre burgers. Matt wasn't particularly interested in talking about the events of the last couple of days and the seemingly impossible enterprise on which they were about to embark. Fortunately, Alex didn't seem inclined to rehash those matters either. Matt was in the middle of what he regarded as a particularly charming anecdote about sixteen-year-old Megan Tincher, his first love, when he noticed Alex's eyes widen. She was looking at something behind him.

Matt turned around to see a grainy image of himself on the large television that was sitting on a shelf in the corner. Matt recognized the picture from one taken in the Middle East. His hair was longer and he had several days' worth of beard growth on his face. It would be hard to take the Matt sitting there today for the same person. This picture was suddenly replaced with that of a youthful, clean-shaven Matt. The picture on his driver's license. On the bottom of the screen, a banner silently screamed "Breaking News" and "Miami Murders."

His stomach tightened when he saw the screen cut to a female reporter standing outside Keg South. The woman was young and beautiful. On her face was a look that resembled a cross between the naked ambition of a hungry reporter just catching her first big story and the shell-shocked look of someone who had just witnessed something terrible. The volume was down so they couldn't hear what she was saying. The camera panned to the crime scene investigators who were wheeling out two gurneys. Each had a black body bag on top.

Matt scanned the room. Several people at the bar were staring at the television. The couple at the next table was leaning into one another and speaking in hushed tones. Matt couldn't make out what they were saying, but paranoia took over and he assumed the worst.

"I think I'd better head back to the room," Matt said as he put on the baseball cap sitting on the seat next to him. "Why don't you take care of the bill and see what you can find out."

"Okay." Alex replied as she pulled out her wallet. "I'll meet you back there in a few minutes."

He gathered his belongings, nodded to Alex and dropped his chin low as he headed out the door.

When Matt returned to the room, he locked the door and drew the blinds. He picked up the remote and powered on the television as he lowered himself into the chair by the bed. He flipped through the channels. It didn't take long to find the local news.

The reporters were describing in dramatic detail the gruesome findings at Keg South and the deaths of two men. The anchors reported that a journalist by the name of Matt Connelly was wanted for questioning in connection with the murders. He was identified as a person of interest ~ not a suspect, although Matt had generally found the distinction between the two to be a matter of time. He sat there for several minutes listening to the limited details provided about the murders of his two friends. Soon the reporters were simply repeating the same information over and over.

Matt stripped off his clothes as he headed for the shower. He turned the dial hard to the left, flinching when the water practically scalded his body. Facing the shower head with both palms pressed against the wall, he leaned in to the torrent coming from the shower head. His head fell down and the hot water cascaded over Matt, drenching his bowed head and plastering his hair to his face. Finally, he tilted his head up and felt the hot water sting his face before pouring down his body. His face burned from the assault. With his eyes squeezed shut, he struggled to shut out the images of Dan, Patrick, Stephen and even Aamir that were swimming before him.

He lifted his head weakly when he heard the bathroom door open. He hadn't heard anyone enter the motel room. He turned just in time to see Alex walk into the bathroom with just a towel wrapped around her. Without a word, she dropped the towel and slipped into the shower behind him. The sight of her naked body was all too fleeting.

"Alex," he began.

"Shhhh," she interrupted as she stepped in close behind him.

With a slight pressure on his right shoulder she gently turned him back to face the wall. She reached past him and adjusted the temperature to something more bearable. As she did, he felt her breasts brush lightly against his back.

"I've got your back," she said softly from behind as she reached for the soap sitting on the shelf affixed to the wall in front of Matt. Again, her breasts made an agonizingly brief contact with his back.

He held his breath as he waited for her next move. He didn't have to wait long. Her soapy hands were gentle on his back. She expertly massaged his back and shoulders before moving lower. With her palms resting on either side of his waist, she pressed her thumbs deeply into the small of his back.

She hesitated briefly before her hands moved around his hips and to his stomach. Matt shuddered. Still without saying a word, Alex stepped forward and pressed her body against his. One hand slid across his abdomen. He could feel Alex's full breasts against his back as she pressed deeper into him. Her other hand moved lower. A small groan escaped his lips.

Matt slowly turned around and looked at her. Her wet hair ran in shiny dark sheets down her face and covered her shoulders. Water droplets ran down her neck and chest. She opened her eyes. He took her face in his hands and kissed her, tentatively at first and then more deeply.

Desperate to escape the madness of the last few days, he pressed against her. He pushed his tongue deeply into her mouth. He felt her hands against his back. He moved one hand down her body and to her back. With his hand on her lower back he pulled her closer. With his other hand, he cradled her head as he took two steps forward, pushing her back against the wall.

She was returning his kisses hungrily, her hands pressing deeply into his back. She lifted one leg around his hip, welcoming him, begging him to come closer.

Not taking his mouth from hers, Matt reached out and slid the shower door open. He stepped out first and then pulled her with him. She followed him as he guided her to the bed.

Later, Alex and Matt lay in bed watching the shadows cast by the moonlight that peeked through the blinds. The red numbers from the clock shed the only other light in the room. The bed sheets covered their feet and nothing else. Alex's head rested comfortably on his chest, her body pressed against his side, her right leg stretched languidly across him. With the index finger of her right hand, Alex absently traced circles and figure eights on his chest. His right hand rested on her hip while his other hand gently stroked her arm.

"What are you thinking, Matt?" she asked.

"I was actually thinking about Commissioner Suarez," he responded.

"What?" She playfully pinched him.

"I assume you wanted the truth," he replied.

"Okay, what's the deal with you and this guy?" she asked.

He described Commissioner Suarez, his hard-partying past and the rumors that he had made his money by associating with some very unsavory people. Matt explained that the commissioner's real estate development projects were fraught with complaints about shoddy workmanship, undocumented day laborers working for below minimum wage and worse. Yet the commissioner's company was able to obtain with little difficulty all the zoning and building permits and approvals needed to move these projects along.

He described the commissioner's run for county office and then the seemingly unchecked political power that he had been able to amass, despite his questionable reputation and history. Alex laughed softly when he got to the part about Matt's public run-in with the commissioner at the charity event.

"And this man has the power to jeopardize your career?"

He explained the commissioner's sphere of influence within the local Latin American community as well as the national star power of the commissioner's brother who was a member of the Senate Intelligence Committee and one of the most promising Hispanic leaders in Congress. Both men were Cuban-American Democrats in a state with a significant Hispanic population, a state that had proven itself critical to any national political election. The commissioner's brother was considered by most to be the Democrats' only chance at securing Florida in the next Presidential election.

"That's one of the reasons I've been so reluctant to go to the police about what's going on," Matt explained. "I am a prime target for Suarez, and he has the local police on his side. Once the commissioner and his brother hear about my involvement, especially with allegations against another high-profile and highly connected corporation that contributes so significantly to our local tax base, the commissioner, his brother and all of the minions at their disposal are going to be coming at me with guns loaded. So

I know that I better be damn sure about the facts before I go to the police."

"But, what then, Matt? Assuming we are able to get some proof and expose the truth, what are you going to do about these brothers From what you tell me, it seems like you'll always have these guys threatening your career?"

"Well, it would be nice to expose the commissioner for what he really is, but I tried that and it didn't work out so well for me," Matt conceded. "So, second option ~ since I do really like living in sunny South Florida - is to stay under the radar with him and play nice, at least until I have something really concrete."

"I see," Alex said as she sat up, pulling the sheet up with her to cover her body.

She didn't say anything for a few moments. "Well, speaking of making nice ..." she said as she let the sheet fall down around her and began to lower herself toward him.

CHAPTER TWENTY-THREE

MATT AND ALEX DEBATED late into the evening whether they should show up for their appointment at Protegere. The news bulletins had only indicated Matt was a person of interest and wanted for questioning. There was no mention of a warrant out for his arrest or even of Matt being a suspect in the murders. Matt and Alex figured that even if the guards did run his name through some database of convicted felons or wanted criminals it was possible that nothing would come up.

And it was Sunday, Matt reasoned. The compound would probably not be fully staffed, and the guys assigned to the weekend detail probably watched more *Dog: The Bounty Hunter* reruns than local news. At least that's what Matt and Alex hoped when they ultimately decided they would just show up at the designated time for their appointment.

They had to travel several more miles through the Everglades to reach the compound in the middle of the swamplands. The facility was strategically located in this remote location in order to allow Protegere to train its employees and law enforcement professionals far from prying eyes. It had long been speculated that the relationships with these government agencies had enabled the company to avoid the otherwise strict regulations associated with operating a large commercial enterprise in the federally protected National Everglades.

From the front of the facility it was difficult to see what lay beyond. They pulled up at a guardhouse made of concrete block squatting solidly at the entrance to the compound. A dense fichus hedge at least fifteen feet high spanned one-quarter mile across either side of the guard station. Matt noticed a solid-looking metal gate behind the foliage that seemed to cover the entire perimeter. The metal gate was topped by concertina wire, with Xenon Stadium lights perched above.

Four men were stationed at the entrance. They were dressed uniformly in black T-shirts, green fatigue-style pants and black boots. Their haircuts were short and Matt could make out security earpieces in place. They all wore wraparound sunglasses. Three of the men had goatees; the youngest was clean shaven. They all carried lightweight machine guns. A guard approached the window and instructed Matt where to park. It was clear that Matt would not be permitted to drive the car into the compound.

They parked and walked over to stand in front of the guard station, separated from the man inside by a very thick glass partition with a slot to pass papers back and forth. They had to present two forms of identification, provide their social security numbers and then wait. And wait. Eventually, one of the men standing outside walked over, opened a metal gate and gestured them through the entrance. Once inside, another guard approached them with a large handheld security scanner.

This guard instructed Matt to remove the contents of his pockets and the messenger bag he had strapped across his shoulder. After a slow and thorough search, the guard set aside the cell phone and Swiss Army knife and told Matt he could retrieve them on the way out. He instructed Matt to place his feet wide apart and extend his arms to his sides. He passed the scanner first in front of Matt's face and neck and then above and below each arm. He scanned Matt's front beginning with his chest. The scanner beeped when it passed Matt's belt buckle. The guard paused, briefly inspected the belt buckle and continued down the front of Matt's body. He then scanned on either side of Matt's legs before instructing Matt to turn around and then followed the same process from the rear.

He instructed Matt to move to the side and motioned for Alex to move forward to the spot Matt had just left. After following the same procedure with Alex, the guard told Alex she would not be permitted to take pictures except with the express approval of their guide and that the camera, including memory card, would be inspected prior to her departure. If she violated this rule, the camera and the memory card would be destroyed.

Finally, temporary badges, color-coded to reflect their clearance level and stamped with an expiration date and time, were issued. The tags indicated they would be permitted to stay on the premises exactly two hours from their designated appointment time. They were instructed not to take off their interactive tags. If they did, the tour would immediately end and they would be ejected from the premises.

After they cleared that checkpoint, they were escorted to a Humvee parked nearby and told to sit in the back seat. One of the guards jumped into the driver's seat and started the engine. As they drove through the campus, Matt surveyed the expanse of yard and concrete paths leading to various nondescript one-story buildings. Each of the buildings looked exactly the same as the next one. The landscape was interrupted by fox holes and bunkers throughout the yard. Matt wondered whether these were for training purposes or in anticipation of some type of armed assault on the compound.

They traveled at a fairly brisk pace, but it still took several minutes to reach their destination. The building had a sign out front that read "Administration." It was also only one-story high, an uncompromising hulk of grey concrete with no windows. The sticker in the front window announced that this building was protected by Preases, a large high-tech security company. Another guard waited in front of the building. When the car stopped, Matt and Alex jumped out and headed toward the building.

Once they were inside, the guard inspected their Protegere-issued ID badges closely and then placed a call. As Alex and Matt waited, they settled into a reception area that was clean and functional but devoid of any decoration. The reading material offered on the table in the center of the room consisted of the latest issue of the NRA's *American Rifleman* and *Shooting Illustrated.* The guard stood immobile in the corner as Alex and Matt flipped through the magazines and waited for their escort. The man avoided all eye contact, but Matt suspected he registered their every move.

Finally, the door to the left of the reception desk burst open. A tall thin woman strode in, shoved her hand out to Matt and blurted, "Mr. Connelly, I'm Patty Shaw and I'm going to be conducting your tour of our world-class facility."

"Patty, great to meet you," Matt said as he slowly rose and took her hand. "This is my colleague, Alex Doren."

Patty appeared to be in her mid-20s. Her flaming red hair was pulled back, but several errant pieces had fallen loose and framed a long attractive face dotted with freckles. She blew the hair back as she exchanged greetings with Alex.

"I want to warn you," she said addressing them both. "I don't usually do these types of tours. Typically, visits are coordinated through the North Carolina office and handled by someone else. So you'll have to bear with me."

"No problem, Patty," Matt reassured her. "We appreciate your seeing us on such short notice. We promise not to take up too much of your time."

"Alright, then let's begin." She said as she directed Matt and Alex through the door from which she had just come.

After an uninteresting tour of the administration building, Alex and Matt were led to a large building. The sign out front read "Armory." They passed their identification cards through a security checkpoint and they were buzzed in to a large warehouse-type building. More than half the room was taken up by an indoor gun range with approximately ten lanes set up for target practice. The other half of the building was comprised of several storage rooms filled with the largest collection of weaponry Matt had ever seen. While he was in the Middle East, the United States had proudly displayed its state-of-the-art military technology as a testament to its reputation as an unparalleled fighting machine. But, here, during this tour, Matt saw technology of the likes he had never seen before or even heard about.

"Protegere is one of the nation's largest weapons manufacturers," Patty told them. "And this facility is one of the testing sites for our new technology. Once the weapons have been approved for sale in the marketplace, this facility also serves as a training ground for the end users. You could probably tell driving in that our campus is surrounded by the Everglades so we're able to coordinate the testing and training without the risk of bothering the neighbors."

After leaving the Armory, the trio approached a building designated "IT Building." After passing through yet another electronic security checkpoint, they entered the building. The one-story building was laid out in a wide-open floor plan. From the entrance, you could see clear across the entire floor. Scattered throughout the floor were pods of cubicles separated only by partitions that stood approximately four feet up from the floor. Since it was a Sunday, only a few of the work stations were occupied. The men and women stared intently at their computer screens, ignoring the small group passing through.

The back wall was solid concrete block. Matt thought this was simply an exterior wall of the building, until he noticed two large double doors in the middle. There were no exit signs above the doors. There was a fingerprint pad to the right of the doors. During the course of the tour, they had gone through several doors. All the other entrances required a swipe card to gain access, like the cards Patty, Alex and Matt wore around their necks.

"Patty, what's that area?" Matt asked gesturing toward the two double doors.

"I have no idea," she said looking over. "I've never been in there."

"Well, let's go check it out," Matt said heading in that direction.

"We can't," Patty said quickly. "That section is off limits to me."

"Why?" Matt asked. "What do you mean?"

"I don't have security clearance for that area."

Matt raised his eyebrows.

"Our security system is state of the art," Patty continued more confidently after a moment. She held up the card on a chain around her neck. "This swipe card ~ my badge ~ contains my identification information. The swipe machines you see throughout the campus are connected to the computer mainframe, which has been programmed to know where each person should and should not be. The computer will allow me to open the doors in areas where I've been granted security clearance. For areas I'm not cleared for, my card won't work. Same with your cards," Patty said pointing to their cards.

"There are swipe cards on each of the computer terminals as well." She stopped at the closest cubicle and gestured to a computer with a swipe machine affixed to its side. "The computers can't be accessed until a card has been swiped and the system determines that I'm authorized to operate that computer. Once I'm logged on, the computer allows me access only to the files to which I'm permitted access. The computers track every location I visit and every piece of data I access. The card also has a microchip in it so security knows exactly where I am and what I'm doing at any given moment."

Matt whistled softly. "Impressive."

By this time, they had completed a loop around the perimeter of the IT Building. Matt glanced back at the double doors as Patty directed them toward the exit.

The last building on their tour was the physical training facility, a state of the art gymnasium the size of a large warehouse. In one corner were weight benches and weight-training equipment. In another corner large mats were set up for martial arts and hand-to-hand combat training. In the center were four large boxing rings surrounded by boxing bags hanging from the ceiling. Halfway up the wall was a running track. A lone man was working out in the corner. He bounced lightly on his toes, jumping rope with the grace of a dancer.

"Why are there so few people here?" Matt asked. "Even on a Sunday I would have expected more people."

"Most of the administrative staff doesn't work on Sundays. I don't usually work on Sundays," Patty added pointedly. "And most of our operatives are on assignment."

"In Afghanistan?" Matt asked trying to sound casual. Matt had read a report that the U.S. was moving large numbers of personnel to permanent bases in Afghanistan. It was a deeply controversial build-up. The dramatic increase in American-led military presence in Afghanistan had unsettled some regional powers, not to mention many in the U.S. who continued to oppose the war in Afghanistan. So, rumor had it that the U.S. was staffing these bases with private military contractors, instead of U.S. troops.

"Yes, some are in Afghanistan, but we have operatives serving in a wide variety of capacities throughout the world," Patty responded evenly while watching Matt closely.

Matt decided to try another tack. "And how many of your operatives are engaged in combat?" he asked. "I've read several reports that say Protegere employees are actually engaged in combat, fighting alongside the men and women of the U.S. military and, in some cases, leading them."

"Specific assignments are completely confidential," Patty replied. "However, I can assure you that our operatives are not mercenaries." Patty had clearly understood where Matt might be headed with this line of questioning. "Our operatives serve as valuable resources to the U.S. military and the militaries of our allies in the global war on terror." A very nice, if not outdated, sound bite Matt thought.

"Okay," Patty said clapping her hands together. "At this point, that's the end of our tour. If you will follow me now, I'll take you back to the administrative offices."

With that, Patty turned around and began leading them toward the exit. "Any further questions will need to be addressed by the head of our PR department. I understand that you have a call set up with her for later today. Correct?"

"That's correct," Matt confirmed.

As the trio left the gymnasium and headed back toward the administration building, Matt looked over at Alex, trying to catch her attention. She was on the other side of Patty and staring straight ahead.

Matt guessed the key servers that ran Protégée's toxic programs must be in the IT Building behind that concrete block wall. Matt and Alex were within striking distance of where they needed to be, yet with each step they took the opportunity was slipping further away from them. His mind raced as they walked toward the administration building and likely toward an armed guard ready to escort them out of the compound.

Matt's pace slowed and he began to fall behind the two women.

"Alex," Matt said. "Let me get that camera bag for you."

"It's okay," she replied.

"Really, Alex, I got it."

Alex turned around to reply but must have caught the expression in Matt's eyes.

"Uh, sure. It is kind of heavy."

Matt reached forward and took the bag. He slowed his pace a little so he fell a few steps farther behind the two women. They continued walking.

Suddenly, a crashing sound ripped through the otherwise peaceful afternoon. Birds in nearby trees chirped and fluttered away. Patty and Alex jumped and turned back toward Matt, then down at the camera laying in pieces at his feet.

"Damn," Matt muttered. "Didn't realize the bag was open."

He squatted down and began to pick up the pieces. As he bent over, the open camera bag spilled out its contents in every direction. Matt heard someone sigh heavily and then footsteps as both women walked back to help Matt pick up the mess.

"Well, look who's old school," Patty said as she squatted down next to Matt and picked up a canister of film.

Two pairs of hands joined Matt's to pick up pieces of the now-broken camera, accessories and film. They were shoving everything into the open bag sitting on the ground in the middle of them. Patty leaned across Matt to pick up an errant film canister that had rolled off to the side. Matt leaned in quickly and placed one hand on the back of Patty's head. With his other, Matt pressed one end of the glass camera lens against Patty's neck. She gasped and her eyes widened.

"Up," Matt commanded. "Very slowly," he said. They rose together awkwardly.

"What are you doing?"

"Extending our tour."

The young woman's eyes darted from side to side but no one was around to help. Her eyes began to tear up.

"Let's go," he said pushing Patty back toward the IT building.

Patty stumbled along with Matt leading the way and Alex following closely behind.

At the entrance to the computer building, Matt ordered Patty to use her swipe card to open the door. The building was empty. The two technicians that were there earlier must have gone to lunch or left for the day.

Matt directed Patty toward the back of the room. When they approached the door in the back, Patty stopped.

"Open it," Matt said.

"I can't," she replied.

"I said, Open it!"

"I told you," Patty said weakly. "I can't get in there." She gestured toward the biometric fingerprint pad. "The room has additional security. And I'm not authorized."

"I don't believe you."

"I'm telling you the truth." Patty stammered as her bottom lip began to quiver.

"Do it." He pressed the jagged glass harder against her neck.

Her eyes welled up again. She reluctantly lifted her hand and pressed it against the pad. The light next to the pad continued to blink red.

"Try it again." Matt demand.

She pressed again, this time harder. Nothing happened.

Knowing it was likely futile, Matt nonetheless jerked the handle.

"Damn it!" he said to no one in particular when it did not budge.

"Shit. Shit. Shit," Matt muttered as tried to think of another option.

Patty was now openly crying as he continued to hold her neck and the glass firmly against it.

There had to be another way. His eyes combed the building, looking for a window. Another entrance. Something.

"It's okay," Alex said from behind him.

Matt turned to look at her. She pushed past him, moved in front of Patty and toward the keypad. She pressed her hand against the biometric fingerprint scanner. After a few seconds, the light on the scanner switched from red to green. There was a soft buzz from the door. She turned the handle, pushed it open and walked into the room.

"What? How?" Matt asked as he slowly followed her in, dragging Patty along with him.

"Alex?" Matt said when she didn't respond. "How, did you ..."

CHAPTER TWENTY-FOUR

"WELL, HELLO, MATT," a familiar voice boomed from across the room. "Thank you for joining us."

As the words hung in the air, Jack Rabin stepped from behind the rows of servers and walked slowly in their direction. Following closely behind him, Cole Harrison flashed Matt a grin. Matt was rendered speechless at the sight of the two Department of Homeland Security officers. Matt felt a stirring behind him and turned back toward the door quickly, jerking Patty with him. Two other men walked into the room, both had their guns pointed directly at Matt.

Patty whimpered. One man pointed toward the woman and then toward the door. Matt hesitated for a moment, and it was enough. Patty pulled her arm out of Matt's grasp and raced past the two men and out of the room. One of the men followed her.

"Alex, I commend you," Rabin continued smoothly. "You've brought this much further along than we'd planned."

"What?" Matt said dumbly. He looked from Alex to Rabin and then back to Alex. "What's he talking about, Alex?"

Alex was standing slightly ahead of Matt and to his right. She didn't acknowledge the question or even look in Matt's direction. She was staring straight ahead at Rabin.

"Alex?" The word hung in the air as she continued to avoid looking in his direction.

"What the hell's going on?" Matt demanded as he reached over and grabbed Alex's left wrist.

Suddenly, Alex turned and grabbed the back of Matt's hand, twisting her left hand and wrenching her wrist free. With her right hand, she squeezed his right thumb into his palm while at the same time pressing his fingers toward his elbow. Pain shot through Matt's wrist and down his arm. Alex turned and began pushing Matt's elbow toward his face. Matt fell to his knees.

After a moment, Matt caught his breath and slowly rose. Massaging his wrist, Matt turned back toward Rabin. Alex was now standing to the left of Rabin and staring at Matt, her face devoid of emotion. Rabin nodded to the two men standing on either side of Matt. Each man quickly grabbed one of Matt's arms, dragged him over to one side of the room and shoved him into a chair facing Harrison.

Alex began to walk toward the door.

"Alex!" he shouted.

She never turned or even slowed down as she left the room.

Matt started to rise from the chair, but one man shoved him back as the other took out a roll of duct tape.

The two men strapped him in with well-choreographed precision. Although his legs were free, both his arms were stuck to the arm rests.

"Rabin, what the hell is going on?" Matt raged. "Who the hell are you people?"

Rabin didn't respond. Instead, he turned to follow Alex out the door.

"Where the hell are you going?" Matt yelled after them.

"Rabin!" Matt shouted when the man didn't respond. He pulled against the restraints pinning him to the chair.

As the door closed, Cole Harrison's smiling mug came into view. Using the butt of his gun, he delivered a blow to the side of Matt's head.

"Well, I must say, Matt," Rabin began after Matt came to. "You've been very busy the last couple of days."

Matt had no idea how much time had elapsed between when Harrison knocked him out and Matt had regained consciousness. Shortly after he had regained consciousness Rabin re-entered the room. Rabin was dressed in khakis and a black T-shirt. No jacket this time so Matt couldn't miss how the T-shirt stretched tightly against his chest and biceps. He had a gun strapped to his belt, a 9-millimeter Beretta M9Z, standard issue for the U.S. military Special Operations Units.

Rabin sat down in the sleek black ergonomic chair situated behind the desk directly in front of Matt. He leaned back and stretched his legs out in front of him, casually crossing his feet at the ankles. With his elbows on the armrests and his interlocking fingers resting lightly on his midsection, Rabin was the picture of calm.

Harrison moved to one side of Rabin, never taking his eyes off Matt, and sat down on the corner of the desk. One leg rested on the floor in front of him; the other hung loosely in the air. A semiautomatic weapon rested casually across his thighs. The muzzle of the gun was pointing away from Matt, but Harrison held the grip firmly and his finger tapped the trigger.

"You're a long way from home, Matt," Rabin said in that congenial manner he had previously adopted with Matt. "What brings you out this way?"

"A story," Matt finally said. "And you?"

Rabin paused while he contemplated the fingernails on his left hand. If Matt's sarcasm irritated him, he didn't let it show. "We came here to find you," he said. "You've been avoiding us and we had some questions for you."

"I've been busy," Matt finally replied, deciding two could play Rabin's game.

"Yes, we know. Which reminds me," Rabin continued, "my condolences to you for the loss of your friend Patrick Mullarky. I hear he died quite tragically."

"What do you know about that?" Matt asked quickly.

"Well, for starters, I know that you are wanted for questioning in connection with his murder and the murder of some bartender," Rabin looked across the room at Harrison. "What was his name, Harrison? It seems to have slipped my mind."

"No fuckin' clue," the younger man responded quickly, never taking his eyes off Matt.

"I had nothing to do with that," Matt said through clenched teeth.

"Well, unfortunately, Matt," Rabin continued, "the authorities think otherwise. They know you were there. You left the scene of the crime and now you've disappeared." Rabin clucked in disapproval. "The police aren't looking very favorably upon you right now."

Rabin picked up a pen from the desk and began twirling it.

Matt still didn't respond.

"That was one ugly crime scene, Matt," Rabin continued. "And your friend Patrick ... Well, it looked like he really suffered."

Rabin didn't take his eyes off Matt, even as his fingers continued to twirl the pen.

Images of the crime scene at Keg South flashed briefly before Matt. Dan with a bullet between his eyes. Patrick gutted like an animal. He looked again at Rabin and it was as if he was seeing the man for the first time. His dark shiny eyes watched Matt intently but revealed little. Matt looked over at Harrison. His face was lit up with what looked like excitement as he watched realization slowly creep up on Matt. Confusion turned to shock and then rage. It was clear now that Rabin and Harrison had been behind the murders of Patrick and Dan.

"You sick sons of bitches!" Matt shouted.

He strained against the duct tape, pressed his feet against the floor and lifted the chair up.

Harrison jumped off the desk and strode toward Matt, the butt of his rifle raised high. Just as he reached Matt and as the weapon began its downward descent toward his head, Rabin barked a short "No!"

Harrison stopped, the weapon within inches of Matt's head.

Harrison took a step back. Matt fell backward and the chair hit the floor with a loud thud.

"You have only yourself to blame for this, Matt," Rabin said impassively. "You and Stephen are responsible for what happened to Patrick and that bartender. You were both warned."

The pieces were slowly falling into place. The call from Harrison after Matt had made contact with Stephen. Rabin's seemingly casual question about Stephen's whereabouts at the end of their first meeting. The break-in at Stephen's apartment. Then, hearing from these guys again after Matt met with Marie, Bob's widow, in Maryland.

These guys had been involved from the beginning. Worse. They were likely behind the murders of Bob, Stephen, Patrick and Dan. But why? To simply control the spin cycle surrounding what was going on in the Middle East? To what end?

"Warned by whom?" Matt finally asked.

Rabin didn't respond immediately. He got up and began pacing slowly in front of Matt. Now he twirled the pen with his left hand as he moved across the room.

"Your editor, among others," Rabin finally answered.

"Dave Kagan?" Matt scoffed. "He can't possibly be involved in this."

Rabin clucked softly.

"Matt, you have no idea who's involved or even what 'this' is."

"I know IMS has been manipulating information on the Internet," Matt said sounding more defensive than he wanted to.

"Well, that's a good start, Matt." Rabin said in a patronizing tone. "But that's only a very small piece of the elaborate mosaic we have gone to great lengths to construct."

"You mean the lies created by the PR firm about what's going on in the Middle East."

Rabin continued to pace in front of Matt. "Sure that's right, Matt. But did you ever ask yourself how a PR firm could control the media so completely?"

"I know about the computer program."

"Of course you do," Rabin nodded. "Patrick would have explained that to you. He'd been playing with that program for weeks. It didn't take us long to figure that out. Then it was just a question of letting him think we hadn't caught on to him. And the whole time we were tracking him." Rabin laughed. "He thought he was so fucking smart. Stoned off his own so-called brilliance, he continued to toy with that program while we watched him, discovered what he was up to and who he was working with. He led us straight to Stephen. And then Bob."

"If Patrick could figure out what you were doing, Rabin, I'm sure others will too. You must have stolen that technology from the Department of Defense, and it won't be long before they figure it out and come after you."

Rabin laughed. "Matt, for a journalist who has been through as much as you have, you are still quite naïve."

"Well, why don't you fill in the details?" Matt asked.

Rabin hesitated for a moment before replying.

"Well, for starters, Protegere didn't steal that technology from the U.S. government. The government gave it to them." Rabin smiled when he saw the shocked look on Matt's face. "You see, Matt, the government really saw the benefits of that program, even when the bleeding-heart liberals couldn't and tried to shut it down. The government knew it could get a lot of valuable intelligence using it and didn't want some inconsequential thing like civil liberties to get in the way. So, when Congress said they cut off funding for the program, they really just transferred the technology to the private sector. The government continued funding the research and development efforts and, with that funding, the private sector improved the technology."

"And IMS has been using this technology to destroy information that ran counter to its media message about the Middle East," Matt interrupted.

Rabin nodded. "But IMS couldn't have controlled the news so beautifully, with just some fancy computer program that tracks Internet activity. In addition to identifying information they didn't like, IMS had to get the producers of the information to work with them and develop the messages they wanted."

"But no media company with any real credibility would go along with that."

"Of course, they would," Rabin replied. He must have seen the skepticism on Matt's face. "Come on, Matt. Is it really so unbelievable?" Rabin asked. "I know it was before your time, but does Operation Mockingbird ring a bell?"

It did ring a bell.

Matt had learned about the secret CIA operation when he was studying journalism in college. Starting in the early days of the Cold War, the CIA began a campaign to influence the news by recruiting journalists and other members of the major media outlets. The program had been a stunning success.

At the height of the program's success, it was speculated that the CIA "owned" as many as 3,000 salaried and contract employees who had all been paid to promote the views of the CIA. Some were respected journalists and others were employees of major media companies like the Associated Press, *The New York Times* and all the major networks. Tactics included so-called expert opinions to echo the company line. Reports developed from intelligence provided by the CIA were written by well-known reporters. Once published, these reports were reprinted or cited throughout the media wire services and in various publications. Other tactics included misdirection and smears for those reports that ran counter to the message promoted by the CIA.

The government project was named Operation Mockingbird after mockingbirds, which are best known for their habit of mimicking the songs of other birds and the sounds of other insects, often loudly and in rapid succession. The false reports promoted by the CIA were turned into articles that were then repeated over and over again. Repeated often enough, the statements made in these false reports ~ no matter how outrageous ~ became fact.

"Operation Mockingbird happened more than 50 years ago," Matt said.

"Operation Mockingbird never stopped happening," Rabin responded. "It's continued to attract some of the most distinguished journalists and writers in the world."

Matt considered this for several seconds. "Even if you've got a few rogue journalists on the payroll of some of the local or even national news organizations, you couldn't get too many to go along with this. News organizations aren't going to let the journalists print bullshit or ignore a good story."

Rabin's smirk was pure condescension.

"It's not as hard as you might think," he responded. "Media consolidation over the last several years has actually made it quite simple. In the interest of lowering expenses and increasing profit, media companies have been laying off employees and becoming less selective about where they get their content."

"The government on the other hand," Rabin continued, "has at least 20 different federal agencies capable of producing content that has been broadcast in local stations across the country without any mention of the government's role in their production. Think tanks which used to be a place for intellectuals outside the government to weigh in on important policy issues, are now paid fees by the government to help sell the government's policies to the general public. As newspapers are closing foreign bureaus and shrinking newsrooms, these think tanks have moved in to fill the void."

Matt hated to admit it, but Rabin was right. He knew from what was going on at *The Chronicle* that newsrooms were relying more and more on the public sector to assist them in providing news stories. News stories now originate from PR firms, think tanks, even blogs on the Internet.

"This may be hard for you to accept, Matt," Rabin continued. "But news ~ like advertising ~ has become just another form of self-promotion and the media outlets just another platform for content delivery."

"Maybe. But the public is smarter than that," Matt said. "Even with the media's help, you couldn't manipulate the public for very long."

Rabin laughed. "The public was the easiest part of the puzzle. They gladly eat up whatever information we serve them."

"You underestimate the public," Matt retorted.

"No, you overestimate them," Rabin corrected. "We understand them. My employer has spent years studying them and years feeding them what they want to hear or, more important, what it wants them to hear. People who become obese on the junk food of propaganda are less inclined to be skeptical and ask questions. The news is what we say it is."

Matt considered this and couldn't come up with anything to immediately refute it.

"But why would you do this?"

"Because war is a very lucrative business," Rabin said simply before continuing. "It's also recession proof.

Protegere and other big defense companies have been raking in the dough since the start of the war on terror. But not only the defense industry. All kinds of companies benefit, from those looking through a haystack of phone records and email traffic for the needle that will lead to a terrorist group, to private military companies like the division here at Protegere that trains a country's police in anti-terrorism methods or provides armed military personnel to guard military convoys and installations. With the economy being what it is right now, the war business is one of the few things keeping this country from falling into another recession."

"But the war is over," Matt interrupted. "The President has announced the draw-down of troops in the Middle East. The gravy train is running out for all those companies that rely on the trillions of dollars being spent on the wars in Iraq and Afghanistan."

"Not at all," Rabin laughed. "We're just heading into the next ~ more lucrative ~ phase for military contractors. You see, the government is drawing down U.S. military personnel in the Middle East in an attempt to appease the American people who are tired of this conflict and the toll it's taking on our country. But as we speak, Congress is working on a defense bill of over one trillion dollars. And since the troops will be returning home, that money will be spent on defense contractors and private military companies who will maintain the permanent bases that have been built in the Middle East."

"The American people don't want a permanent occupation in the Middle East. And those countries don't want us there either!"

"That's exactly why the messaging is so critical. Politicians understand that Americans and others want U.S. military forces pulled out of the Middle East. They're getting tremendous pressure from their constituents to get out of that quagmire. But they also understand the importance of stabilizing those regions and the importance of the dollars paid in connection with the war, dollars that ultimately flow back into the U.S. So, defense contractors ~ like my client ~ are prepared to bridge the gap. We have trained personnel that are prepared to occupy the permanent bases that have been created and maintain order and peace until the local governments can step up."

"For a price," Matt interjected.

"Of course, Matt. And it's a pretty substantial price. That's why there is so much riding on this trillion-dollar defense bill currently before Congress. That's why our job was so critical. Too much bad publicity about the Middle East and the American people will start demanding that we give up and have no further involvement there. But if they are lulled into a sense of security, they won't care about a blanket bill with no clear itemization of how the overall trillions are being spent there." Rabin paused and watched Matt absorb what he had just said.

"Not only that, but it's all very good for the economy," Rabin continued. "Defense contractors benefit from the funds they receive. The general public benefits from the jobs created by the defense contractors." Rabin stopped and smiled before continuing. "Actually, I think you could characterize this media campaign as our own little stimulus package."

"Well, you'll forgive me if I don't say 'thank you,' on behalf of the American people," Matt replied sarcastically. "I count at least four Americans that have died from your so-called stimulus package."

"Unfortunate casualties for the greater good," Rabin replied quickly.

"Tell that to the families of the people you've killed." Matt snapped.

Rabin sighed. He checked his watch and then turned his attention back to Matt.

"Matt, we've gotten a little off track here." Rabin sat back down before continuing. "You're in some very serious trouble with some very dangerous people. But I might be able to help you."

"How do you figure that?" Matt blurted out.

"Simple," Rabin responded. "If you tell me everything you know and give me the names of everyone you spoke with about this, I'm sure we can figure some way out for you."

Matt knew it was irrational, but there was some part of him that wanted to believe that there was still some way he would make it out of here alive. He couldn't, and wouldn't, ignore everything he had just learned. But if he could just make it out of the compound alive, he could figure out his next move.

"You know everything I know," Matt said. "The only person I confided in that you haven't killed is Alex."

"Yes, Alex," Rabin said. "She was a bad choice for a confidant."

Rabin laughed and Matt felt sick thinking about how he had trusted her and even fallen for her.

"Who else, Matt?" Rabin asked. "We know you met with the family of your friend Mohammed Al-Ahmed and we know you met with your ex-girlfriend. Dana Fried, is it?"

"They've got nothing to do with this," Matt said quickly. "I didn't tell them anything."

"We need to be sure of that. Tell me what you told them." He continued when Matt didn't respond. "It would save me having to make a trip to see them, although I can assure you that Harrison would very much like to meet your girlfriend Dana."

Matt shot a quick look at Harrison who was smiling again.

"I told you they don't know anything."

Before Rabin could say anything further, though, his cell phone rang. He pulled the phone from his pocket, looked at the number and frowned slightly. He pushed a button and put the phone to his ear.

"Yes," he said in a clipped tone as he stepped a few steps away to take the call. He listened for several seconds before terminating the call. Turning to Harrison, Rabin nodded and gestured toward the door.

"I'll be back in a few minutes, Matt. Think about what I said."

Rabin turned to the other guard. "Keep an eye on him."

He strode from the room with Harrison following closely behind.

CHAPTER TWENTY-FIVE

THE GUARD LEFT TO watch over Matt was younger than Rabin and Harrison, probably in his late 20s. He had an M-16 rifle slung across one shoulder and a Beretta attached to his side along with extra ammo clips for both weapons. Matt also noticed a large knife case strapped to his belt. A few attempts at dialogue yielded nothing more than grunts and, ultimately, a punch to the stomach that left Matt doubled over and gasping for air. So the two men sat in silence, eyeing each other warily.

After several minutes they heard voices coming from outside the room. Both men turned to look toward the door. Matt couldn't make out what was being said, but he detected raised voices and the sounds of an argument. He recognized one of the voices as that of Alex although he couldn't make out her words. Eventually, he recognized the other as Harrison's voice. The voices grew louder as the exchange seemed to become more heated.

Suddenly the door was flung open and Alex stormed in with Harrison close behind. Alex's lips were pressed together, her eyes fixed in front of her. Harrison's face was red but quickly turning to purple.

The guard had risen immediately upon the door's swinging open and he now stood at attention as he watched them cross the room. Alex strode toward Matt and the guard as she motioned for the guard to stand down. The guard continued standing, his eyes darting between Alex and Harrison and then back again.

"I told you," Alex said, raising to her full height and turning to stand within inches of Harrison. "It's my turn."

"And I told you," Harrison spat out, "we wait for Rabin. He wouldn't want us to do anything without him."

"Rabin would want us to do the jobs we were hired to do," Alex replied firmly. "I'm going to do mine and interrogate the prisoner."

"Rabin's still dealing with Central Command," Harrison said tightly. "We wait."

"You wait. We need information and I'm going to get it. I have been handling this guy for the last several days, rather well I might add."

Matt had to reluctantly agree with her on that point. To his consternation, she had manipulated him all along and led him right into their trap.

"You can go or stay, Cole," Alex continued. "It's your call. If you want to stick around, I don't mind. I'm sure you would learn a few things." With that she turned her back on Harrison and her attention toward Matt.

Matt looked past her to Harrison. His eyes blazed with fury as he fingered the trigger of his gun still strapped across his chest. The other hand was clenched tightly in a fist.

"Stay here," Harrison commanded the guard before he stormed out of the room.

The guard looked over at Alex. She gave him a curt nod before moving closer to Matt.

"So, Matt, how are you doing?" she said standing in front of him. She spoke calmly and without any hint of the conflict he had just witnessed.

"Go to hell," Matt replied through clenched teeth.

"Now, that's no way to talk to me after all we've been through," she continued as she began to pace in front of him.

It took everything Matt had to keep from looking directly at her. He wondered what she was up to but avoided her eyes.

She was wearing the same thing she had been wearing this morning when he watched her get dressed. Polished black boots, blue Jeans and a white T-shirt under a fitted black blazer.

Yet the woman standing before him now seemed entirely different. This morning she seemed tentative, unsure about whether they should keep the appointment, concerned about whether she and Matt should go to the police. Now she seemed confident, completely in control. Her stance was taller, more rigid. She had a nine-millimeter gun strapped to her black belt. That was new and definitely added an edge to the woman he thought he knew. Not quite the Lois Lane meets Julia Roberts he had originally thought. Matt cursed himself for having been so gullible.

"You set me up," he spat out.

"Well, yes, but you're not going to let a little thing like that stand in the way of a meaningful discourse, now are you?" Matt caught her flashing the guard a smile at her own joke.

Alex walked slowly around the room touching various items, casually picking things up and putting them down.

Matt had nothing more to say. He looked over at the guard. The young man seemed to be growing bored and he was no longer watching them.

Alex approached the workstation across from Matt and picked up a baseball. Not a typical baseball. This one had the old Florida Marlins logo on it. Matt could make out the markings of an autograph. He tried to make out the name from where he sat if for no other reason than to avoid eye contact with Alex. But Alex soon began tossing the baseball from one hand to the other.

"Trust me, Matt, it would be better for you to talk to me instead of Rabin. He'll make the process much more difficult, more painful, than it needs to be."

Matt didn't take his eyes off the baseball as it was propelled from left to right to left to right in an uninterrupted cadence. He watched her approach the desk where the guard sat, flipping through a magazine.

Alex left Matt's line of vision, but he could hear the ball firmly slap against the palm of each hand as she walked around the room. Left. Right. Left. Right. Suddenly, he heard the ball make one final slap, louder than the rest, then a muffled sound as it fell onto the industrial carpet floor. Then nothing.

Matt tried to turn his body, straining his neck as far as he could. He saw the guard clutching his head as he struggled to rise. Before the guard could stand, Alex delivered another blow to the head, this time with the butt of her gun. The guard crumpled to the floor.

"What the hell is going on?" Matt forgot his restraints and attempted to rise. He brought the chair halfway up with him before he fell back with a thud.

Alex didn't respond. She strode toward him, reaching inside her jacket toward a black nylon sheath hooked on her waist band. She pulled out a knife and pressed a button with her thumb. A four inch serrated blade shot forward, pointing directly at Matt's chest.

"Alex, don't do this!" Matt shouted.

Alex was within striking distance when she reached past him and grabbed the telephone from the desk behind him. In one swift motion, she sliced the cord beginning at the base of the phone and pulled the rest out of the wall.

"Keep your voice down," she hissed as she walked back toward the guard who hadn't moved.

"What are you doing?"

She proceeded to hog-tie the guard in what seemed like record rodeo time.

"I'm getting us out of here. That's what I'm doing."

"Like hell you are," Matt spat out. "I'm not going anywhere with you."

Alex started back towards him, the knife once again pointed towards him.

"Matt, we haven't got much time." With a quick swipe, she cut the electrical tape used to tie his left arm to the chair.

"Harrison will have Rabin back here any minute." Then she sliced the tape holding him on the other side.

She went back to the guard, testing the ties. She then went through his vest pockets, grabbing the extra ammo strapped to his body.

The Beretta was lying on the floor next to the guard, exactly where the guard had dropped it when he was hit the second time. Seeing his opportunity, Matt dove for the gun. Alex must have seen the lunge and guessed his intentions. She quickly followed. Matt got to the gun first. They were both squatting down on the ground, but Matt had the gun and it was pressed against the bottom of her chin.

"What the hell's going on, Alex?"

"I'm trying to get us out of here, Matt," she responded through clenched teeth. "Now, put down the gun."

"How do I know this isn't some kind of trick? Because I seem to recall you're working for the bad guys."

"Actually, I work for both."

"Explain."

She hesitated and Matt pushed the gun hard against her chin. She winced.

"Working for the bad guys got me in here," Alex began. "Working for the good guys will, hopefully, get both of us out alive."

"What does that mean?"

"I don't have time to explain, Matt. The bottom line is that we are both on the same side and we need to get the hell out of here."

"Maybe I'd be better off taking my chances with Rabin."

She smirked. "You really think Rabin is going to let you out of here alive? With everything you know."

Matt's grip on the gun loosened.

"Do you really want to take your chances with him?" Her eyes looked toward the door. "You'd better decide soon, Matt, because we haven't got much time."

Alex was right. He wasn't sure what to believe, but waiting for Rabin to return didn't seem like a very good plan.

"Okay," he finally said, lowering the gun slowly. "Let's go."

Alex nodded and turned toward the door. Matt headed the other way, toward the back of the computer room.

"Wait. Where are you going?" She said gesturing toward the door and the exit.

"I don't know about you, but I came here for a reason," he said over his shoulder as he continued toward the computer servers. "I'm going to finish this." Matt unbuckled his belt and began to pull it off as he walked.

"Matt," Alex said. "We don't have time for this."

Matt ignored her as he disassembled his belt buckle and removed the flash drive he had hidden there. It was the one Patrick had given him. Patrick's greatest hits.

"Matt, we need to get the hell out of here," Alex said again from behind him.

"Go if you want."

Matt turned his attention to the computer monitor connected to the server. He found the switch on the CPU, pressed it and waited for the computer to boot up.

From behind he heard a heavy sigh, a thud and then something splintering. He turned to see Alex standing at the main entrance. The keypad on the wall was in shreds. Pieces of the keypad were scattered on the floor and the light next to the keypad was dark, instead of the green it had previously been. Alex was tucking her gun into the holster on her hip.

She shrugged. "That should slow them down."

Matt turned his attention back to the desktop in front of him.

"What are you doing?" Alex asked as she came up behind Matt and leaned over his shoulder.

"I'm going to load the virus I got from Patrick into the main server." He inserted the flash drive into the computer hard drive. "It's the only way to shut these bastards down and expose them for what they are."

Matt heard footsteps from outside the door, a brief pause and then the sound of someone trying to open the door. This was immediately followed by cursing, yelling and then pounding against the double doors.

"That was quick." Alex muttered, darting a look over her shoulder before turning her attention back to Matt and the computer.

"I can't get in," Matt said. "I need a user name and a password."

"Let's try mine." Alex reached and quickly began typing. The barrage of pounding at the door gained intensity.

They both watched the monitor, but the computer quickly responded with the message "User not authorized."

"Damn," Alex said even as she tried again. "Looks like Patty wasn't lying about the security around this system."

Alex tried again and again her credentials were rejected.

"What now?" Alex asked.

The pounding at the door stopped but was quickly replaced by a rapid succession of gunshots.

The assault on the door renewed with vigor and, unfortunately for Matt and Alex, with better results. As the doors began to swell inward, Matt looked over at Alex.

"Looks like we're out of time," Matt said.

They both jumped when the doors suddenly came crashing open.

CHAPTER TWENTY-SIX

TWO MEN BARRELLED THROUGH the door. With their guns drawn, they quickly scanned the room. It didn't take them long to focus their sights on Alex and Matt, who both started for their weapons but didn't make it in time.

One man barked, "Don't do it!" He turned slightly and pointed his gun directly at Alex's head.

Alex and Matt froze.

After a moment, the other man shouted, "Clear!" and Rabin and Harrison strode into the room.

"Alex, I must say I'm disappointed in you, not altogether surprised but nonetheless disappointed," Rabin said as he walked toward them.

He gestured to the two guards. They rushed forward with expert precision and relieved Matt and Alex of their weapons.

"So what were you two up to?" Rabin asked as he approached them.

Neither responded.

Rabin removed his gun from his holster. He raised it slowly, surveyed both their faces and then slowly pointed the gun in the direction of Alex. "I'll ask you again, Matt. What were you two up to?"

"You're too late, Rabin," Matt responded. "We just inserted a computer virus into the server."

"A virus," Rabin sneered. "The most sophisticated computer system in the world and you think you can just drop in the 'My Doom' virus to shut it down." He shook his head as he chuckled. "Nice try, but I don't think so."

"Actually, this is a Patrick Mullarky original."

With that name, Matt saw the confident smile on Rabin's face dim slightly. Matt counted on the fact that Rabin couldn't be involved this deep, couldn't have known he needed to neutralize the computer programmer and not know the man's level of proficiency with computers and viruses in particular.

"You're bluffing." Rabin said. He was still smiling but his eyes narrowed as he studied Matt.

"I wouldn't be so sure," Matt said with more bravado than he felt.

Rabin didn't respond.

"Go ahead." Matt gestured to the workstation even as he stepped aside. "Check for yourself."

Rabin and Matt stared at each other, neither blinking or willing to look away. Rabin broke first. He roughly pushed Matt aside as he strode toward the computer. He was looking at a blank screen. Matt had turned off the computer monitor just as the men had broken into the room. Rabin scowled and reached for the power switch on the monitor but stopped midway. His hand hung in the air, his finger extended. He was clearly unsure as to whether or not he should touch anything.

"Get one of those computer geeks in here," Rabin finally barked to no one in particular. "And you," he pointed to Matt and then to Alex, "sit the fuck down."

Alex lowered herself into the chair behind her and Matt took the seat next to her. He stared at Rabin and was even able to produce a smug smile.

"You know, Matt, after we've finished checking your lame attempt at avoiding the inevitable," Rabin said in measured tones, "I'm going to enjoy killing you."

Matt knew from the look on Rabin's face he meant it.

"I wouldn't plan your fun so quickly," Matt said with more confidence than he felt. "This is far from over."

"I wouldn't be so cocky, Matt," Rabin said, turning his attention away from the computer and toward Matt.

"See, Matt, I've already planned your death. Do you want to hear how things end for you?"

Matt didn't respond and Rabin continued. "The police will receive an anonymous tip about the whereabouts of a man who is wanted in the murder of two men. The caller will mention that the man seemed agitated and was carrying a weapon. You will be holed up in some cheap motel that will soon be surrounded by police. After several entreaties for you to surrender peacefully, the police will break in. They will find a man who, faced with the prospect of spending the rest of his life in prison, has committed suicide. Of course, they will also find the weapons used in the Keg South murders, thereby neatly cleaning up any loose ends."

"No one will ever believe that I did any of that," Matt replied.

"Really, Matt?" Rabin asked. "After all you've been through? Post-traumatic stress disorder is the excuse du jour. I think that, after everything that happened in the Middle East, you would easily be regarded as the victim of it."

"No way, Rabin," Matt said. "There is no way you can pin that on me."

Rabin ignored him and approached Alex slowly.

"But for you, Alex, I'm going to plan something very special. I haven't made up my mind yet, but I have several options in mind." He regarded her with a leer as he took out a knife that was strapped to his belt. "Do you want to hear them?"

Alex didn't say a word, but Matt saw the knife and began to rise.

"Don't do anything stupid, Matt," Rabin said without taking his eyes off Alex.

Harrison and another man moved in and pressed Matt down with one hand on each shoulder.

He leaned down and pressed the knife against Alex's right cheek. "You see, I don't take betrayal lightly."

Alex looked up, the defiance in her eyes slowly melting away.

"You may find yourself the victim of one of the many car accidents that happen on the crowded roads of South Florida," Rabin continued smoothly, while staring intently at Alex. "This time, the driver isn't thrown from the vehicle. She was a good girl and wore her seatbelt. You do wear your seatbelt, don't you, Alex?"

Alex's lips were firmly pressed together. She stared at Rabin and still said nothing.

"Of course, you do," Rabin said nodding.

"So, this time," Rabin continued, "the beautiful young woman driving is trapped inside the wreckage. You," Rabin emphasized, "are trapped inside. The car will become engulfed in flames." Rabin moved closer to Alex. "You may finally get the seatbelt unbuckled, but you won't be able to open the door. The temperature will begin to climb. Rubberneckers, unable to help you, will watch in horror as you struggle frantically to escape from the inside of the car. But it will too hot for any good Samaritans to get anywhere near you. You will be able to see them, though, standing by helplessly." Alex turned her face away from Rabin. He leaned down, grabbed her by the chin and forced her face toward his.

"Leave her alone," Matt shouted.

Rabin ignored him and continued. "They will see you screaming at the top of your lungs and pounding on the window. But the people around will only be able to watch as the paint begins to bubble on your car. And as you hear the sounds of Fire Rescue trucks in the distance, you will start to feel the flames licking your skin."

Alex was sitting tall in her chair and staring unblinkingly at Rabin. Despite her best efforts, her body betrayed her. Matt could see beads of sweat on her brow. Her knuckles were white as her hands clenched the sides of the chair. Rabin looked at her and smiled. He could see right through her tough façade.

"Rabin, stop this," Matt shouted as he struggled with the two men holding him down.

Rabin ignored him. With the blade of the knife, he traced the outline of Alex's face. She squeezed her eyes shut. Matt saw her jaw tighten. Rabin drew the blade down her neck until he reached her collarbone. There, he pressed the knife down until he drew a drop of blood.

"Take your hands off her, you fucking freak!" Matt yelled.

Rabin whirled, stepped toward Matt and plunged his left fist deep into Matt's stomach. Matt fell forward and landed on his knees, gasping and clutching his belly. He struggled to inhale. Rabin struck him in the back of the head with a blow that took him the rest of the way down. Face pressed against the floor, he anticipated the attack, but there was nothing he could do about it. The man above him coiled his leg and kicked him. Through the ringing in his ears, he could hear Alex scream. The barrage of kicks continued.

The assault abruptly ended. There was nothing. No sound except the ringing in his ears. He was afraid to move, afraid to breath. Matt flinched when he felt a warm breath on the back of his neck.

"Not yet, Matt," Rabin whispered. "But soon. Very soon."

CHAPTER TWENTY-SEVEN

"IT'S ABOUT TIME YOU got here," Matt heard Rabin say from above him.

With the arrival of the computer technician, Matt was temporarily forgotten. Not to be forgotten anytime soon was the beating he had just suffered. His ears continued to ring from the blow to his head. Matt tentatively unwrapped his arms from around his midsection. He started to reach up to his head to see if he was bleeding. Sharp pains in his chest made him quickly reconsider that move. He stifled a groan as he continued to uncurl his body, the process excruciatingly slow and painful.

With his face still pressed against the floor, he slowly opened his eyes. With his eyes only half-opened, he noticed something on the floor. He opened his eyes wider, and the room came into focus. Something shiny. A knife. The knife Rabin had been holding when he struck the first blow to Matt's head. Despite the resistance from his body, Matt rolled over and onto the knife. He fumbled for it, then slipped it up the sleeve of his shirt. Just then, he was picked up and thrown roughly back into the chair.

The technician was short and thin. He wore rectangular-shaped glasses, and his eyes darted around the room as he walked toward Rabin. He seemed confused by the activity going on, yet he made no comment about the men occupying what would otherwise be his domain.

"You need to confirm that this computer has not been tampered with," Rabin commanded, gesturing to the computer at the work station directly in front of them.

The computer technician smiled confidently and raised himself up an inch or two. "We have a state of the art security system. No one could have gotten into the computer."

Rabin turned to look smugly at Matt. "Just check it so we can be done with this matter."

The technician shrugged and sat down at the computer connected to the server.

"For the server computer, we have a separate password that we change every two days," he explained as he typed in a string of characters. "Only a limited number of people have access to that password. So, anyone accessing the server would have to input his identification code, his personal password and the server password." The technician punched in a few more characters. He then gestured proudly to the computer screen which now displayed a menu of options.

"Enough," Rabin barked. "I just need to know if a virus has been inserted into the system."

"Not possible," he replied. "But I'll start a virus scan to confirm," he continued when he received a glare from Rabin.

The technician leaned in close and began to tap on the keyboard. Several seconds later he leaned back as the computer monitor in front of him kicked into action.

"So, Matt, your little bluff seems to have bought you and Alex a few more minutes," Rabin crowed. He looked over at Matt, but the younger man was still assessing his wounds and didn't respond.

"Actually, a thorough examination will take about twenty minutes," the computer technician corrected.

Rabin checked his watch and scowled.

"What's your hurry, Rabin?" Matt asked. "You got some place else to be? Something better to do than manipulate the American people?"

Rabin glowered down at him. "No, Matt. Right now, I have nothing more important to do than manipulate the American people."

"You see," Rabin continued. "As we speak, our Congressional leadership is voting on a spending bill that allocates $100 billion for the recovery and stabilization of the Middle East. If I've done my job right ..." Rabin leaned down closer to Matt. "And I can assure you, I've done my job right. Congress will approve that bill. And after that, the spigot of money flowing to private military companies, including my clients, will be turned back on. And my job will be done."

Rabin checked his watch again.

"How are we doing, geek?" He yelled back toward the computer technician.

"Fifteen more minutes."

"Call me when this is done," Rabin barked to Harrison. "I have to finish that call." He looked over at Matt. "I have to advise our employers that everything is under control and on schedule."

"Harrison, you stay here," Rabin demanded. "And keep your eye on them this time."

He left the room without another word.

CHAPTER TWENTY-EIGHT

MATT WATCHED THE COMPUTER count its way toward completion of the virus scan and possibly toward what could be Matt's execution by these men. 24% complete. He noticed that Harrison and Alex were also watching the monitor closely. 26%. The other guard couldn't see the monitor so instead watched Harrison, likely waiting for instructions. 29%. 31%.

"Harrison, what are you doing mixed up in this?" Matt said, interrupting the silence.

"You're making a big mistake," he continued when he received no response. "The game is over. People are starting to figure out about your little project."

"You don't know what you're talking about," Harrison responded without taking his eyes off the computer screen.

"There's going to be a big shake-up over this and I think you can guess who's going to take the fall," Matt said several seconds later. Harrison was completely focused on the computer and ignored Matt. 42%. 45%. 47%.

"Why don't you make it easier on yourself by letting us go?"

"Matt's right, Cole," Alex piped in. "I can speak to the right people. I can put in a good word for you." 50%. 53%. 57%.

At this, Harrison looked up.

"You can help me out, Alex?" Harrison sneered as he stepped toward Alex. "You?" He was towering over her. "You think you can help me?"

He had his back to Matt as he leaned down to within millimeters of Alex's face. But Matt felt the rancor coming off him like scorching sun off new asphalt. "You'd better think about what you can do to help yourself, Alex, because as I see it, you're in for a world of hurt."

Alex looked away from Harrison and didn't respond. Harrison turned his attention back to the computer monitor. 65%. 70%. 74%.

Matt looked over at the computer. 78%. 82%. It was time. He shook the knife free from his sleeve, almost dropping it as it slipped past his cuff. He winced as he caught the knife by the blade. He looked around. No one was watching him. 89%. 91%.

Matt rose quickly from the seat, faltering momentarily but then dismissing the pain that radiated throughout his body. The guard behind Alex saw it happening first, but he couldn't move fast enough. Alex was sitting in a chair between Matt and the guard. Alex saw Matt make his move and hesitated only a moment before she pushed her chair backward and into the guard. Alex and the man tumbled to the ground.

Harrison turned just in time to see Matt tackle him. Matt's shoulder hit Harrison hard on the left side of his body. The collision caused Harrison to drop the assault rifle he was holding. The impact also spun them both around and they fell heavily toward the floor.

Matt hit the ground hard on his back. Harrison collapsed on top of him. Matt winced from the pain radiating up into his shoulder, but he reached out quickly with his left arm and grabbed Harrison around the neck. Harrison grabbed Matt's forearm and began to struggle. Matt held the knife in his right hand and pressed it against Harrison's neck. The man's body stiffened, then stopped moving when he realized the cause of the pressure.

Matt looked over and saw Alex on her hands and knees on the floor behind the desk. The guard was nowhere in sight. Harrison started to move again. Matt pressed the knife harder against Harrison's neck and the man stopped struggling.

Through the legs of desks and chairs, Matt could see the computer technician. He was across the room on the floor and underneath another work station. Cowering beneath the desk, the once confident computer god had his eyes squeezed shut while his lips moved frantically in a silent prayer.

Matt placed his left hand over Harrison's mouth and pressed the knife harder against his neck. The guard was nowhere to be seen. Turning his head from side to side, Matt scanned the limited view from his position. He looked over at Alex who was doing the same. Then he saw a gun appear from above the desk in front of him.

"Come out!" the guard yelled. "Both of you."

The guard continued to inch forward and the gun moved farther past the desk. With each step, Matt felt increasingly vulnerable. He was shielded somewhat by Harrison's body, but much of him was still exposed. At this distance, any shot fired would likely penetrate Harrison before hitting Matt. Matt was trapped. He wanted to make a move for Harrison's gun but knew that as soon as he released his grip on the knife, Harrison would be all over him. Without the element of surprise, Matt wasn't so sure he could win a fight against Harrison.

The gunman's movements grew more hesitant as he likely recognized that he himself was becoming more exposed the farther forward and past the barrier of the desk he moved. Little did the man know, Matt was powerless to do anything from his position.

Suddenly, Harrison started kicking and thrashing against Matt's body. The gunman standing above heard the commotion and hesitated. Matt watched as the man started to point the gun downward. The gun was now pointed directly at Matt and Harrison. Harrison was struggling frantically now.

"Come out where I can see you!" the guard demanded. "I'll shoot, goddammit!"

Matt began to release his hold on Harrison. But first, he slashed Harrison across the cheek with the knife. When Harrison howled in pain and instinctively reached for his face, Matt quickly grabbed the gun from the man's holster.

Still holding his hands to his face and starting to roll off Matt, Harrison shouted to the guard. "Shoot, dammit, shoot!"

The guard tightened his grip on the gun. Matt dove under the desk, but at the same time reached his hand above the desk and fired two shots blindly. Matt heard a shot come from the other side and then a thump as something fell to the ground.

After several seconds, Matt slowly rose. Harrison's gun was still in his hands. He quickly turned it on Harrison who was holding his cheek and starting to rise. With the gun pointed at Harrison, Matt walked to the other side of the desk and looked at the man he had just killed.

"Matt," he heard Alex say.

It took a moment for Matt to draw his eyes away from the man on the floor.

"We've got to get out of here," she said urgently, breaking his reverie.

He nodded. He reached into his pocket with his left hand, still using his right hand to point the gun at Harrison. He pulled out the flash drive and handed it to Alex. "Here, load the virus."

CHAPTER TWENTY-NINE

ALEX SLID INTO THE chair in front of the computer. Matt pushed Harrison down into a chair and stood over him while both men watched Alex at the computer. The virus search initiated by the computer technician had finished. 100%. No virus had been detected. But more important for their purposes, the computer was still logged on and waiting for instructions.

"What are you doing?" the computer technician asked urgently.

Alex inserted the device into the UBS port, and the computer waited for instructions to upload Patrick's greatest hits.

"Wait! Stop!" the computer technician shouted.

From underneath the desk the technician crept forward and then leapt to his feet. Before Matt could react, the man lunged at Alex, grabbing her from behind. He wrapped his left arm across her neck and tried pulling her away from the computer.

Matt quickly stepped behind the technician without taking his eyes off Harrison. Matt tried to pull the man away from Alex with one arm while at the same time pointing the gun at Harrison with his other. But the technician's hold was firm. Alex clawed at the technician's forearm, which was firmly wrapped around her neck. Finally, Matt hit the technician on the side of the head with the butt of the gun. The technician groaned and fell to the ground.

Matt quickly turned his attention back to Harrison.

He was too late. Harrison kicked Matt, causing him to fall forward on top of the technician. Matt scrambled and then rolled over, the gun extended toward where he had previously placed Harrison.

But Harrison was now standing behind Alex, his arm stretched across her neck. The knife was clenched in Harrison's hand and pressed firmly against Alex's throat. The pupils of Alex's eyes were huge and dark. Her fingers gripped his forearm, her gun sitting impotently on the side of the desk where she had left it.

The flash drive was in the hard drive but the program had not yet begun to run. The computer continued to wait for instructions.

"Put down the gun," Harrison said calmly as his eyes hardened.

"Don't, Matt," Alex pleaded as Harrison pressed the knife tighter against her neck.

Matt looked from Alex to Harrison and back to Alex again. Harrison pressed the knife harder against her neck. He drew blood. But Alex mouthed firmly, "Don't."

"Matt, don't be stupid. Put the gun down."

Matt hesitated for a moment and then slowly started to lower the gun. Upon seeing this, Alex fell to her knees, pulling down hard on Harrison's forearm as she did so. She tucked her head low as her knees hit the floor. Harrison tumbled over the top of her and directly toward Matt, who quickly jumped out of the way.

Harrison rolled completely around and rose easily onto his feet. He was still holding the knife, but now Matt was holding a gun and pointing it at Harrison. The man paused momentarily before speeding toward the door. Matt fired off a shot. The bullet pierced the wall of an office cubicle as Harrison raced out the door.

Matt turned back to Alex and saw her sitting at the chair in front of the computer for the server.

"We haven't got much time," Alex said as her fingers flew across the keyboard with a few commands. Matt stood over Alex as he watched the door.

"Are you finished?" Matt said after a moment.

"Yes." She pushed herself away from the computer. "It's done."

"Then, let's get the hell out of here."

Matt hurried back to the technician and ripped the keys and pass card off the man's belt.

Matt handed Alex her gun, and they raced toward the rear exit. He cautiously opened the door. A shot rang out and slammed into the cement wall within inches of Matt's face.

"Back," he shouted as he jumped back and slammed the door closed. Matt gestured to a steel file cabinet against the wall and together they pushed it against the door.

Pounding immediately ensued. Instinctively, Matt and Alex backed away. The cabinet began to sway under the assault. Their efforts wouldn't keep anyone out for long.

"Now what?" Alex said.

Matt turned in a full circle and scanned the room. He strode over to the computer technician. He knelt down and grabbed him roughly. He slapped him awake.

"How do we get out of here?"

"I have no idea." The technician said rubbing his head.

"Yes, you do," Matt said pointing the gun at the man's face. "Where is it?"

The man's eyes widened. "Don't, please, don't," he begged.

Matt pressed the gun closer. "Tell me."

"Behind the old server," he said quickly, gesturing to the back of the room. "There's a door. It leads to a hurricane shelter underneath the complex."

Alex was already headed over to the old server. He watched as she struggled to pull it away from the wall. From across the room, Matt could see a small space beginning to appear between the server and the wall. He could barely make out the outline of a door.

"How do we get in?"

"You already have the key," he stammered, gesturing to the keys Matt was still holding.

Matt ran to the back of the room. Alex had been able to move the server a few inches from the wall. He handed her the keys, took her spot and pulled the server the rest of the way. He stepped aside and Alex moved in to unlock the door.

She hit gold on the third key and opened the door just as the cabinet slid far enough away from the entrance to reveal a shoulder pushing its way through the small space. Matt shoved Alex through the entryway. He shot one quick look over his shoulder before he started through the door himself. Harrison was forcing himself into the room. Matt stepped through the door out of the room just as Harrison raised his gun and fired off a shot.

Matt slammed the door shut. They were plunged into darkness. He fumbled for the handle. No lock. His fingers frantically ran along the length of the door and located a deadbolt above the handle. He quickly slid it into place. Groping blindly, he continued to explore the edges of the door. He found two other dead bolts to seal the thick steel door. One bolt slid into the concrete block ceiling and still another slid into the floor. He quickly slammed each of them into place.

A musty, pungent smell pinched his nostrils. It took a moment for his eyes to adjust to the blackness, and even then, he could see nothing. He slid his right hand down the wall. Finding the light switch, he flicked it. Nothing happened. Shots reverberated off the door from the other side.

Matt took two tentative steps forward. He almost plunged into darkness before realizing the floor beneath his right foot had disappeared. He grabbed the air and his hand hit a railing. They were standing at the top of a metal stairwell.

"Follow me," Matt said as he descended the stairs into the darkness. "Just hang on to this railing."

Despite Matt and Alex's slow and cautious movements, the metal stairs echoed loudly. The pounding on the other side of the door had stopped.

When he reached the bottom of the stairs, Matt reached out with one hand. Holding the banister, he turned and walked under the stairwell. If this was a hurricane shelter, as Matt suspected, there had to be an alternate power source. Matt searched the darkness tentatively with his hands. Hurricanes had been known to take out the power anywhere from days to weeks in South Florida, and a military installation such as this would undoubtedly be prepared. Finally, he found what he was looking for. A generator.

"What are you doing, Matt?" Alex called from behind him.

"Just a minute," he said as he continued to maneuver in the darkness underneath the stairwell. Within moments, he had the diesel generator roaring to life. The lights flickered on weakly.

The area was cavernous, like a fallout shelter designed to withstand a nuclear attack. The Florida limestone served as a natural floor and as walls for the underground compound. Cases of bottled water and canned foods, medical supplies, sleeping bags and flashlights lined the walls. This was hurricane preparedness in South Florida post-Hurricane Katrina style.

"There must be another exit," Matt began. "One that's some distance away. They would have been concerned that the entrance would be blocked if the building was completely leveled."

Alex nodded.

Matt scanned the room. On the far wall, a map of the facility hung prominently. A red arrow helpfully pointed out their current location. He walked over and ripped the map off the wall. It showed a sweeping labyrinth that appeared to span the entire complex. Passageways led to each of the buildings and beyond. There were several different exits. Matt quickly identified two passages that led to exits outside the complex.

As Alex looked over his shoulder, Matt traced one of the passages with his finger. "This route will get us closer to the car but we'll still be inside the gate so we'd still have to get past the guard station."

Alex pointed to another route. "This exit will get us outside and away from the complex," she noted before turning to Matt.

"They'll expect us to take the route that gets us out of the complex and the farthest away," Matt said with more decisiveness than he felt.

"I say we go with this one," Matt continued as he pointed to the map.

Alex nodded.

Matt looked at Alex and then reached toward her. He grabbed the visitor's tag hanging from her neck and ripped it off.

"You won't be needing this anymore," Matt said before ripping off his own. "Let's get the hell out of here."

CHAPTER THIRTY

THE UNDERGROUND COMPLEX was being powered solely by the emergency generator so the eerily quiet passageways were dimly lit. But Matt knew that the light and the silence would be relatively short-lived if ~ or more likely when ~ Rabin and Harrison figured out where he and Alex were in the underground maze.

He had identified several exits on the map, most leading to other buildings on the campus. Rabin would know, as Matt did, that in light of the sophisticated security system, Matt and Alex could be trapped at any of those exits without the proper ID badges. The security clearance designations on their badges were limited before, but likely more so now that they had revealed their true intentions. Only two exits were not inside a building, leaving few options for Matt and Alex as well as few exits for Rabin to cover.

"So, Alex, tell me who's side are you on now?" Matt couldn't resist asking Alex as they moved quietly through the tunnels.

"Matt ~"

"And, will you be switching teams again anytime soon?" Matt interrupted before she could respond. "I'd really like to know before we come face to face with Rabin and his goons again."

"Let me explain."

"You can understand why I might be a little confused."

"Listen, Matt." Alex grabbed his arm and he was forced to slow down. "The stuff I told you about me ~ my family, college, the Army ~ that was all true."

This time he didn't interrupt but he kept walking.

"Two years ago," Alex continued, "my unit was deployed to Germany. From there we were sent to the front lines in Afghanistan about once a month, usually for two to three weeks at a time." She hesitated. "For most of our missions we were dropped into hot zones, given a target and told to get in and out as quickly as possible. We'd been doing this for over a year."

"I've heard all this before, Alex," Matt interrupted gruffly. "Incredibly intense times. I get it. But what does that have to do with your lying to me, Stephen, Bob and who knows how many other people?"

She turned away from him and started walking again.

"On our last mission," she continued slowly, "tensions were particularly high. We'd just received word that the military had postponed ~ yet again ~ the date that we'd be returning stateside. CNN was also reporting on a suicide attack that had killed ten soldiers. It was on that note that we were asked to carry out yet another night raid."

Matt recalled that night raids were regarded as the most effective tool against the Taliban insurgents. Commanders and whole groups of fighters had been killed or captured during these missions. They were also highly dangerous, with many coalition lives lost during these nighttime skirmishes.

"We were a relatively small group," Alex said. "All Special Forces. We were sent into a village called Mian."

Matt knew the village formally named Mian Poshteh. It was a farming community located in a remote district in Southern Afghanistan. It was used by the Taliban fighters as a supply route. The Marines spent several long months attempting to clear insurgents from the volatile region.

"The attacks were typically very quick and precise," Alex explained. "More so now ... you know, since the U.S. military started taking a lot of heat for operations that resulted in civilian casualties. On this one we were instructed to go in hard and fast. We were told that there was a militia meeting going on, that the men inside were heavily armed and that there were no civilians in the house. This was supposed to be good intelligence." She paused for a moment. "But that turned out not to be the case."

Matt felt sick to his stomach. He continued listening.

"We did just as we were told." She continued slowly. "We went in hard and fast. But the insurgents must have gotten wind of us." Her breathing grew harsher and the words now began to tumble out. "They had their weapons locked and loaded. Bullets started flying as soon as we crashed through the door." Alex shook her head at the memory. "One of the insurgents raced to the back of the house. My captain and I ~ we followed him. My captain, Rick was his name, had already been hit once. He didn't even realize it until later."

She stopped now, but she looked straight ahead, not making eye contact with Matt. "The room in the back was full of women and children. And there was no way out ~ not even a window. The guy we were chasing had grabbed one of the women. She was across the room holding a baby. And this guy was pointing his gun at her threatening to shoot." Alex caught her breath.

She turned to look at Matt now. He could see shock and horror in her eyes even at only the memory.

"We were screaming at him. The woman was screaming and the baby was crying."

Alex paused.

"What happened, Alex?" Matt prodded.

"Rick shot him. The man fell to the ground. Dead, I'm sure now. No return fire." She paused before continuing. "And then Rick shot him again. And again. He kept firing. I shouted at him. I punched him, but he kept screaming and firing all over the room. I hit him again. Finally, after Rick had emptied his magazine, he stopped. And then he just stood there."

They were standing now, neither moving, Matt looking at Alex and Alex looking at the floor.

"After he was done, after I could breathe again, I looked around the room and saw that he had killed the mother. The child too. He had cut them to ribbons.

"Oh my god, Alex."

"It was an awful scene, Matt. Like nothing I'd ever seen before. And I'd seen some terrible stuff." She shook her head before continuing. "The woman. The baby. I'll never get that scene out of my head."

Matt reached out and touched her hand. "I'm sorry you had to go through that, Alex."

She nodded her head, turned away from him and began walking again.

"And that's when my trouble began," she said softly from his side.

"What trouble?" Matt grabbed her arm, stopped her and then turned her to face him. "What are you talking about? The guy cracked under pressure. Extreme pressure. That wasn't your fault."

Alex paused and looked away. "By the time we had contained the situation, all the insurgents were dead, but so were two civilians. This was a nightmare situation, Matt. The President of Afghanistan was already threatening to kick U.S. forces out of the country. He was just looking for an excuse. Any excuse. And we had just given it to him."

"So, Rick wanted to ..." she faltered and heaved a heavy sigh before continuing. "On the way back to base no one said anything. When we finally got there, Rick immediately pulled me aside. He said we needed to get our stories straight."

Matt didn't ask what that meant. He didn't have to.

"The insurgent he killed had a gun. On this point, we agreed. Rick wanted me to say that the man had held the woman and child in front of him and started shooting. And that Rick had no choice other than to return fire. He had to injure the woman to get to the insurgent and then to keep shooting until the gunman was immobilized."

"What did you do, Alex?"

"I told him I wouldn't go along with it," she replied. "I was reporting the events as I had witnessed them. I figured that by telling exactly what I had seen, he might get some help. I thought I would be doing the right thing."

"So what happened?"

"Well, my captain wasn't happy, to say the least. He tried to convince me to change my story, to confirm that he had no choice but to fire and then keep firing. I think he actually had convinced himself of that. He also said that by telling my version, I would be ruining his career. When that didn't work, he threatened me. I still wouldn't agree."

"So, ultimately, it came down to his word against yours," Matt said.

"Exactly." Alex nodded. "But, he had the higher rank. More importantly, he had the story everyone really wanted to hear. The story that would keep the U.S. military out of trouble with the Afghan government. I should have known I would take the fall."

Alex shrugged her shoulders. "Shortly after my report, I was approached by the FBI for a special assignment back in the United States. At this point, staying with my unit wasn't an option so I accepted."

"What kind of assignment?"

"The FBI knew about some ex-military personnel who were working for private military companies and, in some cases, engaging in illegal activities. They must have assumed

I was the kind of operative the PMC would like – particularly after the stories that were circulating about what happened in Mian. So they wanted me to infiltrate the group, to find out exactly what they were doing."

"That couldn't have been easy," Matt said.

"It was easy getting inside. Back then, PMCs were hiring like crazy. With my military training ~ combined with the stories the FBI planted about me being not afraid to get my hands' dirty ~ I was an ideal candidate. So after sending out a few resumes to companies that said they were looking for former military personnel for some consulting work, I was contacted by Rabin. He told me he worked for a newly formed company that was looking to do some domestic and foreign private military work. After a couple of meetings and a background check, they hired me."

"But this doesn't explain what happened with Bob and why you set me up, Alex." Matt looked over at her quickly.

"I was assigned by Rabin to keep an eye on Bob. I used my cover to get to know him and he introduced me to Stephen. Even after I figured out what was going on, why I had been asked to watch Bob and Stephen, I had no idea they would actually kill Bob."

"Well, they did," Matt said angrily. "And now his wife is raising two small children by herself."

Alex winced.

"You're right, Matt. And I have to live with that for the rest of my life. I'm not making excuses," she continued quickly. "But once I knew how deadly serious these guys were, I tried to find Stephen before Rabin did. Clearly, I didn't. So, yeah, their deaths are on me."

She didn't say anything more for a few seconds and then she continued. "Your name came up a few times when I met with Bob and Stephen. So when you came back into the country and popped up on our radar, I got as close to you as possible. I convinced Rabin that Stephen would likely contact you and by getting close to you, we'd be able to track down Stephen. At first I did that because I wanted to protect you. But later," she looked up at him, "it became more personal."

Matt didn't say anything.

"I was undercover, pretending to be something I wasn't, working for that sociopath Rabin and his sidekick Harrison. When I was assigned to watch you, it was business at first ~ ideally, a means of exposing what they were doing and ending this assignment." She paused and then turned to look at him. "Last night was real, Matt. That wasn't me doing my job."

Matt looked over at her and knew that she meant it. He could also tell that after all she had told him, she wanted him to say something, maybe some words of forgiveness or at least kindness. The words didn't come. The master of the English language was once again at a loss.

"Let's just get the hell out of here," Matt finally said. "We'll figure the rest out later."

By this time, they had reached the end of the hallway leading to the exit. They were in a large room with more supplies, another generator and some commercial pruning equipment. On the other side of the room, the concrete flooring rose up to a steel door that had a red exit sign above it. They headed toward the door. When they reached the landing, they looked at the keypad. Instead of a solid red or green, the keypad flashed on and off.

Alex looked at Matt, her eyes wide. "It looks like the system is down," she said.

"Probably a by-product of Patrick's nasty little virus," Matt replied. "Let's get the hell out of here."

The door was bolted from every conceivable angle. He started with the top, then the bottom and finally the side. He turned the door handle slowly. He tensed, fully expecting an alarm to go off. Only sunlight greeted him as he pushed open the door. The brightness momentarily blinded him, causing him to squint and reach up to shield his eyes. Fresh air, the hushed and tranquil light portending the end of the day and the soft buzz of insects greeted him. He turned to smile back reassuringly at Alex.

He was still looking at Alex when he heard what sounded like a firecracker. He felt a sharp pain in his left thigh and looked down. He watched as blood began to darken his jeans. He looked back up at Alex. Her eyes were wide. Her mouth, unsmiling. His leg gave out and he fell to the ground.

"Back. Back," Matt said from the ground. Alex and Matt both scrambled back into the safety of the room they had just attempted to leave.

"Lock the door," Matt shouted after he kicked it closed with his good leg. Alex reached across his body and quickly slid a steel bar into place.

Once safely in the room, Matt slumped heavily against Alex. The urgency of the last several seconds had distracted him from his throbbing head and leg, but now the pain threatened to overwhelm him. Spots appeared before his eyes. The room began to spin. He felt Alex grip him under both shoulders. He saw her dig her feet into the floor and watched as his legs were dragged along the concrete floor and toward the wall opposite the door. After he had gone a few feet, Alex fell to the ground behind him.

Matt shook himself alert. He gingerly reached up and touched the back of his head and then moved his hand to the front of his face. Squinting in the light, he saw there was no blood. He peered down at his leg. The bullet went clean through his thigh, but the wound was bleeding profusely.

Matt's eyes scanned the room. He spotted a half-opened box of clothes.

"Alex, grab me something from that box."

She quickly rummaged through the box and handed him a long-sleeved T-shirt. He rolled the shirt up and wrapped it hard around his thigh, tying the sleeves together into an improvised bandage. He groaned as he tightened the sleeves.

Alex jumped up while Matt rose unsteadily. "Can you walk?" she asked.

Matt attempted a few steps. "Slower than I'd like but, yeah. Let's go."

WHAM!

The sound was deafening. Matt grabbed Alex and pressed her against the wall. He wrapped his body around her, absorbing most of the impact from the debris flying around them.

After a few seconds, he turned to look back at the door. Through a curtain of dust and debris he saw light flood in where the door hung open on its shattered frame.

"What was that?" Matt asked.

"Sounded like C-4 plastic explosives. Probably at the hinges."

Matt fumbled toward the boxes of supplies that he had seen earlier stacked against the wall. He upended the first one and when it fell down to the floor next to him, he ripped it open. Inside was an assortment of tools. A wrench. A screwdriver. Rummaging through the contents, Matt finally found something useful. He handed Alex a pair of safety goggles before putting a pair on himself. Covering their mouths against the dust that filled the air, they both watched the doorway, waiting for what was to come.

Two men with bandannas tied around the bottom halves of their faces rushed in. Both men tightly gripped handguns, their arms fully extended. The men scanned the room wildly. Their eyes hadn't adjusted yet from the bright sunlight to the dimly lit room. Matt grabbed the wrench sitting on the floor next to him and threw it to the opposite corner of the room.

Muzzle flashes erupted like strobe lights. Bullets ricocheted off the walls. Smoke and the smell of cordite swirled around them. Simultaneously, Matt and Alex both raised their guns. They each fired off a shot at the nearest man. Both shots hit their marks, and the men went down.

Matt and Alex scrambled over to the men and reached for their weapons. When Matt reached down for the gun on the floor that the man nearest him had dropped, the man reached up, caught Matt around the neck and flipped him onto his back. Matt looked up and into the face of Cole Harrison. The other man's face was red with rage, his lips pressed into a sneer. He improved his hold around Matt's neck and then began to squeeze tightly.

Blows by Matt to Harrison's body seemed to have no effect. Matt clawed at Harrison's hands, but he couldn't release the vise grip. Harrison continued to squeeze firmly around Matt's neck while at the same time pressing his head hard against the concrete floor. Dark circles swirled before Matt's eyes.

Matt frantically scanned the floor with his hands for something to use against Harrison. His fingers slapped, brushed and scraped against the cement floor in search of something. Anything. Finally, his fingertips brushed against the cold steel butt of the gun Harrison had dropped. He took one last gasp of breath and stretched until he was able to grab the handle of the gun. He pulled it toward him.

"Step back," Matt croaked weakly as he looked past Harrison and to Alex who had come up behind him. She hesitated and then slowly stepped back. Matt pulled the trigger. Harrison's face immediately registered rage, and then shock. And then nothing. He collapsed heavily across Matt.

From underneath, Matt pushed the body off and scrambled away. He heaved himself into an upright sitting position on the ground. Alex came over to him while Matt continued to gasp for breath. He looked up to see Jack Rabin slowly emerge from the shadows.

CHAPTER THIRTY-ONE

RABIN STOPPED DIRECTLY behind Alex and pressed his gun firmly against her cheek. "Drop your weapons," he commanded.

"Do it," he urged when neither one of them moved.

Matt slowly put his gun down on the floor. He looked over and saw Alex follow his lead.

"Kick it over to me, Matt," Rabin commanded. "Now!"

With both of their weapons now at his feet, Rabin shoved Alex toward Matt, who caught her before she fell to the ground. Matt stumbled on his week leg but then regained his balance. Rabin reached down and picked up both their weapons. He removed the clips from both guns and placed them in his vest pocket. He checked the weapon chambers to confirm there were no unspent cartridges and then threw the useless weapons in the corner.

Rabin then stepped back. He looked them over while at the same time scanning the room. His gaze briefly stopped at Cole Harrison lying dead on the floor but quickly moved on.

"Rabin, it's over," Matt finally said. "The virus has destroyed your network."

Rabin didn't respond. He walked over to a workbench along the wall.

"By now, the program we loaded has exposed your little project," Matt continued.

"You can't take back what's on the Internet," Alex said. "Thousands of people know the truth. Millions will know by morning."

"I know that, Alex," Rabin stated as he surveyed the contents of the workbench, occasionally picking up things and putting them in his pocket.

"My job is over," Rabin continued. "But I always knew it would come to an end at some point."

"Then why don't you just let us go?" Alex asked.

"Why would I do that?" Rabin asked with what sounded like a touch of amusement. "Particularly, when we have some unfinished business."

Rabin turned around. In his hands, he held a roll of electrical tape, a pair of needle-nose pliers and a box of industrial razor blades.

"Alex, I'd like you to tie Matt's hands together with this," Rabin said as he tossed the roll of electrical tape to her. She instinctively caught it.

"And if I don't?"

"I'll shoot Matt in the head," Rabin replied as he raised the gun and pointed it at Matt.

After a moment, Alex stepped behind Matt. He heard a ripping noise as she unrolled and applied the tape. Rabin checked her work and then grabbed the roll of tape from her. As Rabin turned to toss the roll of tape onto the worktable, Matt felt Alex slip something cool between his wrists. Cool and smooth. Like glass. It was the camera lens he had used earlier to get them into the computer building.

Rabin turned back and shoved her away. Stepping closer to Matt, he delivered a powerful kick to Matt's right leg. Matt doubled over in agony. Blood started to ooze down his thigh from the re-opened wound. Matt fell to the ground, and Rabin roughly dragged him to the corner of the room.

The pain was excruciating. Matt was lying on the floor jackknifed at the waist. He smelled the coppery odor of blood and felt a spasm in his stomach. Opening his eyes, Matt stared into the dead eyes of Harrison lying next to him on the floor. He quickly turned his face away.

"Despite your admirable efforts," Rabin said from above him. "I suspect we have some time before the authorities make their way here to the compound and even longer before they find their way to this location."

Matt looked up to see Rabin grab for Alex, catching her around the waist and dragging her toward a table on the other side of the room. Rabin used the other arm to grab the tape sitting on the table and then sweep the table clean of the remaining debris sitting on it. Rabin threw Alex on to the table. Alex grunted when she hit the table hard.

Rabin was ignoring Matt now, no doubt aware that he was no threat. Matt tried to rise again. This time his leg responded by screaming in protest. Matt brought his hands underneath his body. Now using fingers and abdominal muscles, Matt pushed himself upright. He was finally able to rise to a sitting position. He used his legs to push himself closer to the corner of the room. Using his good leg, he pushed his back against the wall and attempted to inch his way up. The one leg wasn't strong enough, and he couldn't put any pressure on the other leg. Matt fell back down to a sitting position, groaning when he felt the impact reverberate throughout his aching body.

When Matt opened his eyes again, he saw Alex struggling from atop the table. She was kicking and screaming, her body flailing about the table, while Rabin attempted to subdue her. She was losing the fight. Rabin was much stronger and only seemed to enjoy her efforts.

Matt decided to try another tack. He pulled his wrists against the tape. The binds were tight and his wrists were separated by only a few millimeters. He twisted his wrists and rubbed the heels of his hands up and down against each other. There was very little movement. The bindings were simply too tight. He continued pressing his hands apart, straining against the binding, until it was enough. With his fingers he pushed the lens between the palms of his hands and against the tape.

Alex struggled out of Rabin's grip and off the table. From the other side of the table, she stared wide-eyed at Rabin. She then made a charge for a screwdriver that was in the open box sitting on the floor. She now stared at Rabin from across the table with a weapon in hand. Rabin pushed the table hard toward her and slammed Alex against the wall. She doubled over.

Rabin quickly reached across the table and grabbed the hand with the screwdriver. He twisted. With his other hand, he easily deflected a weak blow Alex attempted with her free arm. Rabin twisted harder. A guttural sound erupted from Alex before she dropped the screwdriver.

Rabin pulled her to his side of the table and slammed her down again. Her head pounded the hard surface and a moan escaped her lips.

"Alex, you don't have to make this so difficult." Matt heard Rabin say.

Matt held the lens in the heels of his hands and began to slice at the electrical tape. With the effort, the room began to sway in front of him. He had lost a lot of blood. He didn't have much time.

Rabin grabbed Alex's hands and pulled them over her head. Alex began to flail about and kick her legs. Rabin punched Alex hard in the face with his closed fist. Her body immediately sagged and she stopped moving. Rabin placed his gun down on the table beside her and used the electrical tape on her arms. He methodically tied each of them to one corner of the table.

"Let her go," Matt said as he continued to struggle furiously with the piece of glass. "It's over. You've got nothing to gain from this."

"Ah, but that's where you're wrong, Matt," Rabin said as he moved down to Alex's legs, which were hanging lifelessly over the edge of the table. Alex moaned when Rabin touched her left leg but Rabin was able to easily secure it to the table leg before moving on to her right leg.

The pressure from the camera lens against the tape kept pushing the glass back into the palm of Matt's hands. Each time, though, Matt inched the sharp edge of the lens back up toward his wrists and moved it urgently against the tape.

"Come on, Alex, wake up," Rabin said after he had firmly secured her to the table. He gently slapped her face. She groaned weakly, but her eyes remained closed. "Matt, how's your view?" Rabin said over his shoulder.

"I'm going to get a tremendous amount of satisfaction from what I'm about to do to Alex and then to you." Rabin said as he grabbed a bottle of water from the hurricane supplies. He twisted the top off and splashed the water in Alex's face. Alex's head rose from the table and she began sputtering. Now fully awake, she struggled frantically against the bindings.

"You aren't going to get away with this," Matt said as he continued to saw furiously at the electrical tape.

He pulled his wrists apart and felt less resistance. The lens slipped from his palms. The soft clink when the glass hit the concrete floor was deafening to Matt. He looked over at Rabin.

Rabin had taken one of the razors out of its sheath. He ripped the protective cover off and tossed it aside. Alex's eyes widened as he flashed it in front of her. It glittered in the dim light of the dank hurricane shelter.

Matt's fingers combed the concrete floor until he found the lens. He didn't take his eyes off Alex and Rabin as he furiously resumed his attack on his bindings. His hands were slick with blood. His own. The result of miscalculating his target. He didn't feel the pain as he continued his work.

"Matt, are you catching this?" Rabin said as he ran the blade of the razor softly against Alex's quivering sternum.

Matt felt the last piece of tape fall away and slowly pulled his hands apart. He pushed himself up and took one step forward ignoring the excruciating pain emanating from his thigh.

"Catch this," Matt raged as he flung himself at Rabin.

Both men fell across Alex on the table and Matt felt her squirm beneath them. Rabin roared as he stood up with Matt clinging to his back. Rabin took one step back, stumbled momentarily and then regained his footing. He took two more steps back, slamming Matt against the nearest wall. Stunned, Matt released his grip and fell to the ground. Rabin turned around and faced Matt, a small smile on his face. In his hand, he still held the razor. He moved slowly toward Matt.

Matt struggled to remain upright. He looked past Rabin and saw Alex struggling frantically against the binds. The table jumped and scraped across the floor with her efforts. The gun that Rabin had placed on the table fell to the ground. Rabin heard it hit the floor and turned around. He hesitated a moment before heading back for it.

At that moment, Matt launched at Rabin again. Using the jagged edge of the lens still in his hand, he sliced Rabin on the neck before the man drove an elbow into Matt's ribs, knocking him to the floor.

Rabin turned back toward Matt as he reached his hand up to press it against the side of his neck. Blood seeped from between Rabin's fingers. Finally, at last, the sick grin was no longer on his face. Instead, it was replaced with a look of shock and then confusion.

Matt grabbed the empty semiautomatic handgun Rabin had earlier flung to the corner and stood weakly. With the last of his strength, he stepped forward and swung at Rabin using the handle of the gun as a hammer. The blow struck Rabin soundly on the jaw and he fell to the ground.

Matt limped over to Alex. He used the razor Rabin had dropped to cut the electrical tape binding Alex's hands. He smiled down weakly at her. Her eyes filled with tears. He softly touched her cheek before moving down to release her legs.

Before Matt was able to get even one leg free, a shadow appeared across the floor. Matt looked over his left shoulder to see Rabin standing above him. Blood flowed freely down the man's neck. His jaw was misshapen, his eyes glassy but resolute.

Matt dropped the razor. He lowered his right shoulder, pushed off with his feet and rolled under the table. As his right shoulder hit the ground, Matt grabbed the gun that was under the table. With the gun in hand, Matt continued to roll over his upper back and left shoulder and out the other side of the table. He stood up just in time to see Rabin reach toward Alex, who was now sitting up but still tied by her legs to the table.

Matt squeezed the trigger and fired two rounds into Rabin's chest. Two large holes blasted deep into the man's body as he fell to the ground. Matt and Alex watched as the puddle beneath Rabin spread out in a pool on the concrete floor.

CHAPTER THIRTY-TWO

ONE WEEK LATER, Matt brought a borrowed Boston Whaler to a stop in the middle of Biscayne Bay. Carlos at the Coconut Grove Marina had once again come through for Matt. He shut off the engine, jumped to the bow of the boat and dropped the anchor.

When he returned to the front bench, Alex had already retrieved a bottle of white wine from the cooler. She handed him the bottle and rummaged around for two glasses. Matt popped the cork and filled both glasses before they settled to watch the sunset as it dropped behind the City of Miami.

"This is gorgeous," Alex said softly.

Before Matt could reply, his cell phone sounded. Matt stood up, reached into the pocket of his jeans and pulled out his phone. He looked at the device and saw it was the call he had been waiting for. He handed Alex his wineglass, quickly pressed the receive button and put the phone to his ear.

"Hey, Dana," Matt said quickly. "Any news?"

Matt held his breath.

Alex perked up and her eyes bored into him.

"Yes. Good news, actually. Mo will be released this afternoon. He should be back in the States by tomorrow night. I've called his parents, told them the news and they'll be waiting for him at the airport."

"Outstanding!" Matt replied as he gave Alex the thumbs-up signal.

"Dana, you're the best! I can't thank you enough."

"Well, thank you, but I couldn't have done this without a little help," she continued hesitantly.

"Okay, I understand. Just let me know what I can do to thank you and ... uh ... whomever."

"I guess that would be me," a male voice boomed in Matt's ear.

"Matt, I have you on a conference call with Senator Raul Suarez," Dana quickly interjected. "He heard about the situation with Mo and volunteered to help me arrange for his release."

Matt's eyes widened. Raul Suarez was the brother of Commissioner Carlos Suarez, the local politician Matt had been at odds with over the entire course of the commissioner's career.

There was a brief pause until Dana jumped in. "Matt, as you know the senator sits on the Senate Intelligence Committee. He used some of his contacts to ensure that the entire investigation of Mohammed was terminated and we were able to bring him home."

"Senator, I'm really at a loss for words," Matt stammered.

"No problem, Matt, no problem at all," Senator Suarez said briskly. "I'm happy to do what I can for my loyal constituents."

"Well, thank you." Matt hesitated. "I can't tell you how much I appreciate this and ... if there's anything I can ~"

"Well, actually, Matt, there is one small matter on which I could use your help."

Matt should have known. "And what might that be, Senator?"

"I've been briefed on what happened down at the Protegere compound. I'd like you to come up and speak before a panel I am putting together regarding cybersecurity."

"Does this mean you're conducting an investigation?" Matt asked anxiously. "Looking into who authorized the release of the technology used to commit these acts? Who paid Jack Rabin and Cole Harrison? Can we expect that whoever is responsible will be ~?"

"Wait, Matt. Hold on a minute," the Senator interrupted. "As you know, it's up to the Attorney General to determine whether a crime has been committed and, if so, whether charges should be filed. It's my understanding that the AG's office is looking into this and will determine the appropriate action."

So far, no one had been willing to conduct any investigation about the release of the technology originally developed through the government's Total Information Awareness program, or the authorization of the PR firm to conduct its own Operation Mockingbird, let alone who paid the PR firm or the military contractor and who was behind the whole operation.

Payment alone should be easily traceable. Instead, mid-level officials with the government claimed the Total Information Awareness technology was not sold and, to their knowledge, was not being used. The PR firm disavowed any knowledge of Operation Mockingbird, the computer technology or any media manipulation.

Protegere, the defense contractor that directly or indirectly likely employed Harrison, Rabin and the other men at the compound, was arguing that if Harrison and Rabin were employed by them ~ and it wasn't admitting to that ~ then its contracts and actions were a matter of national security and could not be disclosed. Protegere maintained that its contractors were extensions of the U.S. military and, as such, were immune from liability.

"Senator," Matt began firmly. "You do have the authority to call for an investigation. You could investigate Protegere, the PR firm IMS and even those two mercenaries that were hired to kill people ~ that tried to kill me. You could investigate who authorized Rabin and Harrison to murder innocent people."

There was a long pause.

"Matt," the Senator finally began, "off the record, Protegere and IMS are denying any knowledge of the activities of those two men. IMS confirms that it had an interest in monitoring news reports and even generating press releases in favor of its different clients; however, they deny any involvement in media manipulation and this computer program you describe. Protegere refuses to say whether Harrison and Rabin were in its employ and denies any knowledge of any murders on U.S. soil."

"That's bullshit," Matt shot back.

Alex shot him a look. They had already been through this. She had warned him about the intelligence industrial complex. It was a business that was fast-growing and hiring more new employees than any other business sector in the United States. In light of the vast amount of money and jobs involved, both the government and the private companies would do anything to protect their monopolies on intelligence-gathering and war.

"Senator, with all due respect," Matt began in what he hoped was a conciliatory tone. "You could start looking at your own house. Track down the Total Information Awareness technology. Find out who had access to it. And who allowed it to be used for this purpose. Start there."

"There's no evidence that government technology was stolen or tampered with, Matt."

"That's bull—"

"Matt, as you know, the White House was recently forced to defend the National Security Agency's spy programs. After that public relations nightmare – not to mention the hit the Administration took on the polls for that debacle ~ they certainly aren't going to admit to this. We can't even track down the computer technology you say was used to perpetuate this media manipulation. If it did exist, the virus that you loaded apparently destroyed any evidence of it. I'm afraid there isn't anything I can do."

Matt paused to consider the situation he found himself in. He was relieved that Mo was returning home but disappointed that it appeared nothing was going to happen to punish those responsible for the deaths of so many friends and colleagues. Sure, Rabin and Harrison were dead, but those executives higher up at Protegere who hired the killers and gave them their marching orders were going to get off scot-free. Nobody in the government seemed terribly concerned about that.

Matt looked over at Alex and saw her watching him carefully. Alex's record had been cleared but only on the condition that she never speak of the matter. She understood Matt's desire for justice – not for himself but for Bob and Stephen and their families. But she wasn't prepared to sacrifice her future – and potentially her life – to go public.

Matt looked past Alex and saw that the sun had dropped considerably since he had begun this call. The bottom quarter of the sun was now obscured by the largest high rise in Downtown Miami.

The Senator interrupted Matt's thoughts. "I need your help, Matt. As I mentioned before, I'd like you to come up here and speak with my team."

The Senator continued when Matt didn't respond. "Perhaps you and I can work together to ensure that something like this never happens again.

And," the Senator continued, "while you're in D.C., Matt, I'm sure that there will be some opportunities for you and me to get together for some additional face time and maybe chat about some other topics."

Maddening as it was, Matt wasn't naive. He knew that there were limitations on what you could do as a journalist.

You could investigate and report events, issues and trends to a broad audience. That had been done. Thanks to their success in installing Patrick's virus and sending out Stephen's message, a lot more people had been able to read the truth about private military companies, the U.S. war on global terror, the U.S. government's involvement in regime change and the U.S.'s infringement of civil liberties in pursuit of those activities. What the citizenry did with that information was something Matt had no control over. He could only continue to inform and hope that people became aware and that positive change came from it.

"Matt?" The Senator was still waiting.

"Of course, Senator," Matt replied quickly. Then, after pausing for a few moments. "And, perhaps while I am there, we can talk about how we can persuade your brother Carlos to be a little bit more discriminating about from whom he accepts campaign contributions? Convicted felons are not the only ones with deep pockets who have a vested interest in influencing our democracy."

Alex winced. An awkward silence followed, during which Matt held his breath.

"Perhaps we can talk about that too while you're here, Matt," Senator Suarez finally said.

"And one other thing, Senator. Perhaps you might be so kind as to arrange a few introductions to some of your esteemed colleagues? I'm working on few other stories and their input could be helpful."

"I'll see what I can do, Matt. How about coming up a week from Thursday?"

"Sure," Matt replied. "I'll be there."

Dana, Senator Suarez and Matt said their good-byes and the call was over. Matt put his phone back in his pocket and turned to Alex.

"What do you say, Alex. Want to come up to D.C. with me next week? It shouldn't be too hot this time of year."

"It's always hot in D.C., Matt," Alex said. "Even when it's cold, it's hot."

She had moved to the back bench of the Boston Whaler. From there she was smiling at him. She gestured to the falling sun and beckoned to him with his glass of wine.

Acknowledgements

To my family and friends, for their love and support over the years. I have been truly blessed in so many ways but none more so than by the amazing people I have in my life. To Trey and Megan, I have no words but if I've done anything right, you know. To my husband George, the love of my life, without your support this labor of love would never have seen the light of day.